Flycatcher

Flycatcher

◆

Elleston Trevor

A TOM DOHERTY ASSOCIATES BOOK
NEW YORK

FLYCATCHER

Copyright © 1994 by Trevor Productions, Inc.

This book is printed on acid-free paper.

A Forge Book
Published by Tom Doherty Associates, Inc.
175 Fifth Avenue
New York, N.Y. 10010

Library of Congress Cataloging-in-Publication Data

Trevor, Elleston.
    Flycatcher / Elleston Trevor.
       p.   cm.
    ISBN 0-312-85647-4
    1. Serial murders—New York (N.Y.)—Fiction.
    2. Police—New York (N.Y.)—Fiction. I. Title.
PR6039.R518F55   1994
823'.914—dc20   94-26026
                                      CIP

First edition: October 1994

Printed in the United States of America

0 9 8 7 6 5 4 3 2 1

To
Link and Sterling

Flycatcher

One

The scream came shrilling into the silence of the warm Manhattan night, jerking Tasha awake.

Staring at the pale wash of light thrown by the street lamps across the ceiling, she felt the thudding of her heart as she held her breath and waited for another scream to come.

But there was just silence now.

The night air stirred at the windows, sending a silk curtain rustling. Tasha went on waiting, not sure now that the scream hadn't been part of her dream; but it would have taken a nightmare to produce a sound with so much terror in it, and she never had nightmares.

Letting out her breath at last she dragged the bed sheet aside and went to the windows, staring out across Fifth Avenue to the massed trees of the park. It had come from there, the scream, and the sound of it was still going through her, piercing her nerves as she watched the lamplit trees with the sweat creeping on her temples, itching on her face.

Still silence, except for the rustling of the curtain.

There wasn't going to be another scream. That would be the only one—the first and the last. Whatever had been happening in the trees over there was finished now. But she spun away from the window and went to the telephone by her bed, dialing 911 in case she was wrong and it wasn't too late.

"Emergency."

Tasha started at the sound of the woman's voice.

"Yes. I—I just heard a scream." Her mouth was dry, her tongue clumsy. "From Central Park."

The line was silent for a moment, then the dispatcher said, "A scream." It wasn't a question. The voice was deadpan. "Just one?"

Tasha felt a flush of embarrassment, realizing what the dispatcher was thinking—only one scream, Jesus, from a place like Central Park? Things were real quiet tonight.

"It sounded," Tasha said at last, "as if somebody . . . I mean it sounded quite desperate." It was the best she could do. How could she be expected to describe in mere words something that had left her shaking like this, the phone slippery in her hand from sweat?

"You are Miss Tasha Fontaine," the dispatcher said as she checked her screen, "at Temple Mansions, on Fifth. Is that correct?"

"Yes." She could feel her pulse beating where her ear was pressed to the phone.

"Okay, Miss Fontaine, I'll send a unit to check out the area."

The line went dead.

Tasha stayed where she was for a minute, leaning her back against the wall, her bare shoulder blades sensing the raised flock of the wallpaper, her fingers fretting at a nail she must have chipped, her heart slowing a little but only a little, because that desperate, agonized cry had come to stay with her, was suddenly a part of her experience, her life, connecting her like an unbreakable thread to something monstrous that had happened just now in the park, the sound of it bringing her out of her dreams to face its terrible reality.

The light from the street sparked on the silver top of the decanter across the room, where she kept some cognac and a bottle of Perrier and some crackers for when she felt like a nightcap after a rough day's work. She needed a drink right now, for God's sake . . . but she didn't go over there to pour one. It would simply deaden her nerves, and she needed them to remain alert; she wanted to share in what was happening, what had happened down there among the trees, to share in its appalling reality. She had to acknowledge it, and not turn away. The opposite would be to ignore it, to forget it, and that would be almost obscene, a denial of an undeniable truth.

Go back to bed, and leave it to the police.

No way. She'd never left things to other people, even the police: it was too easy. In any case, there wasn't a hope in hell of getting back to sleep; it was gone three in the morning by the small gold bedside clock, and most of her sleeping was done: she'd turned in early last night after a long day at the boutique.

Okay, Miss Fontaine, I'll send a unit to check out the area. Had she meant it, or was that just a polite brush-off? But there might have been murder done! Or was it just a rape going on? Oh, God . . . had it come down to *that* in this city, that you were lucky if you *just* got raped?

She moved suddenly, going across to the closet and pulling out her navy tracksuit and a pair of Nikes, struggling into them as rainbows began flashing across the ceiling, floating and flashing as a police car moved into the area. So it hadn't been a polite brush-off: they had taken her seriously. She suddenly let out the breath she'd been holding for a long time without being aware. You could crab all you liked about the cops, but you felt a whole lot better when they finally turned up.

By the time she got the zipper of her suit unstuck and her track shoes on there were more lights coloring the ceiling, and she could hear the crackle of a radio as a car turned off Fifth Avenue into the park. She shook her dark hair back and tied it with a ribbon and went out to the elevator, wondering why she was doing this but knowing she had to do it.

Lewis, the night doorman, was at his little mahogany desk in the lobby with a newspaper spread out under the green-shaded lamp when the elevator doors came open. He got up in a hurry, his elbow knocking against the lamp as he looked at his watch.

"Jogging, Miss Tasha, this time of night?" His gaunt, mottled face was full of surprise.

"Something happened in the park," she told him as she crossed the lobby, her shoes squeaking on the marble. "I heard a scream." She pulled open the door before Lewis could get there. He realized that the top button of his uniform was undone, and fixed it with shaking hands. They were always shaking—he had Parkinson's, as all the residents knew, but pretended not to.

"A scream?"

But Miss Tasha was already going down the steps onto the sidewalk, her ponytail bobbing, and Lewis stood bent-backed at the open doorway, watching the flashing lights. He hadn't heard any scream.

Another car swung into East 65th past the Children's Zoo as Tasha crossed Fifth and kept on through the trees along Transverse Road, turning onto the bridle path as she saw more lights in the far distance, moving down the West Drive. The summer leaves drew overhead as she jogged steadily, shallow-breathing now as the acrid smell of exhaust gas came drifting on the air.

And then, halfway along the bridle path, she broke her stride and stood leaning with her hands on her knees, getting her breath as she watched the cluster of flashing lights a quarter of a mile away through the trees.

Time to go back now.

Yeah.

She shouldn't have come here anyway—it could only have been morbid curiosity, a thing she despised in people when she saw them gathering like ghouls around an accident in the street.

Time to go back to the calm and safety of Temple Mansions, the door closed, and good old Lewis on guard.

Sure.

Leaning on her knees and watching the rainbow-colored scene over there among the trees, hearing the faint crackling of radios, voices in the night.

Turn around and go back, yeah. She'd seen enough— whatever had happened, the cops were there now, and maybe there was still time to do something for the woman who had screamed; drag the guy off her or stop the bleeding or whatever was necessary. They'd do a good job; this was nothing they weren't used to, couldn't handle.

Leaning on her knees, staring through the trees in the posture of a primitive animal, a shaggy primate crouched on the watch, suddenly disgusting herself as she realized this, straightening up but not turning around, not going back.

Because she couldn't.

She had to get closer than this, had to see what had happened over there, why the scream had been so desperate, so full of terror. She had to go on sharing in this hideous, outrageous event, had to accept it as something that already had become part of her life.

Okay. If that was how it had to be.

Okay.

And then she was suddenly on the move again as if someone had pushed her, and as she ran toward the lights she knew she ought to question why she was doing it, why she felt she had to share in this thing, but there wouldn't be any answer, she knew that too.

Turning left at the far end of the bridle path, she stopped again in the knoll of trees as an ambulance came moving in along 72nd Street and swerved toward the cluster of lights, halting with a squeal of tires as a door snapped open.

The patrol cars, a good dozen of them, were standing

near the trees like bright, scattered toys, their lights coloring the spread of leaves overhead. Dark figures moved, some in uniform, unreeling yellow tapes and running them around the trunks of the trees as someone called out and one of the cars was backed and turned, coming in to flood the center of the scene with its headlights.

"Jesus *Christ* . . ." someone said, his voice carrying clearly in the sudden silence.

At the center of the scene Tasha saw the brightness of something red—a lot of it, glittering richly in the glare of the patrol car's lights before it was blotted out by the canvas screen they were setting up.

The ambulance crew had brought a stretcher from their vehicle, but no one seemed to want it, and they just stood there with it propped against a tree.

Tasha watched.

She watched with the awe and the stillness of revelation, her breath held and her eyes wide, unblinking, still seeing the glittering redness that was now hidden by the screen, knowing that this was what she had come here to see, for whatever unknown reason, by whatever unknown bidding, and now that she had seen it she could go back.

The dark figures, now frosted with a sheen from the car's lights, were gathered around the canvas screen, none of them talking but just looking down, their heads bowed, until one of them turned away and lurched into the trees and began throwing up.

"O-*kay* . . . " a man said, and the group broke apart, one man lifting a camera and sending flash after flash into the shadows as he moved around the screen.

"Bernie?" someone called.

"He's over there."

The patrol lights flickered . . . flickered in silence, throwing their rainbow colors across the men as they moved about their business, one of them unreeling a tape measure, another swinging a flashlight to study the grass underfoot.

Another car swung in from 72nd Street, and a man in dark clothes came down into the trees carrying a black bag, noting the canvas screen and going straight over to it. There were other figures, Tasha saw, standing in the distance, with only the blur of their faces showing among the shadows. They would be what Lewis the doorman called 'the denizens'; the people who slept here in the park when it was warm, who lived here, a lot of the time, in the never-ending twilight of the drugs they used, stole, and traded. Had any of them seen what had happened tonight? Had one of them *made* it happen?

A shiver went through Tasha and she turned away, walking at first and then starting to jog, watching the trees as the light grew less and keeping clear of them, having to brave the no-man's-land that lay between the safety of the bright police cars and the haven of Temple Mansions.

Fifth Avenue was deserted as she jogged across it, but the doorways were in shadow, and she ran up the steps and reached for the bell, leaving her finger on it and letting it go on ringing and ringing as she became aware of how dangerous it was to be alone out here in the night, how dangerous for any woman in any street of this city, of any city, but how much more dangerous for *her,* on *this* night, with only the little round bell and the word *Press* her only passport to safety, because she hadn't brought her keys.

It had been so red, so glittering, the thing out there in the trees.

Pressing and pressing until her finger was numb and she began calling out in her mind: *Lewis . . . Lewis . . . Come on, for God's sake . . .*

Had she been jogging, the woman who'd been turned into something the very sight of which had made a seasoned city policeman throw up? Had she been crazy enough to go into Central Park alone at this time of night? *Lewis . . . For God's sake, where are you? . . . Lewis!*

Tires squealed somewhere as a car swung onto Fifth

Avenue, and the shock went through her and this time she called his name out loud: *"Lewis!"*

The door was jerked open and she caught her breath again, shaking with nerves and already ashamed of it—but the meaning of what she'd seen out there was only just starting to hit her in a wave of delayed shock.

Lewis was staring. "Miss Tasha! Are you okay?"

She pushed past him, hiding her face. "I'm fine," she said, and pressed for the elevator. Over her shoulder— "There was a—an accident, that's all, and I guess I'm not good at things like that."

Safe again in her apartment she leaned her back against the locked door and closed her eyes and tried to blot everything out, but it was worse like this because all she could see was the glitter of red in the darkness. In a moment, she went into the bedroom and poured a jigger of cognac, and tossed it back, to hell with any guilt about giving in to Dutch courage—when you needed a drink, for God's sake, you needed a drink. Period.

And then, as she pulled off her Nikes and got out of her tracksuit with its twin fancy white stripes, she saw a leaf on the carpet, from one of her shoes—a small, yellowing leaf—and she went on looking at it, not moving anymore and not wanting to pick it up and drop it into the wastebasket, because the chances were it had come from there, from that exact place in the park, had been lying on the ground under the trees where *she* had been walking, the woman— at the time when she'd still been a woman, alive and presumably well—and maybe her foot had even passed over it, this leaf on the carpet here, as she'd walked toward her death or had run from it as hard as she could, hearing the footsteps behind her closing in, closing in all the time, then hearing his breath, the animal grunting of his breath, until she knew it was too late and she couldn't run anymore so she'd screamed . . . screamed in the night . . . just once, before it all began to be over.

Tasha looked at the leaf, knowing she ought simply to pick it up and take it to a wastebasket, but knowing also that it was more than she could even force herself to do.

So on her way to bed she picked up a copy of *W* and dropped it over the little yellowing leaf, but she went on seeing it just the same as she finally lay in bed with her eyes closed, knowing it was still there, her very own memento of the unthinkable that she had brought in from the night.

Two

Detective **Behrens looked** at the condom through the transparent plastic of the envelope, turning it over a couple of times. It had been used, that was all you could see, there was some stuff still inside.

"How many of these fuckin' things could we find any summer morning in this fuckin' park if we looked hard enough?"

Detective Baker shrugged. "Maybe a hundred?"

He waited, not intending to say more than that. Every time Bernie used a four-letter word more than once in one sentence—even though he always spoke quietly—it was a reminder to the squad that he was ready to bite their heads off if they spoke out of turn. Ten "fucks" a minute rang the bell: he was in a towering rage, and that was the only way you could tell.

"Maybe a hundred, right." Behrens held out the envelope by one corner with his thumb and forefinger. "But file it. Find any more, file 'em. But remember it's *semen* you're looking for—on the grass, without any gift wrap."

"Yes, sir."

"Where's McOwen?

"He went to grab a bite at the Spoon."

"Beep the creep. Tell him if he's not back inside of five minutes I'll have his ass."

Behrens looked down again at the single sheet of paper in his hand. The first light of the day was strong enough now to read without his flashlight.

Tuesday August 4th, 3:17 A.M.
Received a call from Detective Bernard Behrens requesting that an investigator and Medical Examiner's rig be dispatched to an area in southwest Central Park. Informant indicated that an apparently white female body was at that location.

'Apparently' white, yeah, they weren't kidding—the poor bitch looked like she'd been bathing in ketchup.

3:29 A.M. Medical Examiner's Field Investigator and Ambulance arrived on the scene. Met with Detective Behrens. The body of a white female tentatively identified by her possessions as Christine Courtney Wittendorf, age 32, was examined.

Behrens heard running footsteps and looked up, saw a girl in a tracksuit jogging through the trees near the end of the bridle path, her ponytail bobbing. They should never come into this fucking place on their own, for Christ sake, even in daylight, didn't they ever read a newspaper?

The victim had been completely stripped and most of the clothing was found in the immediate area; one shoe was found sixteen feet, six inches distant, as if lost while running. The decedent's dress, camisole, panties and stockings were severely torn. A sharp instrument had been inserted with considerable force into the vagina, anus, mouth, and both eyes. A dead leaf and traces of soil were found inside the mouth. Blood loss was also considerable and it appeared that blood had been deliberately smeared over the entire body surface. No body parts seem to be missing.

No souvenirs, a finger, a nipple . . . sometimes they took souvenirs. The sheet of paper was quivering slightly in Behren's hands; he noticed it, and tried to hold it steadier. Bastard.

Bastard.

You were expected to have gotten used to this kind of thing after fifteen years on the job, right? Right. So you'd gotten used to it, right? Wrong. You never got used to it. The thing was to hide it from the others. And the only thing you could do to get rid of some of the rage and the despair and the disgust was to try and find the bastard and run him through the courts and into the slammer and hope the other bastards would take a healthy dislike to him and ram a broken-off broom handle up his anus as far as his throat and see how he liked it, the *bastard,* before those fucking bleeding-hearts paroled him after he'd served fifteen years of his life sentence—life, are you serious?—and sent him back onto the street to find another poor bitch and do it again. And again.

Bastard.

"Bernie?"

It was Woodcock. Only Woodcock could call him anything but "sir" when he was in a towering rage.

"I'll be there," Behrens said, and finished his reading, holding the paper as steady as he could.

Informant advises that a patrol unit was dispatched to the area at 3:07 in response to a call from Miss Tasha Fontaine, (no middle name), of Temple Mansions, Fifth Avenue, who reported hearing a scream. All items of clothing and possessions found at the scene were recovered by the Police Department and are on inventory. The undersigned locked the doors of the Medical Examiner's Ambulance at 4:32 A.M. this date.

6:05 A.M. B of I Tech Eberhart arrived at the Morgue and there took 15 B-and-W photographs and 6 color photographs of the decedent, Christine Courtney Wittendorf. Detective Woodcock called to report that at the time the body was removed from the scene a temperature reading of the soil was 51 degrees F.

Gordon J. Sikorsky (SAS)

When Behrens looked up and folded the sheet of paper, he saw that the girl in the tracksuit had stopped near one of the yellow tapes and was just standing watching.

He went over to see what Woodcock wanted.

"We file this, Bernie?"

It was pretty small, looked like something vegetable, maybe the remains of a flower petal, something like that. It was quite a way from where the body had been, twelve or thirteen feet, but between there and where they'd picked up the lost shoe, right in the same directional track.

"Oh, Jesus," Behrens said softly as his memory flashed him a clue from an earlier killing, eighteen months ago and right here in Central Park. "Oh, Jesus, yeah . . . yeah . . . And listen, Woody, the first thing you check when you're back at the base is whether the victim had any orchids sent to her recently, and when exactly, and who by—the works, you reading me?"

"Sure. Orchids? Sure, Bernie. And file this?"

"In the safe." The earlier case had broken before Woodcock was moved in to the Apple from Washington, D.C., so it wouldn't mean anything to him.

Behrens looked across at Baker, who was dropping another goddamn rubber into a goddamn bag, wasting his time, it was traces of semen in the grass they were hoping to find—sometimes the guy would jerk off after he'd killed,

when killing was the only way he could get it up. Clues
... clues ... clues ... was what Behrens needed, before
they dried up or got moved around by feet or buried in the
grass; once those yellow tapes were taken down they could
pack up and go home as far as any new physical evidence
at the crime scene was concerned.

But they'd be here all day, yeah, you bet, they'd sift
every single fuckin' blade of grass, till they were ready to
drop and he requested a change to the day shift so they
could follow this thing through. And he'd been hoping to
finish the house today. Forget it, there were more important
things.

She was still standing over there, the jogger with the
ponytail, and Behrens went slowly across to her, ducking
under a tape to keep clear of the killing area. She was older,
he saw now—it had been the cute little ponytail that had
given her the teenage image. Maybe thirty-four, thirty-five,
but still a head turner, look at those eyes. But the thing was,
she didn't look like a gawper; not often you saw women,
anyway, looking for a thrill like this one, blood still all over
the grass. So why was she here?

Then she told him, before he could ask.

"I heard the scream."

She watched him steadily.

"Oh. It was you who called in last night?"

"Yes."

"Fontaine," Behrens said. "First name Russian, right?
Tanya?" He'd asked the dispatcher who'd called—he always did; sometimes it was the killer himself, did it for the
thrill, wanted to see the pretty lights move in, hear the
sirens, all because of him.

"Tasha," the young woman said.

"Yeah. Tasha. That's nice. Temple Mansions, that right?"

"Yes." She went on watching him steadily, wanting
something from him, he thought. What would she want
that he had?

Behrens looked past her, across the trees and the Mall and the East Drive and Fifth Avenue to where Temple Mansions stood in the early-morning haze.

"How loud was it?" he asked the young woman. "The scream?"

"It sounded—quite desperate."

She wasn't looking past him to the mess on the grass; it held less for her than he did. "Oh. But how loud was it?"

In a moment she said, "It woke me up."

"I see." But it looked a long way from here to Temple Mansions. More than a half mile. It was something he'd have to check out.

"We didn't have anyone else call in," he said, "from places nearer than where you live. Nobody reporting a scream." He swung his body a little, taking in the buildings along Central Park West, a quarter of a mile from here, some of them less than that.

The woman, Tasha Fontaine—no middle name—didn't answer. Maybe she thought it wasn't a question. It was.

Did she really hear a scream, from that distance? Could be. But if not, had she imagined it? Right at the time when that poor bitch was getting herself screwed with a bread knife? Be a coincidence, oh, sure. But Behrens believed that life was a very complicated web, and that if you touched a part of it you set up a vibration that touched other things, other people, right up close or a thousand miles away, ten thousand. He'd never told anyone he believed this because they wanted to call it coincidence, and he didn't want to argue. When you know something is true, you don't need to argue about it, right?

"Woke you up," he said, in case it would draw her out a little bit.

She didn't come back with anything, so he asked her, "That was the only reason you dialed Emergency? Because you heard a scream?"

"Yes."

Okay. It could be true, but it didn't have to be. She could have known the victim, could have been, say, to a party with her, earlier last night, seen her with a new date, a guy acting possessive, aggressive, when they'd left there, could have been worried about her and finally woke up at three in the morning thinking she heard a scream, and called in. A long shot, sure, but take that *kind* of situation and pick out any one of a thousand permutations, the right one, and you'd have the killer.

Try one.

"How well did you know," Behrens asked, looking away, tongue prodding a hollow tooth, "Christine Wittendorf?"

And waited.

"Who?"

He looked back at her. "The victim."

"Was that her name?" She glanced behind him now at the mess on the grass.

"Yeah." He hadn't made a hit. He believed what Tasha Fontaine said. He didn't believe everybody he listened to, but he believed her.

"I didn't know her at all," she said.

Behrens tried again.

"Is this the first time you've been down here, since you heard the scream?"

"No. I came down here last night."

Hit.

"Oh," Behrens said. "Why?"

A siren went wailing along Central Park West. The town was waking up to its same sweet old refrain, and the heat haze was thickening between here and Temple Mansions. By noon you'd need another shirt. He went on waiting, watching Tasha Fontaine. She was taking her time.

"I don't know," she said at last. But didn't look down or away, trusted herself with him, trusted him with a silly answer.

And because of that, Behrens didn't turn on any heat,

didn't raise his voice. But he had to let her know he wanted to get it straight. "So you heard a scream or you thought you heard a scream at three o'clock in the morning and called Emergency but that wasn't enough for you, you had to put on a coat or whatever and come down here, half a mile, alone through a shark-infested area, to see what had happened. And you don't know why. Is that right? Miss Fontaine?"

Her body didn't move but she backed off with her eyes, upset, watching him warily now.

"Yes," she said, her mouth tight.

Learn from this, Bernie. She needs help. She's drowning, and all you can do is push her fuckin' head under? Mad at himself.

"Well I guess it's understandable," he said. "You called the police out, saw their lights moving in——" swinging his body to look across at Temple Mansions——"What floor are you on?"

"The third."

"The third," Behrens nodded. Low in the building, then, with all those trees in the way, a small forest of them in full leaf between here and Temple Mansions. Yeah, he'd have to check it out.

"What were you dreaming, can you remember? When the scream woke you?"

"What was I dreaming?" It was a strange thing to ask. In a moment, Tasha said, "I think it was about a taxi——a taxi, yes, in the rain." Then she got it——he thought she might have heard the scream in her sleep.

"Was it a nightmare? Something scaring you?"

"Look," she said, "that scream was real. I didn't just dream it up. And now we know who it was, don't we?" She glanced behind him again.

"Sure," Behrens said, "sure." He swung his body to look across at Temple Mansions again, swung it back. "What kind of work do you do, Miss Fontaine?"

"I run a fashion boutique."

"That's nice. I—"

"Why did you ask?"

She had questions, too. "I just wondered," he said, prodding his hollow tooth, "if I was keeping you."

She didn't look at her watch.

"No."

Still wanted something from him. It was tantalizing. And important.

Try another shot. "You didn't fall," he said, "for the reasons I thought up. Right? The reasons for you coming down here in the night?"

She took a while, looking down—which was rare—and toeing the grass with her small, expensive Nike. Then up, suddenly—"No."

"The thing is," Behrens said, "you really don't know what made you come down here, what"—he looked for the word he wanted—"what *compelled* you to come down here."

"No." The wide, attentive eyes watching him openly now, trusting him again. "No," she said, "I don't."

Getting close now, Behrens thought.

"And does it worry you? That you don't know?"

"Yes."

Straight off the bat. "Sure," he said, nodding slowly. "I can imagine that." He knew what she wanted from him now. She wanted to know if he was going to catch the guy. The guy who'd made all that mess on the grass behind him. She wanted that man caught, wanted it very badly.

Why?

Because, sure, he killed people, right? Yeah, but there was something more than that. And she didn't know what it was. And it worried her.

Oh, Jesus. He was hitting an absolute blank now. This was something new. With anyone else he would have taken them along to the precinct and put them in the interrogation room and kept them there until either they talked or he was pretty damn sure they didn't know anything. But there was no point doing that with Tasha Fontaine because she wanted to help him anyway, wanted badly to help him.

And didn't know how.

Or was too scared.

Another siren started wailing on the far side of the trees, bringing its joyous morning song to the newborn day.

Behrens pulled out his card and gave it to Tasha Fontaine. "If you feel like a cup of the worst coffee in town, here's where to find me."

She took the card, reading it, not just glancing at it, reading all of it, like it was important, maybe a straw she could clutch at when she was too tired to swim any further. That was his impression.

"Thank you," she said, and tucked the card into the pocket of her white-striped tracksuit. "And if you find who—" she broke off, glancing again across the grass behind him. "Anyway, I'll see it on the news, won't I?"

"You'll be the first to know," Behrens said. "I'll call you."

Three

C andie came on the intercom just after ten.
"It's Al Padolini."
"I'll talk to him," Tasha said.
"I was there!" He sounded aggrieved.

Tasha glanced across at the open page of her appointment book and saw *9:00—Al P. here.* "I'm sorry, Al, I got held up and couldn't call you." She'd stayed too long in the park talking with the police detective, and then forgotten her meeting.

"You're nice," Al said. "Other people don't apologize when they miss an appointment with me. They consider that since I'm trying to sell them something they don't need to have any manners. But it's fabulous. *Fabulous!*"

"They showed you the dress?"

"But of course. I said you wouldn't mind, because we need to hurry. You—"

"Look, Al, I'm still not sure, you know?" La Botica hadn't offered perfume before, and she still felt she should keep strictly to clothes. "I mean, if we do this, next we're into jewelery."

"So why not?"

"La Botica isn't a supermarket, is why not. I need a little—"

"Tasha, give me two minutes, okay? Then I'll get out of your life, at least for today."

She glanced over the rest of her appointments. There were only five important ones—society wives in from the Hamptons to look at the fall lines, two of them coming here together.

"Shoot," she told Al Padolini.

"You are an angel. And wise. Okay, I know you haven't offered perfume before at La Botica, but a lot of people are doing it and this is why. I tell you I can give you a perfume for a particular dress, so you tell me a perfume is for the body, for this particular customer's unique and peerless *body*—and that's absolutely right. So I say, sure, but you're not offering this perfume to complement the charm and the style of the *dress,* but the charm and style of the woman who has *chosen* it—or has had you choose it for her, since she can't always make up her mind. So—"

"Just a minute, Al." Tasha had heard the call-waiting tone, and pressed for Candie. "Who is it?"

"Mrs. van Cleef. Can she come tomorrow instead of today?"

Tasha turned the page of her appointment book. "Yes. In the afternoon, her choice of time."

"Okay."

"Sorry, Al."

He didn't miss a beat. "So what you are offering is not a perfume for the dress, but something to complement it—something *else* that will perfectly suit the woman who is buying it. Like shoes. What's the difference? Is she going to buy green shoes to go with her blue dress?"

Tasha realized she wasn't listening. Al Padolini's emphatic, persuasive voice had faded as another voice came in—Detective Behrens's.

How well did you know Christine Wittendorf?

Who?

The victim.

Was that her name?
Yeah.
I didn't know her at all.

But she did, Tasha remembered now. Not *known* her exactly—but she'd met her once, and only a few weeks ago, on the night of the pouring rain.

"Is she going to buy a simple little black cocktail dress," she heard Al's voice coming in again, "and splash on something sophisticated like Chanel No. 5? So this is the whole point, Tasha. She buys that absolutely *fabulous* Ralph Lauren I saw this morning for the fall and she needs the perfume to complement it. And you know what I'm going to create for you? Tasha?"

"I'm listening, Al."

She had met Christine Wittendorf on the night of the summer rainstorm, when Tasha had just got into the taxi outside Sabatini's and someone had brushed past the doorman and ducked her head in and said, "Could you take pity on a poor girl? I'm drowning!"

Only a few weeks ago . . . and Tasha remembered the extraordinary shock of recognition she'd felt as Christine Wittendorf had gotten in and given her a brilliant smile of thanks, the raindrops sparkling on her black velour coat and her perfume lacing the air—and then the smile had changed, as recognition had come into her eyes too, with a soft flash of surprise. For a moment they'd studied each other, then decided not to say anything because it might have been embarrassing.

"I will give you a soft, mellow top note," Tasha heard Al saying, "of guaiac wood and wallflower, nothing too floral, just a sense of nostalgia for the passing of the year. Then a middle note of fougère, but very discreet, to avoid any hint of masculinity—or maybe chypre, to make quite certain. And finally a base note of cyclamen and tuberose—and here we get the nostalgia, you see? The suggestion of falling leaves and early twilights, with finally the slightest touch of cedar to suggest wood smoke."

She would have told the detective, if that flash of memory had come to her at the time.

I didn't know her, but I met her once. She looks like me.

"Tasha?"

"Al," she said, "why don't you put that on paper and fax it to me? I know you're in a hurry to give me exactly what we need, so I'll check it out and call you back with a decision. Today. Deal?"

He ignored that. "And listen, Tasha, the idea is not for you to offer perfume at La Botica to make money. That would be cheap. The idea is to present the dress with panache, with a flourish, with a hint of its very essence floating on the air. And that will be expensive. But if it worries you, simply add the cost to the dress. We have to be practical." Tasha heard a sigh on the line. "I wish I could have hung on there and seen you this morning, Tasha, but I had to be at the airport. That's where I'm calling you from."

"We both had our problems, Al. And anyway, I can't concentrate when I'm talking face to face with handsome Italians—it would have been counterproductive."

"What can I say?"

"*Arrivederci!* And fax me."

Tasha hung up and sat for a moment, seeing the sparkle of raindrops on the black velour, the brilliant smile, and then the flash of recognition.

She looked like me. I look—I looked like her.

Christine Wittendorf.

The victim.

A new, official title for all that life with its brilliant smile and its husky, intimate voice. . . . "You've been an angel of mercy," she'd said when the taxi pulled up in Sutton Place. She was searching her purse in the faint rainy light, pulling out a twenty-dollar bill when Tasha stopped her, saying it was perfectly okay, and then there was the flashing smile again and Christine was gone, running up the steps to the house.

"What were you dreaming?" the detective had asked Tasha this morning. "Can you remember? When the scream woke you?"

"I think it was about a taxi—yes, a taxi, in the rain."

And Christine, she remembered now. Christine had been there. It was the second time she had dreamed about the girl in the black velour coat, her memory having been impressed by all that shimmering vitality, and by the quiet shock of recognition. Christine, her look-alike, the victim, as the detective had called her, as she would be called in the noon editions today, on the street in just an hour from now. The deceased . . . the dead woman . . . the late Christine Wittendorf . . . Whatever they called her, it had such a funereal ring.

Tasha pressed the intercom for Elizabeth Segal, her junior partner.

"In deep?"

"Shoot," Elizabeth said. "Or shall I come over?"

"Yes, if you like. It'll take a few minutes." Even as Tasha said it, she found herself surprised. At La Botica she had the reputation of making lightning decisions, but this was something else.

When Elizabeth came across the passage from her office Tasha already had the Milan file out of the drawer and on her desk.

"Sorry I wasn't here in time for Al this morning, but you showed him the Ralph Lauren, right?"

"Sure, no problem. He loved it—and wasn't faking." Elizabeth swung her long blond hair back, perching on the arm of a chair. "Traffic?"

"What?" Tasha looked up from the file, then down again. "Oh. Yeah, and I was talking to someone difficult to get away from."

Elizabeth said nothing, and Tasha heard the silence. It had sounded lame, she knew, and Elizabeth also knew that if the president of La Botica, Inc. was stopped on her way to work by someone difficult to get away from, she'd get away—no problem.

"Want some coffee?" Tasha asked.

"I'm fine." Elizabeth, lanky and fine-boned, a former model, swung a slender leg from her perch on the chair and waited. Tasha didn't normally take this long to get to the point.

"How about going to Milan on your own this time around?" Tasha asked at last, looking up.

Elizabeth lifted an eyebrow, the closest she ever got to registering surprise. "On my *own?*"

"Be great for you, don't you think? Great experience."

Elizabeth stirred her limbs just a very little. "Well, sure, I guess."

"I know it's short notice."

"I'm packed anyway. But what happened?"

"I have to go to a funeral."

"Oh." Elizabeth was concerned. "Anyone close?"

"Not really."

"Anyone I know?"

"No. Just a cousin." Tasha looked down; unused to lying, she found she couldn't meet Elizabeth's eyes. "I didn't know her well, but it's—kind of a family obligation for me to be there." And before she could change her mind she went on quickly—"And anyway you know the ropes and they'll be all the same people we met before, so you won't need introductions." She managed to keep her eyes on Elizabeth's at last. "You'll be a real hit—again. Remember Antonio?"

"Look," Elizabeth said, "I wouldn't be going to Milan on my own to get laid by Antonio. I'd be going there to find the best styles for us to invest in—for a whole season. It's a hell of a responsibility!"

Tasha let a couple of seconds go by, timing the coup de grace. Then she said quietly, "Chicken?"

"Of course not," Elizabeth said, and her cool blue eyes met Tasha's head-on.

Tasha handed her the file. "You know most of it, but here's the rest. I'll tell Candie to fix everything up for you, and we'll talk before you leave." She put on an encouraging smile. "And the weather's going to be a whole lot more bearable, now they shifted the date. Give my best to Pat Cromer—she'll be there for Bloomie's, with their president. I'll see you get a reservation for the *Vogue* party and a table at Granelli's for the first night. It'll be fun for you! Now get outa here before I change my mind."

Staring at the closed door after Elizabeth had gone, Tasha was aware that for the first time in her life she'd decided to do something without knowing why. She could hear Dad's voice, coming over the years: "You get an urge to do something, sweetheart, check it out first; and if it looks okay then you just go right ahead and do it, and to hell with what other people say."

And that was how she'd managed her life, right through college and into the fashion field, doing what she had an urge to do—once she'd checked it out and knew it was right—until at thirty-four she was head honcho at La Botica, one of the smallest but most exclusive, most expensive, most successful boutiques in New York.

How many times had she dropped an idea stone-cold because it hadn't checked out? Your guess, but it was in the hundreds. How many times had she gone right ahead with a project because it *had* checked out? Hundreds more. It had become part of her reputation. "Show it to Tasha," people said, "she'll check it out." She just told Al Padolini on the phone, "I'll check it out and give you a decision."

So this was a first, and she got up from her desk and walked around, looking at the big flashlight glossies thumbtacked onto the walls—*Tasha Fontaine of La Botica, New York, sharing a joke with Oscar de la Renta . . . Chatting with Yves Saint Laurent in the lobby of the*

Gallia . . . Deep into girl talk with Betsy Bloomingdale— looking at them and through them into the different kind of world she'd just walked into, where she'd stopped checking things out.

I have to go to a funeral.
Anyone I know?
No. Just a cousin.

Not even that. Not even a friend. Just someone she'd seen only once, talked to only once, in a taxi in the rain.

Christine.

Tasha turned away from the glossy photographs, going behind her peach colored fiberglass desk again and sitting down, because this was where she always worked things through.

How important was it that she went to Milan with Elizabeth? Not very. In fact, it was something that had been in her mind for a year or two now—one day letting her junior partner handle a big show on her own for the experience. Elizabeth was good at what she did, and could sometimes spot a really important dress before most other buyers had noticed it—before Tasha herself, more than once. And when Elizabeth walked into the showroom downstairs at La Botica to greet a customer with that breathtaking swing of the hips she'd learned on the runways, that customer would *not* leave the boutique without ordering something as close as she could get to whatever Elizabeth was wearing at the time. In the past six months they had sold three Ralph Laurens and two Armanis that way, totally unrehearsed.

So the time had come to push Elizabeth out of the nest and send her to Milan solo, right? Sure. Add to her experience, develop her authority, turn her into an even bigger asset to the firm. That alone was reason enough for Tasha's decision.

Plus, after a dozen shows in New York, Paris, and Milan, Tasha was finding the pace a little too wearing—the traditional *Vogue* party for a thousand fashion hounds and the show itself for double that number, people surging into the huge marquees like a football crowd with the noise of a first home win killing conversation dead in its tracks while the blizzard of flashlight sent you reaching for your sunglasses and the press fell over each other trying to crush your brand new python-skin Guccis if you were even a fraction slow with your footwork. . . . That was also reason enough to send Elizabeth to Milan.

So where was the problem?

There wasn't one, really. She had just made a decision before checking things out, that was all. Or maybe she *had* checked them out subconsciously, and the decision had simply leaped into her mind as a result.

Okay?

Tasha pressed the intercom for Candie. "Ask Joe to get me a copy of the first noon edition to hit the street, will you? I don't mind which paper."

She felt a stranger in a strange land, with the tall white candles burning on the high altar and the heavy scent of incense filling the air as the light fell from the stained-glass windows, coloring the silk of the altar cloth and spilling across the marble floor.

She had not been invited here. Not only a stranger, then, but an intruder. *The funeral is to be private,* it had been announced in the press two days ago.

It was a small church, tucked away between apartment buildings on the Upper East Side, and Tasha had apologized to the man in the dark suit—presumably an usher—who was guarding the door, telling him that a traffic accident had delayed her. He had let her through without a word, and she was now sitting behind the twenty or thirty mourners, halfway down the nave, with no one next to her. She was in a simple black dress, and this worried her, because most of the women had chosen colorful clothes, and it made her conspicuous. Maybe it had been at the suggestion of Christine Wittendorf's mother, who had just given a brief eulogy on her daughter's talents as a painter, "which had brought so much color into the lives of all who had known her." If that was why nearly all the women were wearing florals, Tasha admired Mrs. Wittendorf's courage in bringing some of that color even into her daughter's funeral service, despite the ghastly circumstances of her death.

As the final psalm ended, Tasha heard weeping from the front rows, and the voice of the priest rising above it.

"Now shall we vouchsafe our respects and our undying love for Christine, whose memory will live on in our hearts forever." He turned to look down at the front row on the left, and a silver-haired woman, beautifully coiffed, rose from her pew and walked slowly toward the casket, holding the hand of the man beside her.

As Tasha stood and followed the tail end of the mourners, she was surprised and disturbed by a feeling almost of eagerness, of impatience to look again upon the face of the young woman she had last seen in the taxi on the night of the rain, and as she stood gazing down at last into the open casket she was aware that even the muted sounds around her, of weeping and the shuffling of feet, had fallen away into silence, leaving her removed from everything else, isolated in the presence of the woman lying so peacefully among the flowers, still so much alive to Tasha that they could almost have greeted each other again.

"Could you take pity on a poor girl? I'm drowning!"

In the stillness of everything, in this strange other-world silence, Tasha looked down at the face of Christine beneath its heavy veil, seeing it not as it must look now, despite the work of the cosmeticians, but as she had seen it before, the eyes soft and shimmering, the skin flushed with life, the smile sudden, brilliant.

"You've been an angel of mercy . . . " Her voice came

quite clearly in the stillness, low and a little husky, confiding, almost intimate.

"You're very welcome," Tasha said quietly on an impulse, and felt her lips moving as if she were speaking aloud—as maybe she was. "It was nice meeting you. . . . " And as the stillness began breaking up she heard someone coughing discreetly—the priest, she supposed—and realized that all the other people were filing out of the church, leaving her alone with Christine. But she lingered still, her eyes drawn to the card on a small bouquet of gardenias nestling among the other flowers.

To Christine, from Tasha.

Then the voice of the priest broke in. "She'll be sorely missed," he said, his head bowed, trying to give her comfort, Tasha supposed, with an appropriate platitude.

She didn't answer, but turned away and followed the others out of the church and into the bright heat of the day.

Four

A private reception, the newspapers had announced, *will be held immediately following the funeral service, at the home of the deceased.*

It was more like a one-woman show, Tasha thought as she looked around her, with pictures everywhere, some mounted on easels, most hanging from the walls, and all of them with the same signature in the bottom-right-hand corner: *Christine.*

Tasha had arrived late again, having grabbed a taxi round the corner from the church and gone first to La Botica, slipping out of the black afternoon dress and choosing a new Claude Montana with a colorful flower theme, so that she now looked less conspicuous.

And, once again, she was a stranger here, an intruder. The policeman on the sidewalk had given her a steady appraisal as she'd gone up the flight of steps to the house, but hadn't stopped her.

The house itself was beautiful, judging by the great high-ceilinged entrance hall where everyone was gathered. The white-on-white decor and molded paneling made a perfect background for the paintings, bringing their colors out with an almost three-dimensional effect. The address hadn't been in the papers, of course, but Tasha had found the house easily enough, remembering it from the night when she had dropped Christine off in the taxi on Sutton Place—the mullioned windows, the two bronze lions on each side of the steps, the row of small box shrubs that on that night had been glistening in the rain.

This was the room Christine had entered . . . that was the door she had come through when she'd hurried up the steps from the sidewalk as the taxi had driven away. . . .

Tasha felt a shiver as she thought of it, looking around her at the things that Christine's eyes had seen, at the people she'd known so well. It was as if Tasha hadn't driven away in the taxi after all, but had paid off the driver and followed Christine up the steps and into the house—into the house and into a different life, caught up suddenly in some kind of time-warp, reincarnated into this other-world that was Christine's.

Okay. A fantasy is a fantasy. They too make the world go round, along with the other things.

"Would you care for something to drink, madam?"

"Not right now, thank you."

She wanted to concentrate on exploring this new other-world, getting to know the people in it, the people who'd known Christine. The woman over there with the elegant ash-white coiffure would be her mother; she'd been the first of the mourners in the church to rise when the priest had invited them to view the casket. She was standing near the huge Adam fireplace, taking people's hands in both of hers as she spoke to them, a warmth in her face and a light in her eyes that would have been impossible, Tasha thought, in someone of less courage. Or maybe Mrs. Wittendorf was going through the first stage of grief—denial—convinced that with all these colorful pictures in the room Christine would make her entrance from the curving staircase at any moment.

Oh God, how must it *feel* to people like this? To be faced

suddenly with the truth of *their* new world, where there was now just an empty space where someone they had loved used to be? She'd been helping to make the arrangements, this brave, elegant woman, for Christine's trip to Europe, or her birthday party, or whatever, and then the telephone had rung at four o'clock in the morning, just a few days ago, and she'd heard a formal, toneless voice on the line: *"Do you have a daughter named Christine?"*

How did they survive, the survivors?

That would be . . . her brother, over there? Mrs. Wittendorf was comforting him, her arm around his shoulders, her eyes brilliant with unshed tears. And the older man standing near her would be . . . Christine's father? Not holding a drink but just standing there, his handsome face pale and drawn and his eyes hidden, looking at nobody, wishing they'd all go, wishing to God they'd all go.

Tasha turned away suddenly, not wanting to watch them, to watch their grief. It was too intimate, too private; she was a stranger here. And, in turning, she saw a short, softly lit passage off the entrance hall with another staircase leading upward, much narrower, maybe for the staff. There was nobody near, so she went along there as far as the stairs, looking upward for a moment, hesitating, then climbing them, telling herself that if anyone came along she'd say she was looking for a bathroom.

The passage at the top of the stairs had small silk-covered lamps glowing along the walls, even though hazy sunshine was in the windows. Maybe another sign of Mrs Wittendorf's denial? There must be lights everywhere in the house, no shadows, no depression?

All the doors were closed, and Tasha went on past them, her feet making no sound on the rich white carpeting until she reached the end of the passage, where a landing opened out onto the grand staircase she'd seen below in the entrance hall. And here was a door that was unlike the rest, and she stopped. It looked just the same, with its molded paneling and its heavy gold handle in the form of a lever, also molded with a pattern of leaves; it was different, Tasha knew without even thinking about it, only in her mind.

Because this was Christine's room.

Are you sure?

Oh, yes . . . yes.

How can you be sure?

I just know.

Subdued voices came from below where the guests were gathered. No one was coming up the staircase. In the other direction the passage was also deserted, a perspective of soft shaded lights.

She put her hand on the heavy gold lever, found the door unlocked, and went quickly inside, closing it after her.

Christine's room, yes . . . with her presence everywhere, in the colorful drapes and the pictures on the wall, in the glowing rose-pink bedspread with its abstract floral theme, in the long ivory-white dressing table with its silk-shaded lamps, her face suddenly in the mirror as Tasha went across to it and stared at herself . . . at Christine.

Could you take pity on a poor girl? I'm drowning!

Her low, husky voice came softly into the silence, and Tasha stood very still, hardly breathing as she felt herself being drawn farther, so much farther into the other-world that was this other woman's, watching the face—their face—in the mirror, their eyes meeting, their mouth parted as if about to speak.

You've been an angel of mercy.

The flashing smile, then her black velour coat flying as she ran up the steps to the door . . . to the door down there in the entrance hall, where Tasha herself had come in a few minutes ago.

This room was where Christine had slept, where she had sat at the dressing table here on this silk brocade stool, brushing her hair, watching herself in the mirror, thinking, only a few weeks ago, how odd it was that she looked so like the young woman in the taxi who'd given her a lift home in the rain . . . the young woman who sat here now on the silk brocade stool, picking up the same silver-backed brush and drawing it through her hair as the two images merged, their lives coming together again, this time for longer . . . maybe forever . . . as the room held still, embracing them in its silence as the brush whispered through their long, dark hair in the mirror, here on the stool and in the mirror, whispering . . .

A soft sound came and Tasha started, whirling around, watching the door, watching its long gold handle, expecting it to move, for the door to open, for a voice to ask her, *What are you doing here?*

But nothing happened . . . nobody came . . . and she let out her breath, looking around the room and seeing one of the white filmy curtains moving a little, just a very little, as if stirred by a breeze. Her scalp was drawn tight as she watched the curtain become still, so still that she wondered if it had ever moved; but there'd been that soft sound a moment ago . . . Was there a cat in here?

Of course not . . . I hate cats, I always have.

Tasha tensed as the voice came, so softly that again she wondered if she'd really heard it.

She should be going. Her nerves were acting up in this room, giving her weird ideas. Yet she longed to stay just a few more minutes; she would never come here again.

Among the things on the dressing table was a low silver bowl, near the telephone, with some business cards in it, and she took one out. MAISON DE JACQUES, HAIR STYLISTS. The address was Park Avenue and 55th, not too far from here. She drew out another one. QUALITY LIMO SERVICE, BY VINCE FISHER. TWENTY-FOUR HOUR, SPECIAL WEEKEND RATES. Just over on the West Side, on Columbus Avenue. The next one was from a beautician's: *ANGEL FACE.* MASSAGE, MUD PACKS, REVITALIZATION THERAPY. On Madison, near St. Pat's.

Tasha read them twice, three times, committing them to

memory before she dropped them back into the bowl and got up from the stool, moving around the light, airy room and sometimes touching things—a small photograph of Christine in a silver frame, a brocade cushion on the window seat, a crimson scarf draped across the back of a chair near the door.

The sounds from below in the house seemed louder now, or she imagined it—maybe it was a warning for her to go before someone found her here. She picked up the scarf from the chair and moved to the door, surprised to find something in her hand but paying it no attention, pushing it into her purse and opening the door carefully, ready to explain herself if there were anyone in the passage—she was looking for a bathroom and became a bit desperate when she couldn't see an open door . . .

But nobody was there, and she went along the passage to the narrow stairs, going down them with the knowledge dawning on her of what she'd just done, something quite outrageous, totally inexcusable as a guest in this gracious house.

That was stealing.

The stairs creaked under her feet.

No, I—I just felt attracted to it, and she won't ever know.

Robbing the dead.

Oh, God, it's nothing like that, you don't understand.

She hurried now down the narrow stairs, reaching the short, softly lit passage and seeing people in the hall at the end, people talking, holding their drinks, ordinary civilized people who knew how to behave in someone else's house.

Don't worry. It's yours now . . . I wanted you to have it.

Not the voice of her conscience this time; a different voice, less than a whisper, just a vibration in the air, in the mind, and as Tasha heard it—or thought she heard it—she stopped dead and leaned with her shoulders to the wall of the passage, tilting her head back and shutting her eyes for a minute, wondering if she were going to pass out—because she hadn't imagined that voice in her head; it had come from someone else, from the only person it could have come from, and that was crazy, she'd better get out of here, get out of this house, run down the steps and away and away as fast as she could before anything, anyone could come after her.

"Can I help you, madam?"

Tasha leaned away from the wall, turning her head. It was one of the maids on her way to the hall, a tray of canapés in her hands.

"No, I—I'm fine. I was just . . . resting."

"It's been a real shock," the maid nodded, "for all of us."

"Yes." Tasha let her go by and then followed her, joining the others, the ordinary civilized people who didn't steal.

"Would you care for something, madam?"

"What? Yes, is that scotch?"

"Yes, madam. Chivas Regal."

Tasha took the glass, felt more herself, standing with a drink in her hand like the other people, one of them again, almost. Then she drank, letting a whole shot go down because she needed it.

Don't worry. You just wanted something to remember me by.

Christ, these voices in her head. Was she going crazy? Was this how it happened? You started hearing things?

Tasha moved around, restless, listening to the snatches of talk, noticing that one or two people did a double take when they saw her, because she looked so like Christine, of course, Christine suddenly among them, back from the dead, she wasn't surprised they looked at her twice. Then she found a quiet corner below the great staircase, and saw a small picture on the wall, tucked away and not much thought of, apparently, a self-portrait by Christine, clumsily framed—the mat was too big. But Tasha couldn't look away from it, until suddenly she heard another voice—this time a real one, thank God.

"She didn't like it."

Tasha turned, seeing a young woman with large, attentive eyes and a mass of coppery hair, a drink in her hand.

"She didn't?"

"No. But I told her not to throw it away. It'll sell, one day."

"Are you with her gallery?"

"No. But I know them, of course."

"Are you British?" Tasha asked. She needed to talk, to feel normal again, and she'd caught the accent.

"English."

"There's a difference?"

"It's just more specific. If you're British you could be English, Irish, Scottish, or Welsh. But regardless of all that, I'm Audrey Symes."

Tasha guessed this woman would have a generous smile, if she weren't still in shock. "I'm Tasha Fontaine."

"I know." She watched Tasha with interest, never looking away; but it wasn't a stare.

"You know?"

"You've been pointed out to me. La Botica?"

"Yes."

"I'd go there, but I'm unwisely faithful to a Russian refugee who moved here from London. She doesn't know the designers."

"I think she does," Tasha said dutifully. "Vivienne Westwood?"

"Yes, darling, but not one of her best."

"It looks charming on you."

"You're so nice."

Tasha turned back to the picture on the wall. The Englishwoman looked striking enough, with all that coppery hair, but Vivienne Westwood clothes were always a bit eccentric. "Why didn't Christine like her self-portrait?" she asked. "It's a fine little painting."

In a moment Audrey said, "One day I'll tell you. Yes, it's fine enough work, but of course there's so much more to a painting than the paint."

Tasha looked around, and saw there was nobody close. She felt a generosity in this woman that made it worth taking a risk. "Look, I know this isn't her gallery, but . . . you say you know them."

"George Fabius. He's over there. It was his idea, bringing all these paintings across for the reception—I think it saved Marjorie her sanity, turned the whole thing into a celebration of Christine's talent instead of a wake."

Marjorie, Tasha thought, would be Mrs. Wittendorf. She was suddenly terrified of making a slip: this was a private reception for relatives and close friends, and she was a stranger here and knew almost nothing about Christine or her family. A stranger, an intruder, and a thief.

Don't think about it. She said she wanted me to have it. "She's brave," she told the Englishwoman. "Marjorie."

"She's in shock, darling."

"We all are."

"Yes." Audrey Symes was watching her with a certain curiosity, Tasha noticed. "Christine kept you rather a secret, didn't she?"

"A secret?"

"I haven't seen you around, like her other friends." Then in case that sounded too curious she went on quickly, "But then she was like that, wasn't she? So many different lives."

"I—hadn't known her long."

"It's not my business anyway, darling." A perfectly manicured hand with freckles on the back touched Tasha's arm and then withdrew. "Now as to the picture . . . you mean you want it?"

"Yes."

Audrey turned casually, glancing across the crowd. "I can get it reserved for you, if you like."

"I'd really appreciate that." The risk had been worth

taking, of fetching a cool rebuff—this wasn't, as she'd said herself, a gallery.

"I'll talk to George," Audrey said, and something like a smile moved her mouth. "I told you it'd sell one day, didn't I?"

"I can't think why no one's bought it already."

Audrey looked as if she weren't going to reply, then said quietly, "Christine didn't like it because she didn't like herself, as I'm sure you know. And that comes through in the painting. But I'm glad it works for you. Leave it to little Audrey." It was then that Tasha realized that someone had come up to them from behind her and was standing quite close, because Audrey exclaimed suddenly, "Fido—I didn't expect you here!"

"I gate-crashed."

"Couldn't keep away?"

"I guess that's it, yeah."

"Fido, this is Tasha Fontaine. La Botica."

"Oh," he said, turning to look at her. "Fido Hamilton." He went on watching her intently, his eyes dark and serious, a lock of black hair curled across his forehead, his mouth expressionless, his breath smelling of scotch. "Is that a gallery?"

"Oh, God, Fido," Audrey said, "you're so terribly one-track-minded. La Botica is one of the *really* important boutiques in New York."

"I see," he said, and looked away from Tasha at last, swinging his dark head to gaze at Audrey. "I'm not hanging in there very well, as you notice."

"Most of us have had a drink too much, darling, don't worry."

"I mean Christ, it would've been quite bad enough, but happening the way it did . . . "

"The crunch is going to come," Audrey said quietly, "when we all sober up and suddenly realize it's true." She watched Fido downing his drink, waited a moment and then took his glass from him and put it onto a side table. "As soon as you like, we'll creep out by the back way and I'll put you into a taxi."

"What?" He swung his head to gaze at Tasha again, and she felt the tension rise, as it had before when he'd looked at her: he was so intense. "Are you leaving too?" he asked her.

The question was totally out of context, she thought, but then he'd had a bit too much to drink. Or was he picking her up? At a place like this, a time like this?

"Someone's coming for me," she said.

"Oh."

"Fido," Audrey cut in, "let me take your mind off things for a moment. Tasha wants the little self-portrait. Be an angel and tell George."

"Who?"

"George *Fabius,* darling."

"No, I mean who wants——" Then he turned to Tasha, his dark eyes taking their time to focus. "*You* want the picture? Tasha, right? Is that spelled the Russian way?"

"Yes."

He nodded slowly, looking back at Audrey. "Itsh——it shall be done."

"Wonderful," Audrey said, "and now I'm going to smuggle you out through the back——"

"No," he said with sudden firmness. "I'll be okay. But you know what? If they ever catch that *bastard* I'm going along there to smash him up. Smash"——his voice broke suddenly and he squeezed his eyes shut——"*smash him up,* like he did with *her.*"

"We all feel like that, Fido."

For a few seconds he didn't answer, just stood there hunched over with his face clenched in a grimace, then nodded his head, once, twice, three times, and opened his eyes and looked at Audrey again. "I know . . . I know . . . Smash him up." His head swung to look at Tasha, his red eyes blank now, as if he'd never seen her before. "I'm glad—glad to have met you. Excuse me."

Audrey made to follow him but he waved her back. "Fido," she said, "you're not driving, are you?"

"What? Christ, no. Taxi."

They watched him go down the short passage past the stairs, bumping the wall only once; then Audrey turned to Tasha. "Christine's current boyfriend, darling." She flinched slightly. "I mean her latest, last, whatever. Marjorie thought he was too wild for her, and wouldn't acknowledge him; that's why he had to gate-crash. But they were all pretty wild, weren't they? Or perhaps you wouldn't know. Anyway, he's at the Fabius Gallery, as you've gathered. He's not always like that." She was watching Tasha with her large amber eyes. "You're holding up rather well, darling. Thank God someone is."

"I hadn't known her long."

"Oh yes, that's right. Well then, you were lucky. To have known her, and not for long."

Tasha didn't know what she meant, but left it. "I have to get back to the boutique," she said.

The longer she stayed here the more she was aware of being an intruder, an impostor, feeling nothing of the grief these people had come here to share. Stranger, intruder, impostor, thief . . . wasn't there a nursery rhyme that went something like that?

"All right, darling," she heard Audrey saying, "trot along any time to the gallery and it'll be there waiting for you. It's on Park Avenue and 79th. I'll phone them tomorrow, in case poor Fido forgets about it—he's pretty cut up, as you saw." She let a warm hand rest on Tasha's sleeve for a moment. "I do hope I'll see you again."

Moving carefully through the crush of people to the great fireplace, where Marjorie Wittendorf was still standing, Tasha saw Hanif Khattak, who also had an apartment in Temple Mansions; but she didn't stop to speak; they'd never formally met, had only greeted each other going through the lobby or jogging in the park.

What should she say, then, to Christine's mother? When she left Audrey Symes, she had wanted to explore the entrance hall and find another way out, so as not to attract attention; then the idea had soured suddenly in her mind. She was a stranger and an intruder and all those other unpleasant things, but at least she could leave here with a show of dignity instead of creeping furtively away with her face hidden, like a pariah. Marjorie Wittendorf wouldn't recognize her, had never seen her before; but that wouldn't register, the way she was feeling right now.

You have my deepest sympathy?

Too formal, too trite.

I'm so sorry . . . it's been terrible for you.

Sure, but Marjorie knew that, better than anyone, didn't need telling.

Okay, then, don't rehearse anything, just be natural—and suddenly her hand was in both of Marjorie Wittendorf's and she was looking into the endless pain of her deep, haunted eyes and saying simply, "She'll always be with us, for as long as we go on loving her." So as not to burden the poor woman with the obligation to reply, she turned quickly away and squeezed through the people again toward the vestibule. Waiting impatiently for the butler to open the door for her, she went down the steps to the sidewalk, turning along it and hurrying through the heat of the day in a hopeless attempt to escape the new and frightening world that had begun to close around her like a trap.

Five

S hit, Bernie!" **Woodcock** said. "Haven't you got a home?"

Behrens looked up from the mess of pizza crusts and empty soup cans and Styrofoam cups on his desk and looked at Woodcock as if he'd forgotten who the hell he was.

The digital clock on the wall read 2:36 and the building was night-shift quiet. "Sure," he said, "it's right here."

Detective Woodcock kicked a chair over and sat on it the wrong way 'round, his arms along the back. "You look like shit," he said.

"Well, that could be," Behrens said, "because I feel like shit."

Woodcock rocked on his chair, his own eyes baggy with lack of sleep. "We'll get a break, Bern. Anytime now."

"They announce that on the P.A.?"

Woodcock let it go. They were already four days into the investigation of Case #H9073 and they had come up with nothing, zilch, zero. Most of the cases went down inside of twenty-four hours, for the simple reason that most of the cases involved drug dealers, drug addicts, transients, enraged husbands, enraged boyfriends, drunks, freaks, and fruitcakes, who wouldn't even begin to know how to cover up what they did when the first simple question was put to them and they lied with all the experience of a backward two-year-old and blew their story to shit.

But this one—the Wittendorf case—was sticking.

The whole department had been seething for these past four days because the victim had been a pretty young woman and she had been left out there in Central Park looking like she'd been put through a power lawn-mower, and it had got to everyone. The only thing that could have got them boiling their blood hotter than this was if it had been a kid.

"Want some pizza?" Behrens asked.

"I already ate."

"When?"

"I forget."

"So what are you doing back here, this time of night?"

"Checking if you need a coffin yet. You look like you died."

Behrens knocked back the coffee dregs in the last of his foam cups and dropped it onto the pile in the basket. "There's a technique," he said, scratching his two-day stubble, "by which one can make a fellow human being feel good, feel restored, feel reborn, even, just when he's ready to cut his throat." He looked at his fingernails, saw they were black with accumulated grime, and thought what a rich source of physical evidence they'd make. "I don't think, Detective Woodcock, that you have mastered that technique."

"But I can spit real good." Woodcock flicked his eyes up at the clock. "For Christ's sake, Bernie!"

Woodcock, younger, less seasoned but still good, was making out pretty well as the senior detective's assistant, otherwise Behrens would have kicked him all the way down the stairs; but sometimes, just sometimes, Woodcock found he had to act like a fucking mother to this guy when he went on working till he dropped. You didn't get cases to go down like that; all you did was kill yourself.

"If you're going to stay here any length of time," Behrens said, "say, like three seconds, you will please close your trap and leave it that way. You're disturbing the peace of my private little corner of heaven."

This was worse, Woodcock thought, than when Bernie used a four-letter word six words out of five. That meant he was in a towering rage. When Behrens lowered himself to facetiousness he was in the mood to kill with his bare hands.

They'd been all through this case; they'd been all through it three or four times. They'd pulled in some of the creeps who'd been standing around out there near the scene that night getting a hard-on sniffing at the blood and they'd thrown them into the interrogation rooms and listened to their lies: *I never saw nothin'—Shit, man, can't a guy walk through the park anymore?—Who, me? I'm a churchwarden, for Chrissake!* And they'd turned them loose again.

They'd listened to thirteen—so far—of the usual false-confession freaks, some of them just wanting to play around with the NYPD so they could tell their pals how stupid they made the cops look, some of them wanting to get close to that cute little gal they'd seen in the papers, even though she was now a stiff under the ground—or maybe *because* she was now a stiff under the ground—and some of them so depressed by the way their life was going that they felt as bad as if they'd done this terrible thing, weren't sure whether they did it, but were sure that if they did it they deserved the chair.

They'd sat here, he and Bernie and the rest of the squad, reading the labels on the evidence bags and sifting over the samples sent here from the autopsy room after the DNA and blood-typing was done—caked, blackened panties and shoes and human hair and nail scrapings and samples of turf—and they'd come up with nothing, because they needed someone else's blood and DNA for comparison, and there hadn't been a trace of semen around, none in the vagina, none on the clothes, none on the turf, because this dude hadn't done it for a straight sex thrill, he'd done it at the urge of a hate so fierce he couldn't live with it unless somebody died. They knew *that* much about him.

They'd found out from the lab and a professor of microbiology that the shred of vegetable matter Woodcock had found on the grass at the scene was indeed the remains of a flower petal—from an orchid, to be precise—and they'd asked the victim's mother if they could bring away the eleven orchids they'd seen in the victim's suite at the house in Sutton Place, and decided that Christine Wittendorf might have taken one of them for a buttonhole when she'd gone out that night. They were still working the nearest fifty florists in the area to find out which one of them had delivered a dozen orchids and who had ordered them.

They'd reopened the file on the Marianne Cleaver killing in a different area of Central Park two years ago and looked at the other similarities: Cleaver had been in her early thirties, very attractive, had long dark hair, was an artist—in her case, a minor composer—and had been sent a dozen orchids the day before she was slain—and slain in the same way, with a show of rabid, insensate violence.

And now they were waiting for a break, and Bernie Behrens was sitting here looking like a zombie, up to his neck in cold, greasy pizza and cold, muddy coffee and a degree of frustration that was pushing his systolic pressure up to the 200 mark, sitting still.

"I wanna go home now, Bernie," Woodcock said. "We both go home now, okay?"

"People would talk."

Behrens looked at the beat-up Timex clock on his desk, next to the photograph of Christine Wittendorf he'd asked her mother to lend him. He needed it there to remind him how young she'd been, how pretty she'd been, and how dead she was; to keep his rage on the burn, because when the rage was there he could sometimes leap and find answers. But Woody was right: on the Timex it was 2:20 already. He'd never get the house finished today, either. Would he ever get it finished? Yeah, maybe Sunday—just do the finishing touches.

Detective Woodcock watched Detective Behrens in the silence of the squad room under the bright dead stare of the tubular lamps, wondering why he did this to himself when there was a case come up that wouldn't leave him alone. Bernie needed a wife, for Christ's sake, someone to be there at home for him, someone to cook for him and get his stomach off this diet of cholesterol-free homogenized reconstituted crap, someone to chew his ass when he got home late and wouldn't take time off Sundays to see a movie or drive out to Coney Island or somewhere.

"Bern?"

Behrens looked up from his files.

"You got to go get yourself married," Woodcock said.

"It's funny you should say that." Behrens nodded. "I already decided to call Michelle Pfeiffer first thing tomorrow, see if she's free. But then again, maybe she can't cook."

"You marry Michelle Pfeiffer, you'd wanna take time off to eat?"

Behrens went back to his files.

He had a face, Woody thought, that looked like you'd slipped a latex mask over it that was just a tad too big, so it left a whole lot of very fine wrinkles. Maybe that was what the gals went for—it made him look kind of weathered, experienced in life, knew the ropes, how to look after himself, look after other people; also it made him look like he'd suffered, and that would turn most women on, bring out the mother in them. A good half-dozen chicks had tried to get him into a church already; but like Bernie said, he'd never wish the life of a cop's wife on any woman, so he just dated them till they got tired of screwing and him never buying them a ring. And maybe it was that, too, that appealed to them—they'd like to marry the kind of guy that wouldn't wish the life of a cop's wife on any woman, so it went 'round in circles and got nowhere.

"Have we got anything yet," Woodcock asked, his arms along the back of the green steel government-issue chair, "from the NCIC?" As a routine, they'd given the National Crime Information Center a rundown on the Wittendorf case, see if they could match the killing-pattern with anybody on their files nationwide.

"Not yet," Behrens said.

"Maybe they won't have anything for us."

"Maybe they won't." Behrens went back to his files, picked up a small sheet of paper that had got in among them, glanced at it and dropped it into his wastebasket on top of the stained Styrofoam cups.

Woodcock leaned across and took it out and looked at it, because anything Bernie Behrens did, he wanted to know about—anything he did, said, thought of, looked at and filed or looked at and threw away, Woody wanted to be in on, because that was how he would one day, maybe, get to be half as good, okay, one-tenth as good, maybe, as this dude, who had brought down the Klansky case, with the hairless head found in the laundromat dryer, the Lamarr case, with the 911 call saying there were maggots crawling down the electric lamp wire from the ceiling and a funny smell upstairs, and the Hamilton Bettenheimer III case, with the victim anus-impaled on the gearshift of his $240,000 Lamborghini Diablo in the twelve-car garage of Sheik Ismail M'Barka's mansion in Bay Shore, Long Island—and all three cases within two months, with no witnesses and no more physical evidence than you could shove up a prosecuting attorney's nose.

Looking at the bit of paper Behrens had thrown away,

Woodcock saw it was just a memo from Captain Cascioli, saying the Commissioner wanted to know when Detective Behrens "considered it likely" he was going to wrap up the Wittendorf case, which explained why Bernie had dropped it into the wastebasket, because he wasn't in the mood right now to take that kind of crap from the Commissioner or anyone else. The law in the Homicide Department—and it was sacrosanct—was that the first gold badge on the scene of a killing was the primary detective and henceforth in exclusive charge of the case, and everybody else had better keep away from him if they had any ambition to doing anything except kiss his ass, from the squad supervisor right on up through the shift commander and the captains and the colonels to the Commissioner himself. They better leave him alone, because this was *his* body, and he wouldn't be finished with it until he was ready.

"You know something?" Behrens said as he slapped the file shut at last. "I think we oughta go home."

"Well, now, Detective Behrens, let's not be hasty about doing a thing like that. They find you goofing off after only seventeen hours on the shift and they might—"

"Something I need to do first, though." Behrens said, and dropped the file into a drawer and slammed it shut. "So why don't you go hit the sack?"

Woodcock got off the chair and shoved it against the wall. "So what is it you need to do?"

"Something I didn't get time to check on before." Behrens looked around the desk and saw it wasn't in the kind of condition he could fix in less than six months and decided not to start now.

He was on his way to the door when Woodcock asked him, "Where are we going?"

"It wouldn't interest you."

"Fuck, Bern, we use the same car, or what?" Bernie liked teasing him like this, playing the tight-mouthed private eye.

Behrens turned and hung a sagging, red-eyed face on

him. "You wanna come along, okay, the way we fix it is you meet me on the front steps of Temple Mansions"— he checked his watch—"in twenty minutes—say, three o'clock."

"Hide the car?"

"That isn't necessary. Just don't pick up a ticket for me to fix."

Woodcock took off before Bernie could change his mind.

Making his way through the hall, Behrens stopped at the sergeant's desk and picked up the phone and called the Central Park precinct. "Behrens, Homicide. Look, I need a policewoman, thirty to thirty-five, medium build, to go to the concessions building in the park with her partner, no codes, soon as possible. Can you send one out or find one rolling, whatever? Then patch me in and I'll tell her what I want her to do." He gave them the mobile number of his Buick Regal and hung up.

At this hour there was almost zero traffic—and most of it cabs—along Park Avenue in the vicinity of Temple Mansions; the air was cooler than it had been for several nights, Behrens thought, as he got out of his car and walked the fifty yards to the steps where Woodcock was waiting for him.

"We expecting somebody, Bern?"

"Yeah." Behrens found his eyes were having difficulty focusing as he stared across at the massed trees of the park. "I told Michelle I'd meet her here."

"Michelle who?"

"Pfeiffer. She said she was free."

Woodcock hunched his neck into his jacket, annoyed with himself for having missed the trick—but shit, he was rocking on his feet.

The night, Behrens thought, was as still as he'd ever

known it, just these few cabs rolling past, a tug hooting on the East River, a couple of sirens wailing far away among the tall glass canyons. Nearer, some cats fought. Then it was over, and one of them came loping past with its black head turning furtively left and right—you couldn't ever figure out a cat, Behrens thought; they ran their own game through the night.

He stood there prodding his hollow tooth.

Woodcock was keeping his mouth shut, didn't want any more tricks he'd be too tired to catch. All he wanted was sleep, the deep, dark drowning of the mind and then nothing—wanted it more than a woman.

Another cab came rolling by, saw them standing there and slowed, the driver's face at the open window turning slowly like a whore's, looking for business.

Woodcock moved his feet, and Behrens wondered if he was going to speak. He didn't want that; he wanted to listen, to hear the stillness, and anything else there might be.

It was 3:11 when his beeper sounded and he shut it off and started down the steps to the sidewalk.

"We can go now," he told Woodcock.

"Where to?"

"The sack."

"So what happened?"

"Nothing," Behrens said as they walked to their cars. "Nothing, anyway, that we could hear. Unless you heard anything?"

"When?" There was just one thing Woodcock hated about this guy, and that was when he played this fucking cat-and-mouse thing with him. He didn't always do it—it wasn't a routine with him; he only did it when he was pissed off with himself and needed to take it out on other people.

"Huh?" Behrens asked him.

Woodcock said in a tone of murderous patience, "Did I hear anything when?"

"In the last eleven minutes. You hear anything while we were standing there on the steps?"

"Traffic. A tug on the river. Cats fighting."

"Nothing else?"

"Like what?"

"I'm not going for that, Woody. I tell you like what, and you'll start thinking you heard it." He opened the door of his Buick Regal.

"Shit, Bernie, give it to me, will you? In the past eleven minutes I heard *nothing* that got my ears in an uproar, okay? So what were we meant to hear?"

Behrens got into his car, and the extra weight brought the corner of the door down onto the high curb of the sidewalk, and Woodcock leaned his back to the Buick and heaved, so Behrens could get the door shut. He knew the trick: he'd done it before—this wreck was clean out of springs.

"What I did was," Behrens said, looking up at Woodcock through the open window, "I had a policewoman go out there to the crime scene just now and scream her head off, and you didn't hear it, and neither did I. You remember the woman I was talking to that morning when you were collecting condoms?"

"The jogger?"

"Yeah. The one that called Emergency and got us out there. Lives in Temple Mansions, where we were standing just now. She said she heard a scream from the park, woke her up, that was why she called in." He watched Woody's face through the open window. "Her apartment's on the third floor, not high enough to clear all those trees in a direct line to the crime scene. We didn't hear any scream just now from the steps, so she couldn't have heard any scream from her apartment that night, certainly not loud enough to wake her up."

He waited.

In a moment Woodcock said, "She was lying?"

"Could be."

"So why did she call in?"

"You're not so wrung out as you look, Detective Wood-cock."

Behrens kicked the motor into some sort of life and pulled out from the curb, thinking, yeah, she could have been lying, but she hadn't come across to him like that when they'd been talking that night at the crime scene; she'd seemed up front with it all. The whole wide world had lied to Bernie Behrens in the past seventeen years and by now he could tell when there was a crack in the bell. So maybe he should call her, Tanya Fontaine, no, *Tasha* Fon-taine, right, see if she could—

The ring of his mobile broke into his thoughts.

"Behrens."

"O'Keefe, Communications. We just had a fax come through for you from the NCIC. We send it up?"

Behrens looked through the grime on his windshield and the veil of sleep that was trying to come down over his conjunctiva and thought, well, it could be a break, could be the break they were waiting for.

"Yeah, send it up, and call Detective Woodcock—he's in his car—and tell him we got the fax, okay?"

"Right away."

Give Woody the option, Behrens thought as he turned west toward their base, the option of hitting the sack or showing up in the squad room to read their little billy-doo from the NCIC. Give a guess, that's where he'd be when Behrens got there; that guy never knew when to go home.

A fly buzzed in the silence, circling the lights.

Behrens was slumped behind his desk with his feet on a pile of paperwork and his eyes closed. He'd read the fax. Woodcock was still reading it, leaning with his back against the wall to keep himself upright.

So now they had it, Behrens thought, the acid light of

the tubes playing on his closed lids. They called him Jack, this guy, at the NCIC, for Jack the Knife. Seemed like Jack had done eleven jobs like this one in the past eight years, in New York, Los Angeles, Chicago, and Boston, always the same victim type: around thirty years old, slim build, eyes blue or gray, long, dark hair, and involved in some kind of artistic work—two of them musicians, one a dress designer, one a painter—and all of them well-heeled, and in nine verifiable cases they'd had orchids delivered shortly before the attack. The type of attack was also the same; very evidently by a psychopath with marked sadistic tendencies, great ferocity, used with a knife but no semen in the victim's vagina and none of it around anywhere at the scene. Individual case reports would follow in the mail.

The fly went on buzzing, then after a while Behrens heard Woodcock drop the fax sheet onto the desk, and squinted up at him.

"Fuck," Woodcock said, his eyes drooping shut as he leaned his head back against the wall.

"Yeah. Looks like Jack's back in town. And busy."

Six

The door squeaked as the man came into his little conservatory on the roof, and he remembered he hadn't put any oil on the hinges yet. He hated things that squeaked, because that was the sound that rats made, and he hated rats. But on his way here he was too excited to think of bringing an oilcan, and when he left the conservatory his mind was full of the things that the little plants did—not these plants here, the orchids, but the ones behind the green canvas screen—and he forgot to make a note when he was back in the apartment, a note to bring an oilcan next time.

In one of the seed boxes he saw three or four green tips showing above the black potting soil, thrusting their way into the world like sharp little knives, and this was thrilling. They would soon be orchids, as beautiful as all the rest. It seemed to him a never-ending miracle, the way all this beauty came, just from little brown seeds.

People shouldn't throw orchids down on the ground. They should never do that.

He bent over the seed box, wanting to touch the little green tips, to feel them, to feel the life in them that was just beginning. But that would bruise them, and he restrained himself.

Much though he loved and admired them, he could never stay long with the orchids, because of what was happening over there behind the green canvas screen. And again he restrained himself, this time from hurrying; he just stood looking at the screen and the words stenciled on it: STICKLE'S SEEDS. Stickle was such a funny name—"tickle," but not quite.

As he waited for the moment to come, the moment when he would let himself go in there behind the screen, he watched the first lights coming on in the windows across the street and in the taller buildings beyond, as people came home from their work after another hot day and went straight to the refrigerator to get a nice cold drink.

She'd caught him at the refrigerator once, and screamed at him so hard he felt her spittle on his face, then she threw him down the cellar steps with his bare knees scraping and bumping against the walls as she slammed the door on him, leaving him alone in the dark with the rats.

He'd been seven then.

More lights came on as he watched the buildings and the street below. In a window opposite he could see a young woman on her exercise bicycle; she was wearing one of those shiny clinging athletic suits with colored bands around it; he thought they must be very hot and uncomfortable—how could they sweat in those things? But she didn't seem to mind. He saw her over there whenever he came into the conservatory at this particular time, a few minutes after six in the evening; from this distance and because of the window glass he couldn't see what she looked like, but he could tell she didn't have blond hair. She might be pretty, but he hoped she wasn't. He didn't like pretty women.

They should never say, "I don't think so." They should never say that.

Then suddenly, on the other side of the green canvas screen, he heard a fly buzzing, and a trickle of warmth flowed into his groin and he didn't restrain himself any-more—he'd waited long enough.

The screen had brass rings along the top that he'd put there himself, making it like a real curtain, and he pulled it aside slowly, catching his breath at the faint, thrilling smell of the fertilizer. He saw the fly right away: it was quite a big one, a shiny blue, bumping and bumping at the glass panes against the lights and the rising moon. He didn't look down yet; he could wait a little longer—now that he'd seen the fly—to look down and see what was going on.

He picked up the butterfly net and trapped the fly with-out any trouble—he'd done it so many times—and then, feeling for the fly in the folds of the net, he found it and gave it a gentle squeeze, just enough to stop it struggling so hard. Then he reached inside the net and pulled the fly out, taking care not to hurt it any more than he could help because he wanted it to be as strong as possible when the time came, so that it wouldn't be over too soon.

Then he looked down.

Four of them were hungry, he saw at once—their jaws were gaping. The rest of them were closed. He got the stool and perched on it, watching the hungry ones and trying to decide which should have the big blue fly; it was buzzing with one wing now, trying to get away from his fingers. Which of you, then, shall it be? Who shall be the lucky one?

They had a grand name, his little green animals—*Dionaea muscipula,* the Venus's-flytrap. The "musc" part meant they had muscles, of course. He liked the idea of pretty green plants having muscles, and eating flesh. How many other plants did that? None! It was a good thing; otherwise you'd have to be careful arranging the roses, not to get your fingers pinched!

This one, then, would get this handsome supper . . . because it was the biggest. He'd find some more flies, later, for the other three—it was summertime, and they were everywhere.

He drew closer, leaning forward on the feeding-stool, and looked deep into the sticky, seductive mouth of the big *Dionaea,* the long, shining spines of its jaws looking black, in this light, against the amber palate, like the bars of a cage, or a cellar window. Then he held the big blue fly toward it, wishing, as he so often wished, that his *Dionaeas* had eyes, so they could watch him come through the canvas screen and see what he was giving them for their supper.

"Here," he whispered, wishing, too, that they had ears, "here you are, then . . . here you are . . . " He liked to talk to them just the same, because maybe they could hear him in their own way. "Here's your delicious supper, then." He held the fly closer and closer, pushing it between the long, spiny jaws and waiting . . . waiting . . . as the head of the fly, with its huge, magnificent eyes, touched the sticky nectar, tasting it with its round, flattened sucker and sensing, of course, that here was something really delicious, as good as honey, if only it could free its wings and settle down to enjoy it.

Then suddenly the jaws of the big Dionaea *closed like a trap* and he caught his breath, watching in fascination with the warm stirring of pleasure coming again "down there" as the wings of the fly went on buzzing and then stopped, started buzzing again and then stopped, doing it two or three times, until the glistening amber stickiness held them still at last. It was such a big fly that it filled the whole mouth of the *Dionaea* for a while until digestion began, two of its legs sticking out through the clamped jaws, reminding him, as it always did, of the way his mother's legs had stuck out like that before she was finally swallowed up.

Seven

"Are you doing okay, Miss Fontaine? Just nod if you are."

Tasha nodded, her face heavy with mud.

"Great! You need me, I'm right here—just raise your hand."

Tasha nodded again. They weren't first-class at Angel Face—the mud was too thick, and some of it had run down her neck—but it was closer to Sutton Place than Liz Arden, and that was probably why Christine had come here.

She had sat in this very chair, maybe, would certainly have if she'd come to this place often. Sitting here listening to the same Muzak, her arms lying along the upholstered arms of the chair like this, making indentations, like these, where Tasha's arms were resting now.

It felt strange, and yet intimate. Okay, it felt intimate, then, but strange because the intimacy she felt was with someone who wasn't here anymore.

Someone who was dead.

The mud was itching a little, but that was normal.

She was feeling a sense of intimacy, then, with the dead. But Jesus, *that* wasn't normal. Was it?

Hey, listen. She'd been through this whole thing a couple of nights ago when she'd come home to the apartment in Temple Mansions and found the crimson scarf still in her bag. Earlier that day she'd gone straight to La Botica from the reception in Sutton Place and buried her nose in work until it was past 6:00: Elizabeth wasn't back from Milan and there was a lot to look after. When she left the boutique she thought of dropping in at The Checkered Cloth for a simple dinner, then discovered she wasn't hungry in the least, so went on home, pushing the Seville through the sticky evening traffic bumper to bumper.

In the apartment, when she took the crimson scarf from her bag, she draped it over one of the lamp shades in the bedroom, knotting it lightly to keep it there. Then later, when she got into bed and tried to read, her eyes were drawn to the scarf because of the splash of reddened light it cast on the wall, and she put her book down and did some necessary thinking.

So what was she getting into?

Christine Wittendorf was a woman she had never known, never even met formally, yet today she'd left work to gate-crash that woman's funeral and the reception afterward, and in Christine's house she had invaded the last remnants of her earthly privacy and stolen something that had once belonged to her, in the name of—

In the name of what?

Coming away from that house—*running* away, in her mind—she'd believed there was some sort of trap closing on her. But that was bullshit: she was simply shifting the blame on Christine for her own outrageous behavior, trying to salve her conscience by believing she'd heard Christine's voice telling her it was okay to take the scarf: *Don't worry, it's yours now . . . I wanted you to take it.*

Pretending that Christine was speaking to her from beyond the grave, excusing her own blatant thieving . . . but the truth was that what she had done was of her own volition, and she was responsible.

Okay, so that was where the buck stopped—but why had she done these extraordinary things at all, of her own volition? It was a question that had been flashing through her mind all day, and by this time she was getting some of the answers.

One of them was this. She had led a charmed life, so far—yeah, and let's touch wood, reach for the bedpost—and everything had gone right for her, with the love of two terrific parents that had carried her through school and college and into the business world where she was already making her mark. It had all been very smooth, and nothing had gotten in her way to challenge her, to bring her face to face suddenly with the flip side of the world where so many people lived their lives in tragedy, desolation, and despair, going down under it and either staying down or getting up and going on, surviving or giving way, learning from it all or screaming their rage at the gods as the night came down for them.

She had been protected from all that—until just a few nights ago, when that scream of terror had ripped into her sheltered life and shocked her into reality, leaving her changed forever.

But instead of running away from that experience, instead of turning her head on the pillow and going to sleep again, denying it, Tasha had felt an overwhelming need to go out there into the terrifying night and get close to the reality that had awakened her, to be with it, opening her feelings to it and letting them share whatever had happened down there among the trees.

And when she had learned what had happened, she had felt the need to grieve, to join those who, later, would not let this young woman, Christine Wittendorf, go from this world without tears, without remembrance—and *that* was why she had sent Elizabeth on her own to Milan, so that she could be here for the funeral and look into the flower-decked casket at the young, beautiful woman who lay there

with her hideous wounds concealed and her face heavily
veiled, receiving the love and compassion of all those who
had known her . . . and of one who had not.

Okay, so could you grieve for someone you'd never
known?

Very easily, if you'd heard her dying, and not far away,
close enough to go over to her and keep vigil for a while;
the first mourner, a stranger, yes, but earlier than the others,
up betimes and the first to grieve, the only one who would
ever have grieved alone, without the hymns and the flowers
and the incense, without the pomp and circumstance, who
would have been there among the trees to experience the
quiet meeting of two minds in the shadowland between life
and death.

And she alone, among all those mourners in the church,
had known the privilege—if that was the word—of seeing
Christine Wittendorf bright with blood beneath the summer
leaves, the manner of her passing unadorned, her poor,
ravaged body unveiled and unashamed.

That was, yes, the word. It had been a privilege.

Surely, then, she, Tasha Fontaine, the first mourner, was
allowed her grief, was allowed, even, to visit the home
where Christine Wittendorf had lived, to sit for a moment at
her dressing table and watch her face—their face—in the
mirror? Was allowed, finally, to take away a small memento
of her, the scarf that was tied around the lamp shade over
there?

*Don't worry. You just wanted something to remember
me by.*

Christine's voice had been very clear as Tasha had stood
there with a glass in her hand among all those people, the
stolen scarf burning in her handbag.

Of course. You knew why I wanted it. You knew I
didn't take it for any other reason. You knew it would help
me to grieve, to stay close to you—because isn't that the

essence of grieving, to be as close as you can to the subject of your grief? You know it is.

Late traffic rolled softly past the building below the open window, breaking Tasha's reverie.

Talking to the dead, now . . . Talking to Christine, using the second person, as you did in a conversation. Was that okay, too?

Sure. Could you grieve for somebody without talking to her in your mind, without letting her know how you felt?

"Okay, Miss Fontaine, I guess you're about ready."

Tasha was jerked back to the present by the woman's voice. Her name was Flora, she had announced with touching pride, and her voice was a bit too loud and her false eyelashes were a bit too long and her navy-blue—almost— eye shadow was a bit too thick, but she meant well, and Tasha did a lot of nodding because whether she was ready or not she wanted to get this mud off her face before the itching got worse; maybe it was an allergic reaction—she didn't have them too often.

And then, as Flora began smoothing in the moisturizing cream, Tasha heard herself putting the first question, and none too subtly. With a gal like Flora you didn't have to creep up on tiptoe.

"It must have been a shock for you, when you heard about Christine Wittendorf. Wasn't she one of your customers?"

Flora's hands stopped moving, and there was silence for a moment.

"Yeah . . . " Her voice was hushed, suddenly. "It was terrible, yeah, a real shock, you wouldn't believe . . . "

There was silence again and, in the silence, Tasha, with her eyes closed against the lights, heard the woman's breath coming shakily, and then felt, with astonishment, something splashing softly onto her face that could only be a tear, and then another, until Flora turned away and got a Kleenex and snuffled into it.

"We don't like to talk about it," she said through the tissue, her voice still hushed. "People ask . . . but we—you know—we'd rather not say anything. I hope you understand."

"Sure," Tasha said. "I can understand that. I shouldn't have mentioned it." And she lay there without speaking again, furious with herself for upsetting Flora, who wasn't as brash as she looked—and even if people wore too much eye shadow, it didn't mean they hadn't got a heart, did it, for Chrissake, that they couldn't let go with a few tears over somebody who hadn't even been a friend? If this woman was brash, then Tasha herself was an insensitive moron. Had *she* ever shed a tear for Christine while she was going through this big grief-fest of hers?

She tipped Flora handsomely and, to her own surprise, gave her a quick hug as she left the salon, getting into her Seville on the second floor of the parking lot and sending a squeal of rubber echoing from the concrete walls, still furious and ashamed.

Stuck in the traffic on her way home, Tasha found herself hoping that Christine would forgive her lapse in grace. It was the first time in her life she had ever grieved, and she didn't have the hang of it yet.

A taxi with a crumpled fender pulled out from the curb and cut across her, and she gave a tap on the horn and got a finger from the driver through the window, sure, that was par for the course; this was New York City.

Waiting at the lights, Tasha found a question still nagging her, something she'd asked herself in the beauty salon. If she were grieving so much, why didn't she cry, too? If this were genuine, where were the tears?

The lights changed and she moved off with the traffic and had to concentrate. Maybe she should take a taxi to work and back, use the Seville just for longer runs in the evening and on weekends. But how many taxis could you find that didn't have a driver who smoked and had his radio stuck at a jazz station that didn't have God-knew-what sticking out from the bottom of the backseat, a dirty handkerchief, an empty packet of condoms—you name it. Maybe she could use a limo, then—not a stretch, just a small one, yeah, La Botica could afford it, no problem, maybe she'd call the people on the business card she'd seen in Christine's room—Quality Limo Service—ask what their rates were for frequent runs.

Waiting at the lights again she switched off the air conditioner; the summer night was warm, too warm, but with the fan pulling in all that carbon monoxide you were sitting in a gas chamber.

And then, as she waited in the traffic, the answer came up from her subconscious, the answer to the question that had been nagging her. She knew now why she wasn't shedding even a single tear for Christine Wittendorf.

Because she wasn't really grieving at all.

What was that thought that had crossed her mind just a minute ago? Still ashamed at her clumsiness in the beauty salon, she'd consciously hoped that Christine would forgive her lapse in grace. As if she were still somewhere around. And that night when Tasha had tied the crimson scarf to the lamp shade and sat against the pillows thinking things out, she'd talked to Christine in her mind, knowing she understood about the scarf—it hadn't been an act of theft, it had been the need for a memento, something to bring her closer, something physical, that Christine had actually worn.

And Christine had voiced that for her, at the reception when Tasha was feeling so appallingly guilty with the scarf hidden in her bag. Her voice had been quite clear. *Don't worry. You just wanted something to remember me by.*

They'd been talking to each other. They'd been talking to each other ever since the funeral, drawing closer as time went by, and today, just a little while ago, Tasha had sat in a chair where Christine had sat, talking to the same woman,

Flora, listening to the same Muzak, leaving the same indentations on the arms of the chair. And then it had happened—for the first time Christine had sent her a sign of her presence there, through Flora, letting a tear splash softly on her face.

The Seville pulled forward with the traffic as the lights changed, but Tasha was driving automatically now as the truth came to her with a rush.

This wasn't grief. She wasn't grieving. Why should she be?

Christine was still alive.

Eight

I t was nearly one o'clock the next day when Tasha found time at last to battle her way through the lunch-hour traffic to the Fabius Gallery on 79th Street. She'd wanted to pick up the little self-portrait the day after the reception, but Elizabeth had flown to Milan and there was a backup of work to get through; there was always a backup of work to get through, for the simple reason that La Botica was successful. That was great, but it didn't make life any easier.

As she found a slot on the second floor of the parking garage, Tasha caught herself and ran that thought through her head again; about life not being any easier. For her, it wasn't typical thinking, wasn't in character, and she had picked up on it. Normally she relished the action at the boutique, never got in later than nine—except for that day when she'd stayed talking to Detective Behrens in the park—and was often still at work until six or seven or even later when someone needed a dress—*the* dress—for a coming-out party or a political reception or whatever.

But now—suddenly—she wasn't finding life so easy.

Getting old?

The hell with that: she worked out three evenings a

week at the Aerobicon and never felt tired, didn't have to use a wrinkle cream yet because she didn't have any wrinkles, not getting old, no, it was just that there was this—this extra dimension to her life that demanded more of her time, more of her energy, more of *herself.*

Christine.

Because, yes, Christine was still alive; she knew that now. Not alive on the earthly plane, but her influence was still here all right. The night she had screamed in the park she'd just been someone Tasha had only met once in her life, briefly, in a taxi in the rain, but today she was someone Tasha had already gotten to know quite well, someone who had come to "live" with her a lot of the time, even most of the time.

But shouldn't that be just a little bit scary?

Maybe, but she preferred not to think so. There was nothing scary about Christine.

Tasha got out of the car and slammed the door and took the stairs down to the street, her shoes gritting on chips of concrete and a beer-can ring and the broken glass of a bottle: when you used your own car you avoided the public unpleasantness of a cab but still had to pick your way through the detritus of the city before you reached wherever you were going.

Fido Hamilton saw her coming through the doors of the gallery and was halfway to meet her as she stood in the middle of the huge main room, looking around.

"I was thinking of calling you," he said. "Tasha, isn't it?"

"Yes."

"Fido Hamilton." He gave her the same intense gaze she remembered from their first meeting at the reception on Sutton Place, his dark eyes set deep under their heavy brows, a Byronic lock of hair hanging down in a blue-black curl across his forehead. But today his gaze was perfectly steady. "He's not always like that," Audrey had told her as they'd watched him bumping the wall when he'd left them.

She liked his looks, Tasha thought, and would probably like them whether he was drunk or sober. "Calling me?" she asked him. "Why?"

"I wanted you to have the picture." He took her arm and she felt the strength in his hand as he led her through the main room and into a smaller one, where her eyes were immediately drawn to Christine's self-portrait, now lighted and glowing against a black background. "I wanted you to have it as soon as possible," Fido was saying.

Tasha half-heard him. Looking suddenly into the face of Christine Wittendorf, she had felt a jolt of pleasure, of recognition. Not of grief, she noted, not of remembered horror or sadness, as others would have felt. And only she knew why.

Or did this man know, too?

"Christine's current boyfriend," Audrey had told her at the reception, and then had flinched slightly—"I mean her latest, last, whatever." Fido Hamilton Tasha thought, had been much closer to Christine than she had. Did he feel she was in some way still alive?

She would ask him, if a chance came.

Taking a step toward the portrait, feeling the need to be closer, Tasha told Fido, "It's even more appealing than I'd thought."

"We reframed it."

"Oh yes, I see now."

"I would have had it delivered," Fido said, "but I wanted you to see it here, more suitably hung. You can still change your mind, of course."

"Why should I?" Tasha asked quickly. The picture was hers, and nobody else was having it.

"It's just our policy."

"Let's go to the office," Tasha said, and realized she'd sounded abrupt. It was just that she wanted to secure the picture with a check and felt defensive, anxious that something might take it away from her.

"We don't need to do that," Fido said. "Shall I have it delivered now, or do you want to take it with you?"

"I'll take it."

Fido beckoned to a young man in the doorway of the main room. "Roger, box this one for me, will you, right away?"

Tasha found it difficult to take her eyes off the portrait, off the eyes of Christine. Opening her bag she asked Fido, "How much do I make the check out for?"

"She'd have wanted you to have it," he said, "as a gift."

Tasha stood awkwardly, one hand buried in her bag, fingers along the edge of the checkbook. "But I can't——" She didn't know how to finish.

"Believe me," Fido said, his dark eyes intent on hers, "she would have wanted that. So it makes us very happy. As soon as it's boxed, I'll get a taxi for you—or do you have one waiting?"

"No. But I . . . don't know how to thank you. Or her. Christine."

As if she were still alive.

Well, sure. Because she was.

"You could take me to lunch," Fido said, and for the first time Tasha saw the trace of a smile and found it attractive: these strong, dark good looks could do with a little leavening.

"That would be nice," she said, and felt a touch of pleasure. She wanted to know this man better, see more of him.

Because he'd been so close to Christine?

Maybe.

Try again. Not maybe. *Yes.*

On their way out of the gallery, Fido asked her to sign the book. "No, the blue one, for distinguished patrons. I'm sorry I didn't know La Botica was so famous."

"A man wouldn't know," Tasha said as she signed her name, "about boutiques."

"We're not all of us beer and baseball."

"I didn't mean it that way." She touched his arm in apology as they went through the ornate doors into the street.

Fido kept his scarlet Porsche parked in the same garage, and opened the door for her. He drove fast through the streets, aggressively, hunting for gaps in the traffic and taking risks, sometimes getting honked at, the energy in his body forcing itself through the machinery of the powerful car to the spinning tires and the noon-hot surface of the pavement.

Marjorie thought he was too wild for her, Audrey had said. *But they were all pretty wild, weren't they?* Her boyfriends.

Fido would also be angry still, Tasha thought, at the man who'd taken Christine away from him, away from them all. Angry and outraged. *I'd smash him up,* he had told them at the reception. It felt strange to Tasha not to have to grieve, not to feel horror, anger. For people like these, the closest of Christine's friends, it was still so recent, just a few days.

"She was a nymphomaniac," she heard Fido saying as the lights changed to green and the tires squealed again, "as I'm sure you know."

"I . . . knew she had a lot of boyfriends." Tasha said it calmly, though Fido's revelation had come as a shock.

"Boyfriends, girlfriends, you name it." Fido turned his head for an instant and gave Tasha his intense stare. "I'm not being disloyal—I mean, *everyone* knew. She told me once, 'I just adore human bodies; that's all there is to it. I was born to fuck, like some people are born to shop.' He gave a short laugh, lifting his hands from the wheel and slapping them down again. "But somehow she managed to keep us all separated. I mean, she'd just call me and break a date, make some excuse, feeling tired or whatever, and I always knew—*we* always knew—she'd suddenly decided to spend the night or the weekend with somebody else instead. And we couldn't get mad at her, because we knew

she might drop us if we did—and that was unthinkable."
He swung the Porsche through an intersection and said, "Is
Gaspari's okay for you?"

"What? Yes. And there weren't ever any . . . shooting
incidents?"

Fido swung his dark stare on her. "Shooting? Oh. No.
But I know what you mean. I suppose it was the way she
handled us, made each of us feel we were really the only
one when she was with us—and now you mention it, there
would have been shots ringing out all over the place if she'd
just been a cheap femme fatale out to work up our pas-
sions." He slowed along Madison toward 74th Street.
"Christine," he said with emphasis, "had *style.*" Swinging
his head again. "As I'm sure you know."

"Yes."

He used to tell me that so often . . . that I had style.

Her voice came clearly, Christine's, and Tasha didn't feel
that once-familiar jolt of surprise. When Christine wanted to
tell her things, she just made contact—though there were
still times when Tasha believed this soft, husky voice was
the voice of her own imagination, its tone and timbre remembered from that night in the taxi. It just wasn't possible
to know the truth, because the voice never told Tasha anything she wasn't already aware of, or couldn't easily make
up. Most of the time she believed it belonged to Christine
because she wanted to.

"What about the room at the back?" Fido asked her as
they crossed the sidewalk into the restaurant.

"Sure, it's quieter. We can talk."

"I've been doing most of that, I'm afraid. She's still so
much on my mind." He took Tasha's arm as they followed
the maître d' between the tables, and again she was aware
of the strength in this man's fingers.

"Do you have the feeling she hasn't really—you
know—gone from us yet?" Tasha asked him casually. "That
she's in some way still alive?"

Fido's brows came together as he stared at her. "Absolutely not. She doesn't haunt me, thank God, if that's what you mean. I don't think I could handle that."

Tasha said nothing. It wasn't what she'd meant; only the dead could haunt. Or was Fido right, after all? Was Christine really dead, on every other plane of existence as well as on this one, and was this voice that spoke to her simply the audible expression of Christine's invisible ghost? Nothing more than a wisp of the original living entity, a whisper from the dark?

Actually, no.

Tasha moved her fork aside as Fido held the small silver dish of zucchini for her, the handle of the serving spoon turned toward her, Fido's eyes attentive, everything so real, so normal.

"Thank you," she said.

"Is it good? The osso buco?"

"It's perfect."

Then the sounds of voices, silverware, porcelain faded again as she brought her mind back to Christine. No, she wasn't just a ghost, an insubstantial trace of someone who had once been real, a shadow, an echo. Because it wasn't only her voice, was it? There was Christine's presence everywhere she went. And there was her influence on Tasha's life, her constant demands on her time, on her energy.

And there was this: Tasha had gone across to the park that morning under some kind of compulsion—and she'd known that, at the time. Detective Behrens had also known. 'The thing is,' he'd told her, 'you really don't know what made you come down here, what *compelled* you to come down here.' And in the same way she'd been compelled to do all those other things, to gate-crash the funeral and the reception afterward, to search out Christine's room, to bring away her scarf, to visit the same beautician in the hope of talking about her, bringing her closer and closer all the time until now, today, this minute, she was sitting here with one of Christine's boyfriends, closer still to her, closer than ever before.

She was here because Christine wanted her to be. She had done all those other things because Christine had wanted her to, compelled her to. But all the time she'd rationalized, making up excuses, letting herself believe it was okay to feel this way about Christine, to want to get to know her even though other people would think it was too late—she was dead, for God's sake—how could anybody get to know her now?

Someone was waving to her from another table, and the sounds of the restaurant came in again as if the volume had been turned up. She waved back, adding a quick smile.

"One of my customers," she murmured to Fido.

"Does she have wall space?"

"Not too much. She lives on her yacht."

"Then I won't ask for an introduction."

The sound faded again.

So maybe it was time for her to face up to what was really going on, while she sat toying with this really delicious osso buco in this familiar restaurant where she had come fifty times before with her mind full of the day's work, something new in from Christian Lacroix, an appointment tomorrow with Elaine Marjoribanks, the problem of Elizabeth's allergy to silk fibers, ordinary things like that, rational, everyday things.

Not her strange, irrational compulsions.

Not Christine, the source of those compulsions.

Face up, then, to what, exactly?

To the fairly obvious fact that she was no longer in charge. No longer in charge of herself, of her mind, of her life.

Christine was in charge.

"Shall I ask Luigi to turn the air conditioning down a little?"

Fido was watching her attentively.

"The air conditioning?"

"I thought I saw you shiver."

"I did?" Tasha held her arms, rubbing them a little. "No,

I'm okay. It's not cold in here." She tried a smile. "Maybe it was just my thoughts."

Fido was still watching her, his eyes serious now. "Thinking about Christine?"

"Yeah."

"It's hard," he said, "to stop." He pushed his plate away an inch. "You wake, nights?"

"Sure."

"I guess we all do," He leaned forward a little. "I think we'll feel better when they get that guy. Wouldn't you say?"

"Maybe."

"It isn't just that we miss her, that she's gone, suddenly, right? It's the way she went."

"Right."

And the way she came back.

Fido looked around and caught their waiter's eye; and when the dishes had been taken away, he leaned forward again and lowered his voice. "I went along to see the detective in charge of the case, the next day. He would've sent for me anyway, I knew that."

"Why?"

"It's one of the first things they do—talk to the victim's relations, friends, especially boyfriends."

"Could you tell them anything helpful?" Tasha saw the detective in her mind, Behrens, with his weathered face and his street-weary eyes, standing with his feet solidly apart and looking at the ground as she answered a question, hands in his side pockets, listening with his whole body. She'd go see him again as soon as she could make the time; maybe there was some way she could be useful, remember something that might have a bearing on things.

Maybe when they had "got that guy," Christine would leave them alone—all of them. Herself especially. Leave her in charge again.

"I don't know," Fido was saying, "if I was any help to them or not. As one of her boyfriends, I gave them my alibi, of course. It's the first thing they always ask."

Before she realized it, Tasha was saying, "And what was it?"

Fido looked at her for a moment. "My alibi?"

"Yes."

"I was on the roof of my apartment, sleeping under the moon."

With Marcia, this time. She's the romantic type.

Christine's voice came clearly, as always—as if she had hushed all other sounds with a soft wave of her arms, so that Tasha could hear her.

With Marcia. Okay.

And I can't Tasha thought, be making it up this time, just picking the name out of my imagination.

Or can I?

She had no idea how the human mind worked, what tricks it could play. Had she been talking to anybody named Marcia today, yesterday? Try this, then: picturing this man sleeping on the roof under the moon, she had automatically assumed he'd been sharing the idyll with a girlfriend, and "Marcia" had popped up from her subconscious because she'd been talking to someone with that name today, or recently.

But had she?

Tasha searched her memory, and it came up blank. No Marcia. In fact she didn't know anybody at all with that name.

So here was the bottom line, wasn't it? And she was going to have to check it out. Ask Tasha, she'll check it out. Sure.

But it was going to be frightening.

"They asked me about her other friends," she heard Fido saying, "of course."

"Yes?" Tasha looked up, her mind forced back to reality. "I guess that's logical." Take a dozen boyfriends of a murder victim, and each of them was liable to suspect any one of the others.

"Sure," Fido said. "In fact, some of them were rather oddball."

"Do you suspect anyone?"

Fido looked away, his eyes buried under his brows. "One has to be a bit careful, with a question like that. So I'll say no. I don't suspect anyone. But"—with a shrug—"I gave the police as much help as I could. I want that bastard caught."

Luigi came with the zabaglione, and they picked up their forks in silence, Fido's last words echoing in Tasha's mind. Then she decided to go for it and get it over with, because she couldn't stand the waiting, the not-knowing.

"So they asked Marcia along, to confirm your alibi?"

"Actually no, they sent a man round to—" And Fido stopped, looking up suddenly. "Who?"

Tasha had to meet his eyes, force this thing through now she'd started it. "Didn't you say it was Marcia? On the roof with you?"

His eyes were so dark, so inescapable.

"No," he said, "I didn't."

Tasha leaned forward, having to act, something she'd never been good at. "But you said you were sleeping on the roof, under the moon. Right?"

Fido wouldn't look down, look away. "Right. But I didn't say who with."

Forcing herself to hold his eyes, Tasha didn't see any anger there, any hostility; he just looked watchful, alerted to something he didn't understand.

"Well," she said, a hand brushing the air, "I'm sorry, I thought you did. And anyway I guess I got it wrong, so . . ."

She waited. It all rested on a word now, and she felt a vibration along her nerves that she couldn't stop.

"No," Fido said at last, "you didn't. It was, in fact, a girl named Marcia."

*   *   *

It was almost three o'clock when Tasha got back to La Botica from lunch with Fido, to find an urgent message from Candie flashing on her desk screen: Elizabeth had tried three times to call her from Milan and said it was urgent.

Tasha was normally back from lunch at two, unless she was entertaining a customer, and today she hadn't been. She'd been entertaining one of Christine's boyfriends at Gaspari's and she'd also been tangling with a taxi in her Seville on the way from the parking garage, because her mind had been so full of Christine that she'd hit the guy's fender and had to stand there in the street for twenty minutes while they worked out a deal for two hundred and fifty dollars before a cop came to ask them what was going on. The repairs to the cab would cost maybe a hundred dollars at most, and Tasha had always prided herself on never being ripped off by *anyone,* but on this occasion she'd wanted to get back to the boutique without a summons for not reporting an accident. It hadn't helped, of course, when the cabdriver had suggested in his own choice idiom that until she took some driving lessons she'd be best off in a taxi with a professional behind the wheel.

She hit the intercom.

"Candie? What time is it in Milan?" She couldn't think whether it was six or seven hours' difference right now.

"Ten at night," Candie said right away. "Should I call Elizabeth?"

"Yeah. And listen, I just hit a cab, so my car has to go in for some bodywork, and—"

"Are you okay?"

"What? Sure, it was just a fender bender, but I'll need a limo to get me home tonight, say seven o'clock." She read the business card again in her mind's eye. "There's a firm called Quality Limo Service on the West Side that—that somebody recommended, so give them a call, will you? I don't need a stretch, just a shuttle."

While she was waiting for the Milan connection Tasha swung her feet up onto the desk—a thing she'd never done before, but she needed to relax, to feel in control again, in charge. And it wasn't going to be easy, because she knew now, was certain at last, that the voice she'd been hearing in her head wasn't dreamed up by her imagination. It was Christine's.

With Marcia, this time. She's the romantic type.

And when Tasha had put it to the test, Fido had looked at her as if she'd been crystal gazing or something, and he hadn't liked it, hadn't liked it at all. With his nerves still raw from the shock of the tragedy, he didn't need an amateur psychic around him, playing tricks. *What if she'd told him it had been Christine herself who had come through to her with the name Marcia?*

The ringing tone stopped.

"Hotel dei Cavalieri."

"I'd like to speak to one of your guests, please. Elizabeth Segal. She's booked in under the company name of La Botica, New York."

"I'll ring her for you."

It could of course have been a coincidence: her imagination had pulled out the name Marcia from a couple of thousand other names, sure. She had been busy disabusing herself of that idea when she'd hit the taxi. Or it could have been telepathy: Marcia had been in Fido's mind while he'd been talking about his alibi, and Tasha had picked it up. Okay? Sure, but wouldn't you think someone who'd been around for thirty-four years would have learned by now that she was an absolute whiz at telepathy, did it at parties and everything?

The time had come for her to get it into her damned head that the voice she'd been hearing was Christine's. No coincidences, no telepathy, no bullshit.

Christine's.

Click on the line.

"Hello?"

"Elizabeth, this is Tasha."

"Oh, hi—"

"I'm sorry I wasn't here when you called. What's so urgent?"

There was a pause. "I guess it's not so urgent any more. Filippo Constante offered to give us a new gown, but time was very much of the essence, and I had to check with you, and I guess we missed out."

"A new Constante? So?"

"Exclusive, Tasha."

"*Exclusive?* Why would he want to give it to little *us?* In the middle of a major international—" she left it, on a sudden thought.

Elizabeth let the silence go on for a moment, and when she spoke, her voice was quiet and measured. "Tasha, I don't do business by agreeing to get laid. Remember me? I'm a pro. He—"

"I didn't mean—"

"He offered it to us because he's more interested in professional relationships and exclusivity than the big-league ballyhoo, and he has a great respect for La Botica and its reputation in the really elite social milieu—I quote. But anyway, Filippo was under pressure and time finally ran out and the whole thing flew over the cuckoo's nest, I guess." A brief pause. "But he sends his regards."

It was Tasha who let the silence go on this time, not because she was in a mood of bitter frustration like Elizabeth, but because she needed time to think. Not that there was anything to be pulled out of the fire, obviously, except for the ashes of regret. With Elizabeth handling the Milan show, she should have told Candie *exactly* where to find her when she was out of her office, and she shouldn't have spent all that time with Fido Hamilton at the gallery and

Gaspari's, leaving her own car at the garage and having to
go back there in the Porsche to pick it up. The brush with
the cab had been an accident, sure, but its true cause was
that her mind had been out in the wild blue yonder with
Christine and the Marcia thing. And don't look now, but if
she didn't get back on track and spend more time at her
desk she'd start losing her grip on La Botica, and it had
taken her more than ten years to put it where it was—
among "the really elite social milieu," that was perfectly
right.

"It was my fault, Elizabeth," she said at last. "Entirely,
and I apologize."

"You're the boss."

"Sure, but this was your first time in Milan, and you got
us the chance of an exclusive Constante and I dropped the
ball, just by not being available. So I'm sorry."

"There'll be other chances. Anyway, you want a quick
rundown on the show while we're on the line?"

"Tomorrow. You've had a hard day over there, so get
some sleep, or whatever. And I'll wire Filippo some roses."

"Did I keep you?"

"No, miss. I'm parked just over there, closest I could
get."

Tasha knew she was a few minutes late, and thought it
was nice of him not to make anything of it, considering the
rush hour was still in full swing.

Sitting in the back of the limo she ran her fingers through
her hair, glad of the air conditioning and the luxury of not
having to battle with the traffic. She was also aware that
Christine had sat here on this black leather seat, her bag and
her gloves beside her, talking maybe to the driver, asking
him what kind of day he'd had.

Across the bench seat Tasha saw the identity plaque on
the dashboard: Vincent George Fisher, his photograph not

much like him, of course—they never were. He looked
younger than that, his fair hair better groomed.

"So this is your own business," she asked him, "or your
family's?"

He tilted his head to look at her in the driver's mirror.
"It's my own, miss. I drove a cab for a few years and then
saved up and settled for comfort."

"Congratulations. So do I call you 'Mr Fisher,' as the
president of Quality Limo?" But even as she said it, Tasha
felt she was being too chatty, too fulsome; and she knew
why.

" 'Vince' is fine, miss." He sounded a little embarrassed.
Making a turn onto Park Avenue he asked her, "It's Temple
Mansions, is that right?"

"Yes. You know where it is?"

"Oh, yes. This is mainly my area."

He shifted in his seat, settling down to fight the traffic.
But after a few minutes Tasha realized he wasn't doing that
at all: he just seemed to turn and flow with it, nosing out a
gap and taking it smoothly without getting anybody mad at
him. Her own average was somewhere around three fingers and a couple of shouts between La Botica and home.
This was a *very* smart idea, using a limo.

"You really have a handle on the rush hour, Vince."

"Thank you, miss."

She was being too chatty, Tasha knew, because she
wanted to loosen him up, get him to talk. And then, just as
she was wondering how to broach the subject, he suddenly
did it for her, unwittingly.

"D'you mind if I ask who referred you to Quality Limo,
miss? I like to thank people, when I can."

"That's nice." But there didn't seem any way to break it
gently. "It was someone I knew. Christine Wittendorf."

The light gray eyes flicked to the mirror, then down
again. "Oh," Vince said with a little moan in his voice. In a
moment; "That was a terrible thing." He moved his shoul-

ders, settling the jacket of his uniform. "A terrible thing. I couldn't eat anything all that day, when I saw it on the news. And I couldn't sleep that night. I went down to the garage and cleaned the motor, polished the bodywork." He saw another gap and took it, going north up Madison Avenue. "It must have been a shock for you too, miss."

"Yes. For all of us." She waited, sitting here where Christine had sat so many times, her bag and her gloves beside her, as her own were right now. But Vince didn't say anything more.

In a moment, Tasha asked, "You—drove her quite a bit?"

"Yes, miss. For maybe, oh, around six months or so. A gracious young lady, very gracious."

And he was silent again, and Tasha remembered Flora, her cosmetician at Angel Face, snuffling into her Kleenex and saying, "We'd rather not talk about it . . . I hope you understand." Tasha didn't want to make the same mistake again: she'd already embarrassed this poor man once.

But it was tempting to risk it, because wouldn't there be just a trace of Infiniti here in the limo, a long, dark hair still curled on the carpet? Tasha was bringing Christine nearer every day, but she longed to finally close the gap between them. And, okay, maybe that was something she ought to examine some time, ought to question. But not now.

"In six months," she said casually, "you must have gotten to know her quite well."

The light gray eyes flickered to the mirror, then down again. "In this job, miss, I only get to know my customers up to a certain point. And I prefer it that way."

In the glow thrown by the crimson scarf across the lamp, Christine looked into the room from her self-portrait; her eyes contemplative, curious, with a hint of the wry, the cynical.

Watching her from her bed, Tasha thought: *Who are you?*

Speaking of the portrait, Audrey Symes had told her, "Christine didn't like it because she didn't like herself, as I'm sure you know."

Why not?

Fido: "She was a nymphomaniac, as I'm sure you know." They'd both used that phrase out of politeness: Tasha had said she'd known Christine, and they didn't want to give the impression that they were exclusively privy to her secrets. But of course she hadn't known Christine at all. Had it shown? Had she fooled them? Maybe not. But it didn't follow that because they'd known Christine they would have known Tasha, too. Audrey: "Christine kept you rather a secret, didn't she? But then she was like that. . . . So many different lives."

Tasha felt her lips moving as she watched the portrait on the wall. "Was it because you were a nymphomaniac that you didn't like yourself? Did it seem a bit sluttish for someone of your style?"

She felt a shiver as she realized this was the first time she'd ever spoken aloud to Christine, to a dead woman, and she tensed as she waited for a reply. But that now-familiar, husky voice didn't come into her head.

Late traffic rolled below the open windows, tires whispering through the dust of the city at the end of the long, sweltering day. Tasha had worked until seven at the boutique this evening, then after Vince had brought her home she had cleaned up and changed and walked as far as The Checkered Cloth for a late supper before turning in.

She wasn't tired yet, but couldn't pick up a book while the portrait watched her from the wall. Tomorrow she'd hang it somewhere else, maybe in the sitting room.

Tonight she had to work things out, get this whole thing straight in her head.

At the reception she'd told Audrey she hadn't known Christine for long.

"Well, then, you were lucky. To have known her, and not for long."

What had that meant?

"Who are you?" Tasha whispered in the silence of the room, this time out loud, not just in her mind. And then, when there was no answer, "*Where* are you?"

She waited.

One of the white gossamer curtains stirred in a window, as it had done on the night when the scream had come.

"I heard you screaming," Tasha said low, "that night. I went down to see what was happening. It must have been terrifying for you; I can't begin to imagine what it must have been like." She remembered the glittering redness among the trees. "The windows were open, like they are right now, and that's how I was able to hear you screaming."

It was easy to talk to Christine, now she was getting the hang of it, but Tasha was beginning to want answers, or at least a word of acknowledgment to show that Christine was listening, could hear her. How did these things go, when someone died? If they could speak to people here on earth, it didn't necessarily mean—did it—that those people could speak back to them, could be heard?

Were there different planes of existence in the afterlife? One of them still close to this one, so the dead could go on communicating, at least for a time? Then why wasn't it a two-way deal? Christine could talk to her, so why couldn't she talk to Christine?

Oh Jesus *Christ,* Tasha thought suddenly, what the hell am I doing?

Trying to talk to the dead.

Yes, but listen, I'm a perfectly normal, intelligent female New Yorker in my right mind and I'm pursuing a very busy career and I intend to go on doing just that, and I don't have time for ghosts, poltergeists or communication with the

dead or anything that smacks of naïve Victorian sensation-
alism. Okay?

Actually, no.

She hitched the pillows up and ran her fingers through
her hair, shook it out, took a deep breath, looked away
from the portrait—forced herself to look away, to deny its
presence, to take charge of her life again if only for a few
minutes. God, it was so hot in this room, in this city! Even
lying naked on the bed without so much as a sheet over her,
Tasha could feel the sweat moist on her skin; but she hated
to switch on the air conditioning: it always played hell with
her sinuses and left her feeling she'd been breathing out of
a can all night: and the leaves through the windows made
a soft green ocean with the street lamps playing on them,
cooling just to look at as the breeze stirred them into waves.

So why wasn't it okay? Because there was the flip side,
wasn't there? Above and beyond the perfectly normal, intelligent New Yorker image—a contradiction in terms, some
would say—she was a real-live human being with a body
and a soul, just as Christine had been. But Christine's body
had been butchered in the night by a still-unknown assailant, and her soul was still around, adrift in the afterlife,
maybe in shock, and needing help. And that side—the flip
side—was a whole lot more important, wasn't it? Life—and
death—amounted to rather more than the ability to tell a
Balenciaga cocktail dress from a Hubert de Givenchy across
a crowded room at the Plaza, to earn a compliment from
Filippo Constante, to sign the distinguished patrons' book
at the Fabius Gallery.

Sure. No question.

Okay. She turned her head and looked back into the
eyes that watched her from the portrait over there, and took
a breath.

"So how can I help, Christine?"

The air conditioning hummed through the rest of the
building. A bead of perspiration trickled inside her armpit,

leaving an itch. She felt, as she waited for the voice to whisper in her head, the rhythm of her heart, faster than normal.

When she thought a minute must have passed, she said, a little louder, "Christine, I want to help you. But you've got to tell me how. So I'm listening."

Watching the eyes in the portrait watching her, and feeling such closeness, because of this, that she felt certain there'd be an answer this time—if it were possible, metaphysically, electrochemically, what the hell, however it was supposed to work.

The silence went on, made up of the sounds that were its essence: the hum of the air conditioning, the faint throbbing of a car along Fifth Avenue, the stirring of the leaves in the park. There wasn't any voice that she could hear. But the memory came of something that Fido Hamilton had said, earlier today in Gaspari's: *I think we'll all feel better when they get that guy. Wouldn't you say?*

Sure. You bet.

So was this it? Was this how she could help Christine?

In one of the windows the curtain stirred again, attracting Tasha's peripheral vision—but okay, we don't have to get into table rapping here, looking for signs and portents. The curtain moved because there's a breeze outside, simple Newtonian cause-and-effect, we have to keep our *marbles,* for God's sake.

But even so, that could be the message, passed to her through her memory of what Fido had said. Then let's take it as read. Let's work on it, because it's all we've got, right?

Tasha was conscious, as she lay uncovered on the bed with her head and shoulders propped on the hot pillows, that this whole building, Temple Mansions, was full of people at this minute, ordinary people, Wall Street wizards and housewives and interior decorators and tax lawyers and retirees, fast asleep or making love or pitching into a late supper or watching *Nightline* or a Danielle Steel saga or just talking, whatever, while Lewis the night porter sat down there at his desk in the lobby with his liver-spotted hands shaking as he read the paper, everyone doing ordinary, acceptable things, while only one of them was lying on her bed on the third floor staring at the portrait of a dead woman and trying to talk to her, ready to cast herself adrift into whatever kind of other-world there was where this same woman, Christine, a murder victim, was also adrift. And because Tasha was conscious of what was going on, of how alone she was, how vulnerable, she felt a sudden and overwhelming wave of fear that brought the sweat springing—the fear of losing her normal way of life, her carefully planned future, perhaps even her sanity, by agreeing to do this thing, to surrender herself to the laws of another world, another plane of existence, the afterlife, in case, by doing so, she could help the woman who had screamed over there among the leaves just a few nights ago, calling desperately for help, as she might now be calling again, hoping someone would hear, and this time save her.

But there's this to be considered: *If I cast myself adrift out there, can I be sure of getting back?*

No way. In a field of systems as ultrasensitive as the human brain and the soul beyond, merging at the limitless horizon of cosmic consciousness, there were no guarantees. You couldn't expect any.

The sweat running on the feverish skin, gleaming in the red glow of the lamp, the breath stifled by the airless night and the bed shaking to the beat, beat, beat of the fearful heart as the leaves stirred again and the curtain moved in the window.

But she suffered so horribly, Christine, so unimaginably, and now she needs help—again. So let's go for it, and don't let up—*make* her listen, *make* her talk, go for a breakthrough, whatever it takes.

Tasha's voice sounded loud in the quiet of the room, but that was okay. She wanted it to be heard.

Watching the eyes in the portrait, holding their gaze, she said as steadily as she could, "Christine, you told me you hated cats. You told me it was okay for me to take your scarf that time. You told me it was Marcia, on the roof with Fido." In the window, the curtain moved. "Now tell me who murdered you."

Nine

Bernie Behrens picked up the screwdriver, getting the thought out of his head that he shouldn't be doing this, he was wasting valuable time. But he'd got to finish the house, for Christ's sake, take just these five minutes out of his schedule on Case #H9073, for the first time in almost a week.

A week without a break—and without a breakthrough.

The screwdriver wasn't long enough, so he got another one and started working on the front-door hinges while the telephone began ringing and he knew it was Flossie again, to ask him why he wouldn't marry her when she'd *told* him she *knew* what it was like to be a cop's wife and didn't *mind*, was ready to look after him like he was a king, welcome him home with open arms at all hours, day and night, see there was good, hot food ready for him, whatever he wanted.

The screws kept falling onto the floor because this screwdriver was long enough to reach through the window and across the sitting room but it was too long to keep control of, so he turned the house onto its side and tried again while the telephone kept on ringing.

Okay, it would be great to have a wife like that, except

for one or two little things, chief of which, in Flossie's case, was that with all those french fries and doughnuts she must be turning the scale already at around one-sixty and she was only twenty-eight yet with a long way to go, and he wasn't looking forward to climbing into bed in ten years from now, if he lived that long, with a sweet and loving balloon full of happy cholesterol, and also he'd need a wife, if he ever worked up the courage to go down that flower-decked aisle got up like a penguin, who'd need *his* little attentions now and then, some woman as thin as this screwdriver with ribs like a washboard and enough weakness in her that would cry out for some of his strength, enough tears in her that it'd take nights of sleepless and tender understanding to wipe away, leaving them both feeling like a patty-melt on special.

The telephone stopped ringing, and when the four tiny brass screws were into the front-door hinges, Bernie turned the house the right way up and stood back and looked at it, smelling the new wood and admiring the way the real glass windows reflected the light.

"One day," his dad had told them, "we'll have a house of our own to live in, someplace out of town, with trees around it and birds sitting in them," some of what he was saying getting lost because of the stabs of sudden pain, while those two kids across the hall kept up their yelling and fighting and the smell of cabbages came up the stairs from Mrs. Goldberg's kitchen.

Behrens prodded the front door gently with his finger, watching it swing open nice and easy; then he pulled it closed with a fingernail on the brass handle, thinking how strange his fingernails looked today, after he'd spent twenty minutes last night with a hard, stiff brush removing the evidence of everywhere his hands had been in the past two weeks.

"One day," his dad had told them, "we'll have a house with a blue front door and a brass handle, and we'll—" But the pain had finally got so bad he couldn't finish anything he started off saying, and that was the first time Bernie Behrens had been to a funeral, and he didn't like it, because his dad had never done anybody any harm and they said there was a God, so what was all this going on? He thought much the same thing six months later, at his mom's funeral, but it seemed like you could do nothing to change these things.

The early morning light streamed into the apartment, and Behrens noticed a hair sticking out from one of the roof tiles of the house, and got the medical tweezers from his toolbox and tried to pull it away, but it was stuck there, so he got a razor blade from his toolbox and cut it off short.

He had painted the front door blue. All the houses he'd made so far—five of them now—had blue front doors. There'd been a guy here one time, a retired cop who'd gone into antiques and stuff, and he'd told Behrens he'd give him a thousand bucks for each of the houses, with all that incredible painstaking work in them, but Behrens had said they weren't for sale, not telling him they weren't his to sell, in any case. They belonged to his dad.

He swung the little front door inward one more time, then let it close against the concealed magnet with a satisfying click, a fragment of memory flashing through his mind, of a little scene at the precinct one day when Commody, a redneck rookie just up from uniform, had come into the office and looked at Behrens and said, "Hey, I just heard you make dolls' houses!" He had a this-I-just-don't-believe expression on his flat red face, and Behrens saw Woodcock look up from some stuff he was going through.

"So what's wrong with that?" Woody's voice wasn't loud, but it kind of bounced around the walls like the knelling of somebody's doom, and the rookie looked at him with his mouth open.

"What the fuck did I say?"

And then Woodcock said, about ten octaves higher, "*It's*

*better than the shithouse you've made of your desk since
you got in here, for Christ sake, now get it cleaned up, you
hear me, you get it cleaned up, and right now!"*

The rookie went white as a stiff and started on his desk,
and Behrens murmured to Woody that the guy hadn't
meant anything by it, and that was the only time in the
whole of their partnership when Woody had told him to
shut the fuck up.

The sunshine in the room was going in one window of
the new house and out the other, and Behrens stood there
for another half minute with something like a thought passing through his mind, not quite a thought, maybe more of
a dedication, *This one okay, Dad?* Then he pulled away and
got his black leather briefcase with the initials almost worn
off and a bright smooth patch on it from where he slung it
into the Buick every day, and by 8:30 he was in the precinct, a ray of something like happiness prodding its way
through the murk of everyday reality this morning because
they all had another house to live in now.

"Bernie?" McOwen called across the room.

"Yeah?"

"You know what happened last night on Fifty-seventh?"

"So tell me."

"Some dame at the Washeteria complained her machine
was stuck, and when the manager looked inside he found
a head."

Behrens saw a report on his desk from Woodcock, and
pulled the paper clip away. "Nobody can ever say crime in
this city ain't creative." He wasn't interested in heads in
washing machines, it didn't have Jack the Knife's signature.

"But Jeeze," McOwen said, "what a way to go!"

"Yeah. Must've made the poor guy's head spin."

So here was the stuff from Woody at last on the orchid
delivery—it had taken some tracking down. Seemed like a
dozen of them had been left on the doorstep of the trades-
men's entrance at the Wittendorf residence sometime after

6:30 on the night when Christine Wittendorf was murdered, and the maid had thrown the florist's box into the garbage after she found it in Christine's room later that night when she went to turn down the bed—that was what had taken the tracking time, because the maid couldn't remember the name on the box and they'd had to scour the nearest municipal garbage dump. Then Woody had gone to the florist—Floral Arrangements on Madison—and they'd said sure, it was their box, but they wouldn't have left a delivery on a doorstep unless it was requested, especially at an address like that where there was a staff in residence.

Behrens looked across at McOwen. "Did Woodcock show this morning?"

"He called in, said he'd be here around nine. Trying to catch up on some sleep."

"McOwen?"

The junior detective looked up from his desk. "Yeah?"

"When anybody on the team calls in, I want to know, and I want to know the minute I get here. Are you listening, McOwen?"

"Jeeze, I—"

"You clean forgot, McOwen, for the second time. Third time they're going to find your fucking head in a fucking washing machine, McOwen."

"Yes, sir."

Behrens went back to the report. So it looked like somebody could have bought some flowers—not orchids—at Floral Arrangements and bought some orchids someplace else and then thrown the flowers away and put the orchids in the Floral Arrangements box and left them on the doorstep at the Wittendorf residence, also leaving a totally cold trail. Woody had traced the only five people who had bought orchids at Floral Arrangements, and none of them remotely resembled a serial killer.

It occurred to Behrens as he dropped the report sheet onto the desk and tilted his chair back that the orchids were the only viable clue he had to work on, and he was perfectly aware that if you still had only one clue to work on after six days of investigating a homicide you were in pretty bad shape, and maybe this was why the orchids stayed on his mind so much—not because they were intrinsically important but because they were all he'd got. Or almost all.

There was the scream reported to the dispatcher at 3:07 on the morning of the fifteenth, too. It wasn't evidence, because it didn't actually exist—except in the mind of Tasha Fontaine. He had proved that. But he couldn't ignore it, hadn't ignored it since the woman had stopped to talk to him in the park that morning at the crime scene.

It was like, Behrens thought as he rocked on his chair, the flash of colored light you sometimes saw on the wall from a prism of some kind, the beveled edge of a mirror, a glass vase standing on a windowsill, whatever—a flash of something that looked like it could have escaped from another world, to play around for a while like a butterfly before it finally vanished as the sun moved on.

The scream wasn't a clue, wasn't evidence, because it existed only in that woman's head.

Behrens rocked on his chair.

But what else existed in her head? He had a few questions to ask Fontaine, but he hadn't called her yet because there'd been all the physical evidence to plow through, plus the stuff they'd had in from the NCIC to evaluate. But now might be a good time to go along to Temple Mansions and talk to her.

As he checked the file for her number and his hand reached for the phone on his desk it began ringing, and he picked it up.

"Behrens."

"There's a Miss Tasha Fontaine here to see you."

Behrens watched the black hairs lifting on his wrist.

"Tell her to come on up."

* * *

"You look right out of a bandbox," Behrens said as he greeted her in the doorway.

"Thank you. That's because the last time you saw me I was in a tracksuit."

"No," Behrens said, "you weren't. But come on in. Let's commandeer that room over there."

It was bare-walled, with just a long metal table and a few metal chairs, and Behrens went across to the big interior mirror and pulled down the blind.

"I wasn't in a track suit," Tasha said, "the last time you saw me?"

"First let me get things organized," Behrens said, "around here. Then we'll be more comfortable."

"Is this an interrogation room?" Tasha had never been in one before, but this was what she imagined they'd be like; almost as bare as a prison cell.

"Yeah, but this isn't an interrogation, right? You came to see me of your own free will." On his way back to the open door, Behrens stopped and looked at her. "It's just so we can get away from the howler monkeys out there. But we could go to the little café round the corner, if you like."

She looked at her watch. "I won't have time. I just stopped off on my way to work."

"Whatever's best for you," Behrens said, and poked his head out of the door and spoke to McOwen, keeping his voice down. "Get some coffee in here, and bring those flowers from my desk." He came back, leaving the door open. "Take a seat, Miss Fontaine, make yourself at home."

He was trying to lighten things up, Tasha thought, but she'd hardly recognized him when he'd greeted her out there. A murder case could do this to a detective in just a week? He looked drained, punch-drunk.

"And I know why you've come." Behrens said, and took the other chair.

"You do?"

"Sure. I told you if you wanted to try the worst coffee in town, you knew where to find it. Guaranteed—I make it myself." McOwen came in and put two mugs on the table, and Behrens took the small vase of flowers he was holding in the crook of his elbow. Flossie had left it for him yesterday, for his desk; there were only a few daisies and things but it was better than nothing in a room like this. McOwen shut the door after him when he went out.

Tasha felt surprisingly touched. The little vase looked almost comical on the expanse of bare metal, but it was a good try, and she hadn't expected a homicide detective to have this kind of imagination. His wife was a lucky woman.

"You take cream?" Behrens asked. "Sugar?"

"Straight up is fine."

She had a nice smile, he thought; a sudden white flash, but behind it she was nervous. Sure, that figured, in a place like this. "Cheers," he said and lifted his coffee mug. "But watch it—it's hot."

"Okay." Tasha wished she'd come here to give him the name of the Central Park killer, but she hadn't. Christine hadn't answered her question last night.

"No," Behrens said, "you weren't wearing a tracksuit the last time I saw you. You were at Christine's funeral."

Tasha looked at him. "Oh. I didn't see you there."

"I know."

"Were you watching for him?"

"For who?"

Tasha's hand brushed the air. "For the man who killed her."

"We just kind of watch for whoever's around." Leaning back, tilting his head, "And when I saw you there, I was interested."

"You were?"

"Sure. Because your name wasn't on the invitation list."

She looked down, and Behrens waited. In a moment she said, "I gate-crashed."

"Why?" It was already too late to take it back. She'd frozen, looking at him as if she was almost scared. He hadn't remembered what she'd been like, how he'd learned to treat her, in the park that morning. She wasn't into giving him a lot of lies; she was out of her depth in some way, even drowning, and she needed his trust—and you don't get people's trust by shooting a sudden question at them. "I mean," he said slowly, "people do that, sure. There's somewhere they want to be, and—"

"I don't know why," Tasha said.

"I see." There was something floating on his coffee, which was par for the course in this place, and he used his pinkie finger to fish it out; with any luck it was just a bit of antique scum from the percolator. "Just like," he said, "you didn't know why you had to go down to the park that morning, when we were there picking over the pieces."

"That's right."

"Some kind of compulsion," Behrens nodded slowly, "that you don't understand, just like you told me." He wiped the bit of crud from his pinky finger onto the edge of the table. "Did you gate-crash the reception in Sutton Place, too? I never did get to see the invitation list."

"I—was there, yes."

"So I guess you must have given it some thought, this compulsion of yours. Come up with anything?"

Tasha took another sip of her coffee. He was right—it really was pretty bad, but it gave her hands something to do. "All I've come up with, Detective Behrens, is—"

"You wanna try 'Bernie'?"

It surprised her, and then, after an instant's reflection, didn't surprise her. Her prefabricated image of a homicide detective was getting in her way—the cold-eyed, square-jawed hunk with a gun at his hip. This man wasn't like that in the least. Watching his finely crumpled face and his quiet eyes, she felt something like compassion for him; until he could solve this case he was going to live with it day and night, losing sleep and grinding his energies into the ground, and even though she wasn't experiencing the burden of Christine Wittendorf's death in the same way, she was experiencing it in ways more subtle, following her compulsion and even now becoming afraid of it, trapped by it, to the point where she felt that the only way to rid herself of this—this haunting that had come into her so-normal, so-rational life was to try helping this man find out who had killed Christine, and avenge her, laying her ghost and leaving her in peace. And that was why she was here: there just might be something she was missing that a seasoned detective would pick up straight away.

"Bernie," she said, "okay. Please call me Tasha." She took a deep breath. "So, all I've come up with that could explain my compulsion is that up till now—up till the fifteenth—my life was completely smooth, easy, and untroubled. So when I heard that scream coming through the open window it was like—I don't know—like I was suddenly being exposed to reality, the real thing, urgent and terrifying and demanding, right out of the dark at three o'clock in the morning."

Behrens prodded his hollow tooth with the tip of his tongue. "It was a shock." He nodded understandingly.

"It was more than that. Much more."

"Oh? In what way, more?"

"I felt instantly *involved*."

"Involved." Behrens played with the word in his mind. So this gal—this very attractive young woman—had been awakened out of a sound sleep by a scream, and felt instantly involved. By a scream she couldn't have heard, any more than he'd been able to hear the policewoman's.

Tell her about the policewoman? Instinct said no. She was already out of her depth with this whole thing and if he told her she'd only imagined that scream she could flip out and go dingbats.

Was she in fact dingbats? Sure, she could be, the bored socialite looking for drama in her life whether she knew it or not, identifying with a torn, bloodied murder victim and letting her imagination go wild. Be easy enough to believe, except for one thing, and that one thing threw out the whole theory of blue sky yonder.

Tasha Fontaine had heard somebody screaming in her mind at exactly the time when Christine Wittendorf would have screamed, as she saw her death coming.

She'd heard somebody screaming so "desperately" that it had woken her up and sent her to the phone to dial Emergency.

The scream was the key.

For the second time today, Behrens watched the hairs lifting on his wrist as he cradled his mug of coffee.

The scream was the key to this whole case, forget the blood-soaked panties and the shoes and the human hair and the nail scrapings and the shred of orchid petal in the grass, forget the report on Jack the Knife from the NCIC, forget the whole goddamned file on Case #H9073. The scream was the key. And this young woman was holding it in her hands, trying to give it to him, and not knowing how.

Behrens took a swig of his coffee, savoring the flavor— which Tasha Fontaine could not—of this whole place, of the phones ringing and the doors slamming and the hands of the deadpan government-issue clock on the wall going 'round and 'round through noon and midnight and into the graveyard hours, the flavor of a direct hit on a case, of watching it go down, the flavor of blood, like that guy said, blood, tears, and sweat, that you couldn't find in a cup of coffee anywhere else this side of hell.

So, okay, the scream was the key.

Great. Let's go tell Woody that. Hey, Woody, you know what? All the evidence is in now, and we're going to bring down this case in a matter of hours. The whole thing depends on a scream, see, that nobody seems to have heard except this gal who's losing her marbles so fast she can't hear them hitting the ground. So, ain't that great? Woody? You listening?

There was something Woody didn't know about Detective Bernard Behrens of Homicide, NYPD. Detective Behrens, noted by all in that critical organization for being good at his job, flew his operation so near the ground, like most successful people, that as he whizzed from triumph to triumph he came close, sickeningly close, to crashing it into the cliffs and outcrops that threatened at every moment to make, on impact, the final kill. And the final kill was failure.

Woody mustn't ever know that. He'd never sleep. And by the same token he mustn't know that his hero, the prince of the city, was right now figuring that the only way to find the man responsible for the Christine Wittendorf killing was to concentrate on an inaudible, nonexistent scream. But maybe that wasn't quite fair: there was a bit more to it than that. He had to concentrate on this woman sitting here at the table with him and find out how she could have heard that scream—if she had, because she could be lying, even though he felt certain she wasn't—and how she could have heard it at the very time when Christine Wittendorf was at the point of death, and why she was locked into this compulsion of hers, and what she was doing here now.

"Okay," he said at last, "so you felt involved, when you heard that scream. Caught up in something." He slid his coffee mug an inch to the left, watching it carefully. "That day in the church, you stood there for quite a while at the coffin, didn't you? You were the last to leave."

In a moment, Tasha said slowly, "I knew it was going to be the closest I would ever get to her again."

"Physically."

"Yes."

"And how close do you feel to her mentally?" Behrens waved his hand. "Spiritually?"

Tasha hadn't expected that. It wasn't a question a hard-nosed cop would ask. "Pretty close," she said.

"Pretty close to somebody you never actually met."

"That's not quite true. It's what I told you in the park,

but I remembered later that I had actually met Christine, just briefly." She told him about the taxi in the rain.

"And that was the only time?"

"Yes." She didn't look away. Maybe he thought she'd lied to him in the park, for some reason.

"Only met her once," Behrens said, "but it shook you up when she was—when she died. Well, sure, it got us all shook up, but with you it's more personal, right?" He moved his coffee mug back to the right an inch, watching it, not her. He'd hear what he wanted in her voice, didn't need to watch her eyes for it, risk intimidating her. "So all you know about Christine is what you've discovered since her death. Right?"

"Right."

"Like what?"

She hates cats. Can't tell him that. "Just things people have told me."

"You want to name any of those people?"

"No."

Behrens looked at her now, allowing himself another smile, making it look kind of rueful. "You're loyal. I like that." He went on watching her, the defensiveness in her eyes, the wariness. "But you'd tell me anything you thought might help us find the man we want. Wouldn't you? Anything at all?"

"It's why I'm here, Bernie." She liked calling him that, felt easier with him in this bleak, unwelcoming room.

"To see if you could help."

"Yes."

"Well that's great," Bernie said, and shrugged himself forward on the metal rattrap chair, bringing his face closer to hers and letting a smile show again, seeing her eyes relax. "That's really great, Tasha, because I was thinking maybe you knew something, but couldn't say so."

"What could stop me?" She sat up straighter.

"Fear."

"Fear of what?"

"Oh," Behrens said, and got off the chair and took a turn, came back, "I thought you might have known there was a chance something could happen that night if things turned out wrong between Christine and"—he shrugged—"whoever. Maybe a boyfriend she was trying to break it off with? A jealous boyfriend? So when you heard the scream, you connected it and called Emergency right away in the hope of stopping something, being in time, you know? Then you were scared of coming forward to tell us what you knew. Because you were scared of him—the boyfriend or whoever. It happens. We get—"

"Listen, I don't scare easy. I would have gone to the police like a shot. You don't know me."

"Well, I'm beginning to," Behrens said, and smiled nicely.

"But what gave you an idea like that?"

"That was just one idea, Tasha. I have a thousand. It's the way we have to think, see. When there's so little evidence to work on that the case bogs down we just have to blue-sky-yonder the whole thing, dream up a bunch of conceivable scenarios and see if any of them fits the physical evidence. And the way I arrived at the idea that you might have known something could happen that night was when I started thinking about this compulsion of yours—to show up at the crime scene and go to the funeral and everything. I began wondering if it could be an expression of remorse. Guilt, even."

Tasha got up from the chair, catching her ankle against a leg of the table and wincing.

"Jeeze," Behrens said, "you better rub that."

"I guess the idea of guilt occurs pretty easily to you people," Tasha said. She stood with her back to the wall, her arms folded, wishing she hadn't come here.

"Sure," Bernie said. "And innocence."

"But what would that have made me, for God's sake? An accessory before the fact or something?"

"Don't worry about it."

"I *am* worried about it. I want your trust."

Behrens went up to her, touched her arm. "You've got my trust. You know the problem? Ninety percent of the people I talk to in this room have got something to hide, and my job is to find it. So when someone like you comes in here, I forget to change the channel and you get the same routine. I'm sorry."

Tasha looked down, half her mind noting the coffee stain on Behren's creased jacket where the button tugged, the shapeless pants, the splits on the worn brogue shoes, sensing the fatigue in him, the weight of the Wittendorf case wearing him down.

"Okay, Bernie," she said and looked up again into his eyes, and saw they'd been waiting. "I've got your trust, but don't you ever renege on me. If I'm to be of any help to you in this case, you have to know that whatever I tell you is true. It can't work, otherwise."

He moved away, not to crowd her. "You're absolutely right. And it's a two-way street—you need my help any-time, you got it." He started thinking about that, but stopped short. He hoped Tasha Fontaine wouldn't ever need his help. "There's something maybe you should know," he said in a moment. "The man who killed Christine has killed before."

"Oh my God!"

"Yeah. He's a serial. There was a woman attacked a couple of years back, same place, Central Park. Her name was Marianne Cleaver."

Tasha shook her head. "I don't remember seeing any-thing about it."

"It didn't attract much attention—she didn't have a Sut-ton Place address. That was his first kill, as far as we know. Then he took off around the country—Los Angeles, Chi-cago, Boston. Now he's back in New York."

Tasha asked, not wanting to, not wanting to hear the answer, "How many?"

"Eleven. As far as we know."

"Eleven"—she stared at him—"and the last was Christine?"

"As far as we know."

"How can you tell it's the same man?"

"Chiefly by his M.O.—his method of operation. It's been identical in every case. Anyway," Behrens said, and picked up his mug of cooling coffee, "I thought you should know. If it had been just Christine it would have been bad enough. Worse, there were others. Worse still, he could do it again. And again. So you'll be helping us, maybe, to save lives. If you can tell me anything about Christine, anything you've heard about her that we might not know, it could help. If you have any intuitions, even—women are good at that—intuitions, hunches, whatever."

He waited. This time she might feel like opening up.

"Christine didn't like herself." Tasha moved across to the table and perched on the edge, sheer silk and brushed-hide Mephistos dangling. "She hated cats. She had 'so many different lives,' quote unquote. She was a nymphomaniac, according to one person. Her boyfriends were all 'pretty wild.' Somebody said I was lucky to have known her, and not for long—I didn't ask what that meant. I think you've questioned one of her boyfriends, haven't you?"

"Fido Hamilton."

"And Marcia?"

"Marcia Fremont."

"She went to a beautician's, Angel Face."

"And a hairdresser, Marcel's."

"Right. She used a limo service—"

"Quality Limo. We've checked those people out. We asked them if they knew anything about Christine's movements on or shortly before the fifteenth. They didn't. Her bookstore, her bank, her couturier, all those people. But go on." Behrens had wanted to save her time, because any minute she was going to look at her watch. She'd told him earlier, 'I just stopped off on my way to work.'

Tasha cast her mind back; was there anything else?
She knows what I'm thinking. She talks to me.

Would that come under the heading of intuition? No, it was too much of a risk: he'd think she was a weirdo, into Ouija boards and stuff, not to be trusted anymore.

Behrens was waiting.

"She used Infiniti."

"Used——?"

"The perfume."

"Oh, yeah." He'd been thinking of the car. "One of the maids told us." He had a half-empty bottle of it in the evidence box, on loan from the deceased's effects; it could be important. If—when—they caught up with Jack the Knife, would there still be a trace of Infiniti on his clothes? Could even be a clincher, if the prosecutor had his back to the wall.

"I can't think," Tasha said, "of anything else right now." She looked at her watch. "I guess I haven't been of much help."

"Sure you have," Behrens told her, "just by coming here. People don't like going too near the police, you know? It's the image we've got—badges and handcuffs and all that good stuff, puts people off. So I appreciate the effort you made today. Really." And she'd helped, he thought, as he moved past her to open the door. She'd confirmed what he already knew: she'd come here today because she couldn't keep away from Christine, or from anyone or anything that had to do with her. And this reminded him that the key to the Wittendorf case was the scream she had heard that night. And the hand that held the key was Tasha Fontaine.

"Any time you need me," Behrens told her as he led her through the office to the elevator, "you'll get instant attention. If I'm not here, there'll be somebody else on the team—Woodcock, McOwen, Baker, Orsini, there's five of us, plus the supervisor, Sergeant Lowenstein. Okay?" His hand cupped her elbow as the doors of the elevator slid open. "Count yourself one of the family."

And then, as Tasha got in and turned to look at him before the doors closed again, she saw that his nice smile wasn't reaching his eyes: they were quite serious. "I mean that, remember? You need us, you got us, anytime."

Detective Orsini was at his desk when Behrens came back through the office.

"Hey, Bernie! You got the hots for that lady?"

Orsini was Italian, born with his mind on spaghetti and sex. He'd seen the door shut and the blind go down in the interrogation room when they'd gone in there.

As Behrens made his way between the desks, Orsini noted there'd been no comeback to the crack, which was unusual. Guy had his thoughts in his pockets, sure.

Going back into the interrogation room for his coffee, Behrens wondered if he was making too much of this thing, or—and this would be dangerous—too little. Here was the scenario: Jack the Knife used Central Park for his kills when he was in New York. Tasha Fontaine lived at the edge of Central Park, just a half-mile from the spot where he killed Christine Wittendorf. It could be the guy haunted the park when he was in this city, even by daylight—killers were often like moths around the crime scene—and he might see Tasha sometime in the area, notice her, follow her. She was the typical victim type in this casebook; young, attractive, long, dark hair, with connections to the art world, mixed with dress designers.

And somehow, strangely, she felt herself involved with Christine, his last victim.

And couldn't keep away.

Behrens stood in the doorway of the interrogation room with the mug of cold coffee in his hand, his eyes in space. Then they focused and he looked across the desks.

"Orsini?"

"Yeah?"

"Put a name on the case computer. Use capitals. TASHA FONTAINE." He gave Orsini her address and telephone number. "Anytime she calls—*any*time—she gets priority attention, sirens and flashing lights. Put it on the board as well; get memos out to the desks, and patch in Operations. Fontaine calls 911 from Temple Mansions, I want wheels rolling the instant her number comes up on the dispatcher's screen. You got that?"

"I got it, Bernie."

Ten

___

The man tested the beets, pressing them. He always tested everything.

Farmer's Market was noted for its quality, but he still liked checking things out for himself; there was nothing worse than a tired beet or limp lettuce, was there? He liked things fresh—but then, who didn't?

There were three supermarkets closer to where he lived, but he went to them only for what one might call the domestic basics: household and kitchen things and cleaning materials, not food. Farmer's Market, with its well-earned reputation, had found the right place for itself, near 56th and Lexington, where it caught the quality trade from the residential areas east of Central Park. People came here from Sutton Place, even, or sent their housekeepers with the chauffeur. Christine had lived on Sutton Place.

This morning there were figs in again from Macedonia, and boxes of Medjool dates, which he loved; he'd heard that an Arab could ride his camel all day through the Sahara on just one or two dates. He liked nutritious things, when he could find them; there was so much junk around these days. Farmer's prices were a little bit on the high side, but—as the slogan on the posters said so cleverly—QUALITY IS A SAVING GRACE.

He needed some walnuts, next to the kumquats, but
there was another customer in that section, a young
woman, picking and choosing, and he held back, testing
the Anjou pears and leaving a little dent in one of them—
well, that was all right, one had to know what he was
buying, and how else could he tell?

She had long brown hair, the young woman, hanging
down over her green silk top, and her tan, bare arm reached
for the kumquats in the top compartment, throwing one or
two back because they weren't ripe yet. He didn't like
kumquats; they were too sharp, and had what somebody
had amusingly called "pucker power."

He didn't like young women either, and with this
thought he felt a stirring in his groin, and turned away to
look at the pomegranates.

I don't think so.

Staring at him with her eyes wide suddenly, almost in
shock, like he was disgusting or something, or crazy for
even thinking he should ask such a thing.

I don't think so.

He touched a pomegranate, feeling its moist curve.

They should never say that.

The young woman moved off in a few minutes, and in
relief he picked out a guava for himself—the ripest—putting it carefully into his shopping cart so as not to bruise it
because it was soft and ripe and expensive, but fruit was
almost all one could think of eating in this dreadfully hot
summer, and he knew others thought the same.

Goat's milk, a small yogurt—plain, with no fruit or
honey, because sugar made the bacillus less effective—and
some Parmesan, and that was about all he needed. He
rolled his cart with a flourish between two others, bringing
a smile from a nice man in a plaid hat, and in a minute he
was down at the checkout with only one person in front of
him.

The young woman.

She stood there in her frayed blue jeans, a girl, really, one foot out behind her with her toe on the ground and her heel way up, trying to look insouciant, one might suppose, tossing her head to make her long hair swing as she watched the checkout clerk pricing the things she was buying—lipsticks and pantyhose and cookies as far as he could make out without staring, typical purchases for such a girl, and as he watched her the scent of her body reached him and the stirring in his groin started again and he turned quickly and looked at the big black headline that said ELVIS TALKS TO WIFE THROUGH DRUGGED ROCK STAR with the picture of a man with his head hanging down like he was out cold, with Elvis in a kind of cloud behind him, but it didn't hold his interest because he knew the girl was still there right beside him and when he turned back to look at her she was putting some money down and the clerk dropped the receipt into the brown paper sack and the girl said cheerily, "Thank you!" and walked away with her long hair swinging.

The clerk looked at him and said "Hi!" and started pricing his things as he stood there watching the girl going through the exit door, but he knew now that he mustn't lose her.

Bitch.

"I'll be right back," he told the clerk as he looked in his wallet, "I need to get some money from the car."

He didn't wait for an answer but made for the exit, not hurrying too much, just walking quickly.

The girl was getting into a battered blue Chevy and he hurried now because he had to, with the feeling very big and hot in his groin and the breath coming fast out of his chest as he reached his Pacer and unlocked the door and got in and started the motor and swung out of the parking lane with his eyes everywhere, looking for the battered blue Chevy, a shopping cart in the way and he bumped it aside, his hands shaking on the wheel and the light beginning to flicker the way it always did when this was happening to him, but there was nothing he could do about it now because it had gone too far and he only just missed another car that was turning into his lane and the driver called out something but it didn't matter—all that mattered was the girl in the battered blue Chevy.

Bitch! You little bitch!

There was a truck lumbering in from the street with its windshield sending a flash of light from the sun across his eyes and he hit the brakes and backed up and turned and took the next lane with the rear tires spinning on the loose surface and shooting grit across the doors of a Mercedes but he couldn't see the Chevy and his breath was blocked in his chest as he gunned up again and swung past a man pushing a shopping cart and heard another shout and a clatter and hit the brakes again and brought the Pacer sliding to a stop.

This is wrong, go back.

But she's—

She's gone, go back now before there's—

But I want that *bitch*—

"Are you fucking drunk or something?"

Face in the window, staring, man with the shopping cart.

"Sick, I got sick." Slumped over the wheel.

Take it easy; go back now—

Sitting in his sweat, she was gone, she was gone, gone, gone—

"You want me to call a doctor?"

"No, I'm okay now, I'm okay, I'm sorry I—"

Go back.

"No problem. Nothing got smashed, I guess."

His breath sawing in and out of his lungs and his eyes squeezed shut and someone tapping the horn, someone behind him, but if he could only have caught up with that *bitch* and followed her, found where she lived—

She's gone—it's too late now.

Tears on his face, smell of his sweat, shriveling down there, shrinking, too late, yeah, go back before there's trouble.

Got the Pacer moving off, the sunlight blinding, heat pressing down from the flat brass sky, her dark hair swinging across and across his eyes through the tears of his dying rage.

Eleven

Silence had come at last in Tasha's office, the kind of exhausted silence that sets in after a late party, when the few survivors can't even muster the energy to go home.

But it was 11:00 in the morning now, and outside the tinted windows the day's heat had begun climbing the walls of the building, its light bouncing off black glass and shimmering on brushed steel surfaces.

Tasha was tilted back in her chair behind the peach-colored fiberglass desk, her glass of Pouilly-Fuissé still untouched because she'd been concentrating with every nerve in her body for the last hour while Elizabeth knelt on the carpet and spread her collection of designs from wall to wall—rough artwork, photographs, cuttings from catalogs, small posters smudged from the copiers, plus a half-dozen menus lying facedown with good wishes to "La Fontaine" scribbled across their backs.

Elizabeth had got into Kennedy from Milan before 6:00 last evening and phoned Tasha from the airport saying she was ready for debriefing, but Tasha had told her there was a limo waiting there for her and she must go straight home and hit the sack, and her junior partner didn't make even a

token protestation. Five days of the Milan show with its
unending tension and hysteria plus six hours' worth of jet
lag was enough to floor the finest.

And now Tasha lifted her glass and tilted it in Elizabeth's
direction.

"I think you did fabulously," she said.

A breath gusted out of Elizabeth as she let her slender
fashion-model body flop prone across the moss-green carpet with her arms flung out.

"Thank God," she said.

Tasha gave a laugh—and a question flashed into her
mind: how long was it since she'd laughed like that, spon-
taneously, out of a free spirit? It seemed like weeks. "You
need a drink," she told Elizabeth.

"Anything except Campari. *Anything.*"

Tasha poured some wine into the other glass for her and
brought it across as Elizabeth sat up, scattering some of the
colored sketches as she looked at Tasha with her eyes still
puffy from too many late nights. "So," she said, "with the
kitty at La Botica three-quarters of a million light, I'm not
fired?"

"I would have spent more," Tasha said, "and some of it
on trash."

"Not really—and not at this year's show . . . it's going to
go down in history. There was so much *talent* around, I
didn't have to pick the plums off the trees, they just fell into
my lap. And I missed you like hell, Tasha—*everybody* did."
She picked up one of the menus—"Giorgio had nineteen
people clamoring for a table and he kept them all waiting
while he wrote you this!"

The maître d' at the Villa Firenze had used a red felt pen,
or maybe—knowing Giorgio—a borrowed lipstick. *Tasha
mia!—This is written with my blood because I stab myself
in my heart when I see you are not here in Milano this year!
You do not come next time and I stab myself again! How
can you do this to me? I will soon need transfusion! Con mi
amore—Giorgio.*

"Those Italians . . . " Tasha laughed.

"They're the only people," Elizabeth said, "who can tire you out and leave you feeling high at the same time. Here's a message from Ungaro himself, and one from Vittorio. Filippo Constante was really nice about the dress we lost, and said he understood perfectly. You should have—"

"He got my roses?"

"Of course—I checked at the desk." Elizabeth sipped her wine, watching Tasha thoughtfully. "They're right, you know. You have to be there next year—and every year. It's where your soul is, at these shows."

Tasha felt a pang of regret. Yeah, the Milan show was the best circus in town, a superspectacular in sequins and silk under the blazing sound-stage lights of the huge marquee as the models whirled and darted through the shadows and the smoke, breaking suddenly onto the runway in a parade of rainbows in their colored gowns while the hard rock hammered from the amplifiers and the flashlights burst like an electric storm as the tide of applause washed in from the crowded seats while the buyers' pens got busy and the barometer rose from fifty thousand dollars to a hundred, five hundred, a million, ten million and beyond, way beyond, as the talents of Armani and Christian Lacroix and Yves Saint Laurent and Scaasi and the rest of them were paraded under the supercritical eyes of the people who really mattered here, massed in the shadows below the dazzling lights, anonymous, the people who'd come here to buy—or not to buy—thumbs up for the Valentino collection, thumbs down for Granelli's, let Lagerfeld hear the roar of the crowd this year for those stunning velvet gowns, a statement in strict tempo the whole length of the runway, and hats off again to Lacroix for those romantic froufrou fantasies set ablaze with diamanté in homage to the madly in love.

And sitting among them all, this year, there'd been the girl whose own flair for line and color and accent had brought her all the way from the feverish grind of the runways to a junior partnership on Fifth Avenue: Elizabeth of La Botica, New York.

"Yeah," Tasha said, "I should have been there with you." And suddenly she felt tears coming, and knew she had to stop them: to break down in front of the serene and supercool Elizabeth would be embarrassing. But already it was too late.

"What the hell," she heard Elizabeth asking quietly, "is this?"

Tasha got off the floor and spun around to a window with her back to her, staring out at the tinted monochrome of the city and seeing unexpectedly her own reflection in the glass, for an instant wondering whose it was.

"You're right," she said in a minute, delving for a tissue, "it's where my soul is. Where my *life* is, goddamn it!"

Behind her she saw Elizabeth's statuesque reflection on the window glass, watching her as her voice came quietly.

"How did the funeral go?"

"What?" Tasha turned to face her, blotting the last of the tears. "Oh . . . It's not about that."

But it was, of course.

It was about Christine.

"Can I help?" Elizabeth asked.

"You just did."

Sure, it was about Christine, the tragic little ghost who'd been haunting her day and night since the real Christine had died, never giving her peace, driving her to the point where she'd started coming late to work and taking time off, making mistakes, misjudgments, sending Elizabeth to Milan in her place while she'd stayed in this hot, sweltering city so that she could shuffle behind those weeping strangers in the church to look down at the veiled face of the stranger in the catafalque.

Why?

I knew it was going to be the closest I would ever get to her again.

Okay, so why did she want to get close?

In God's name, why?

Because it was Christine.

"I—I've been letting myself get caught up in something," she told Elizabeth, "that's all. And you brought me back to where my real life is."

In a moment—"Do I know him?"

"What? No, it's not a man. It's a ghost."

"A ghost," Elizabeth said with an elegant shrug, "okay." Like it happened all the time. But her cool blue eyes watched Tasha without blinking.

"Yeah," Tasha said, and picked up the bottle of wine, seeing Elizabeth lay a pale, long-fingered hand across her glass. Refilling her own, Tasha dropped into one of the deep Copenhagen chairs. "You remember the gal who got murdered in Central Park the other—"

"Christine Wittendorf?"

"Right."

"Of course."

Tasha hadn't realized that out there beyond her obsession with Christine the whole of Manhattan was still in shock. "Okay," she said, "well, I heard her scream, that night, from my apartment. That's why the police got there so fast—I called 911." She drank some wine, beginning to feel better, to feel that she'd reached a critical point in this Christine thing where she had to make a decision. "And you know? It kind of got to me. I felt involved."

"I can imagine."

"You can?" Tasha gave a short laugh. "That, too, helps." She began playing with one of the leather-covered buttons on the chair, moving her fingertips around and around it, not looking at Elizabeth. "But then I—I started getting in too deep, you see. That was the funeral I 'had' to go to."

Elizabeth looked at her. "Wittendorf's?"

"Right. I lied to you. She isn't—wasn't, *wasn't,* for God's sake—a cousin."

"Oh." After a moment, "Was that why you didn't go to Milan?"

Tasha looked up, and her fingers stopped playing with the button on the chair. "Yes."

It sounded crazy.

At the time, when she'd told Elizabeth she was sending her to Europe alone, it hadn't seemed any big deal; she'd rationalized her way through it—good experience for her junior partner, Milan was a great big hassle anyway, let's give it a pass this time around. But now it seemed a crazy thing to have done, *was* a crazy thing to have done, totally insane.

Insane. She said the word over in her mind, listening to it, shivering suddenly. Oh Jesus . . . it was the first time she'd thought of that. She'd been rationalizing her obsession with Christine all this time, too, making it look normal, or at least acceptable.

While she was slowly going insane.

Then Elizabeth was asking quietly, "Are you going to see anybody about this?"

Tasha took a breath. "You think I'm losing my marbles?" She waited, wanting—needing—a quick answer, not getting it.

Sirens sounded from the street below, muted by the windows.

"If I thought you were losing your marbles," Elizabeth said at last, "I'd say no, of course not. It's just that for you, with your whole life centered in La Botica and the fashion world, I thought maybe you'd get back on track faster with somebody's help." She began sorting the stuff on the floor, editing out the catalog clippings and the menus and putting the artwork together. Maybe she was just trying to take the heat off, keeping her hands busy as the silence went on, but to Tasha it made it look like the party was over now, with the curtain coming down on Milan. And she hadn't even been there. She'd stayed behind in New York—with the

humidity in the eighties and the heat around eighty-five—
and gone to a stranger's funeral.

She heard Elizabeth saying, "But, hey, I was in and out
of shrinks myself a dozen times before I was twenty. How
else could I finish up as an overdressed ice goddess without
getting all that childhood shit out of the way? It's no big
deal. Those guys can do a lot of good, if you can find one
who doesn't want to screw you on the couch as part of the
therapy, and charge you for it."

Tasha felt anger rising, and was surprised. Elizabeth was
not only a vital business asset to La Botica, but she'd
become a friend—as far as an 'overdressed ice goddess'
would allow any kind of friendship—and she was trying to
help Tasha now. But she needn't have been so goddamn
quick to talk about seeing a shrink.

Tasha drained her glass of wine and set it firmly on the
corner of her desk. "Thanks for the suggestion," she said,
"but I think I can handle my own problems for the time
being."

"Hanif told me you'd be here, darling!" Audrey Symes gave
Tasha a quick little hug. "I'm so glad. I didn't know you'd
met him."

"He's just a neighbor." Hanif Khattak had a penthouse
in Temple Mansions; they shared the elevator sometimes,
that was all, and acknowledged each other in Farmer's
Market or when their paths crossed jogging in the park.
She'd also noticed him at the funeral reception at the Wittendorf residence, but they hadn't spoken.

"I'm receiving for him," Audrey said, and guided her
through the guests, "but we must let him know you've
arrived." She appraised Tasha with her large honey-colored
eyes. "And you're wearing Infiniti! It was Christine's favor-
ite, did you know?"

"It was?"

Tasha had put it on this evening without thinking. She'd bought it because she'd seen it on Christine's dressing table at the house that time, wanting to get so close that she'd even *smell* like her, for God's sake, how crazy can you get? But in the two days since Elizabeth had got back from Milan and awakened her to reality, she'd come to the decision she knew she'd have to make, to save her sanity.

Cut Christine Wittendorf out of her life.

But it wasn't going to be easy.

Last night, coming home after treating Elizabeth to dinner at the Four Seasons, she'd dropped her coat and bag onto the bed and gone straight over to Christine's self-portrait on the wall to take it down—and the phone had rung, startling her.

"This is Jason."

"Who?"

"Jason Newberry."

Tasha waited, but he didn't say more than that. She didn't know any Jason, either Newberry or anything else.

"I'm sorry, but you have the wrong number."

"No," the voice said.

She waited again, feeling her skin creeping a little, because this guy was so strange, acting like she knew him. Okay, there were some pretty strange guys in this city, so she just hung up.

When she went back to the self-portrait she was still feeling uneasy, so when the phone rang again just as her hands reached for the picture, she cried out this time, and stood there with her skin crawling again as the ringing went on, and on, because she wasn't going to answer it, this must be Jason again, hadn't liked being cut off, well that's tough shit, old buddy, because you've got the wrong number like I already told you, so bug off, okay?

When the ringing stopped she took a deep breath and went into the sitting room and switched on the answering machine, feeling extraordinarily protected by such a simple gadget; then she caught sight of her white-faced reflection in a mirror, and was startled again—hey, listen, people get a zillion weird phone calls in this city every day, especially every night, so what's the big deal? You a New Yorker or not?

To get her mind off it she went across to the television to catch the late news to see if there was anything breaking yet on Bosnia, and it wasn't until she was in bed a half-hour later with the latest issue of *W* and a nightcap by courtesy of Remy Martin that she understood something. It hadn't been the phone call that had gotten her so uptight. It was the fact that it had interrupted her in what she was doing at the time, at the very instant when she'd reached out to take Christine's portrait off the wall. And it had happened twice.

And the portrait was still there, watching her from across the room, because after she'd caught the late-night news she'd gone into the bathroom to brush her teeth and forgotten about it.

Christine, just across the room.

Tasha watched her back.

Christine, will you get the fuck out of my life?

A feeling of shame, of guilt.

Look, what happened to you was terrible, but now I want to forget all about it. All about you. Okay?

Late traffic rolled below the windows. There was no breeze tonight; the city lay slumped in a torpor beneath the haze of the long day's heat.

So you have to go now.

Christine?

You have to go. You're in the wrong world. This is my world, and you have yours. Let's keep it that way.

But the eyes over there just went on watching her, and the worst part came when Tasha threw back the bed sheet and began walking across the carpet toward the portrait to take it down and her legs gave way and she buckled, darting a hand out to save herself but not finding anything to

hold onto, so that she stayed there in a kind of crouch like
an animal in fear, running her fingers through her hair with
her eyes squeezed shut as she listened to the soft insistent
thudding in her chest and came to know, quite definitely to
know that she couldn't take the portrait down tonight, she
was too tired, and as she accepted that idea the strength
came back into her legs and she straightened up and turned
around and got into bed again, switching off the light and
bunching the pillows and lying there with the sweat cooling
on her as she waited for sleep to come, waited in quiet
desperation for sleep to come and save her from thinking,
from having to think, from having to understand.

By morning she was certain only of one thing: that
cutting Christine out of her life was not going to be easy.

"I learned from the Fabius Gallery," she heard Hanif
Khattak saying as he greeted her with a gracious little bow,
"that you'd bought Christine's self-portrait, and that's why
I thought you might like to see some of her other work. I'm
delighted you could come."

Her other work, yeah. Christine's self-portrait, Christine's other work, Christine's perfume, you couldn't get
away from her. She shouldn't have come, Tasha thought;
but then, she hadn't known why she'd been invited.

"I'd love to, of course," she heard herself saying, surprised how eager she was managing to sound. "It was kind
of you to think of me, Mr. Khattak."

"Entirely my pleasure. My first name is Hanif. You knew
Christine, of course?"

"A little. I—"

"Such an appalling, senseless affair," Hanif said. "I was
so fond of her, you know, so very fond. She was already
showing signs of becoming important, even at her young
age." His English was perfect, Tasha noticed, and his trace
of an accent attractive.

She accepted a glass of sherry, going with Audrey and
her host to view the paintings. "Of course," he said, "I have
Audrey to thank for most of these; I'm afraid I hadn't even

heard of Christine until I received instructions to go *straight* to the Fabius Gallery one Saturday morning." A gold tooth glimmered in the warm brown skin "One doesn't question, does one, instructions from Audrey?"

"I found him the Renoir, darling, the one over the hearth. I'm with Reed-Mathieson, did I tell you? Hence my total indispensability to Hanif, among other collectors."

Reed-Mathieson was second in line to Sotheby's in the art-auction field, as Tasha knew; she'd found a dress for Miriam Reed a month ago to wear at what she'd called the shotgun wedding of her daughter to an Austrian prince. "Is there any of Christine's early work here?" she asked Hanif. Having to show an interest, she was aware of a strange feeling of remorse, almost of grief: only a few days ago, when Elizabeth was in Milan, she'd been eager for any new closeness she could find to Christine, going to the gallery and picking up the self-portrait with a sense of achievement, to carry away something that was the very essence of Christine, a portrait not only of herself, but by herself—and as she'd seen herself to be. And now, so soon, she was desperate to put Christine out of her life, to reject her, to forget her.

To let her die, like everyone else had done.

So that was what this feeling was about, of remorse, even grief. She'd let Christine "come through" to her in some weird metaphysical way, had let her talk to her; and she'd been ready to listen, even to start a small, stumbling crusade to help her, by going to the police. She'd given this restless spirit confidence in her—and now she was taking it away, letting Christine down, sending her back to the shadows.

Okay. But it had to be done. Because was it really the truth of things? Was Christine really trying to take over her life like this, or was it all going on in her own imagination?

No. Remember Marcia. You couldn't have dreamed her name up.

Coincidence.

Remember the cats, then. She said she hated cats.

So? I've had no proof of that.

Then get it.

How?

Ask somebody.

I don't want to.

You've got to. Or you'll never know what's really happening. You'll never know the truth.

Listening to Hanif Khattak as he talked about the paintings, answering him, even, and apparently making some kind of sense, Tasha stood there among all these well-dressed, civilized people in this charming, elegant room and saw herself becoming isolated, withdrawn from it all, led away into a cold, silent wasteland where figures moved through the keening wind, a place where only their shadows were real in the lowering light, a limbo, a netherworld, where she'd been brought for a purpose. And that purpose was to give her answer to those whose domain this was, a simple answer to a simple but terrible question, before she could be allowed back into her own reality.

Are you possessed by the dead, or are you going mad?

Oh, Jesus. Oh, Jesus Christ. So I can't win either way?

Answer.

I can't.

You must.

Why?

Because until you know, you can't hope to save yourself. You won't know how.

The figures moved through the half-light, faceless, ageless, their garments flapping in the wind.

Okay. But I need time.

Very well. But hurry, before it's too late.

The light grew suddenly brighter, and as the room swung around her she put a hand out to steady herself and felt Audrey's warm, ample arm in support.

"All right, darling?"

"What?" It was taking time to get things back into focus. "Yes. Yes, I'm all right."

"It's so hot in here." The large amber eyes were watching her in that quiet way they had, that didn't look like staring.

"Is it?" Tasha looked around her. "Where's Hanif?"

"He drifted off. But don't worry, you thanked him very nicely for showing you the pictures."

"I did?"

"Of course."

"God, I don't even remember. I was miles away."

"I know." The watchful gaze was questioning now, but nothing was said, nothing asked, and Tasha realized how glad she was that this comforting and undemanding woman in her eccentric Vivienne Westwood dress was here tonight, because the worst wasn't over yet. The question—the simple but terrible question—had to be answered, and soon.

But it's so scary.

Sure.

"It was—it was really kind of Hanif," she said, "to ask me here." The social graces, thank God for the social graces. They could save your life; okay, your sanity. But only for a while.

"Any man," Audrey said gently, "would be only too delighted to invite you to his party, but they don't all know your telephone number. I think Hanif saw you, though, at the reception for Christine, and at last he had an excuse." A warm, freckled hand touched Tasha's arm. "Don't get me wrong, darling—Hanif Khattak is a charming man susceptible to women, and successful with them, but that is all. His reputation is flawless; you can take little Audrey's word."

Tasha turned away from the pictures on the wall, from the presence of Christine. "I've seen him around, of course. Is he in the art business too?"

"Not professionally. He just loves pictures, so he travels

around the States a lot of the time, buying and selling a few here and there and making a comfortable profit; this is just his New York pad. He's shrewd enough to know that this country's sadly underrated in the arts and antiques field; all the Americans can think about is Paris, Rome, and the Orient." She half-turned as a short, perfectly tailored man moved into their space, a drink in his hand. "Oh, hello, Clive. Where on earth have you been?"

"Florence, looking at the ceilings again."

Audrey looked at Tasha. "What did I tell you? Darling, this is Clive Stuyvesant, who invented psychiatry—Tasha Fontaine, couturiere to the rich and famous."

"A pleasure." His hand was cool, dry-skinned, his eyes critical behind the smile.

"The pleasure's mine," Tasha said, but wasn't entirely sure; she had the feeling she'd just been put under a microscope.

"I was just saying, Clive, how besotted the Americans are with foreign art—including your Florentine ceilings. If only you'd take the Wyeths and O'Keeffe more seriously, we could get the prices up."

"Give them another thousand years," he said with a cool smile, "and we'll think about it."

As small talk turned into a discussion of the veneration of antiquity for its own sake, Tasha let her attention lapse, bringing her mind back to the big, frightening question that she'd have to ask as soon as there was a chance, and then try to think what in God's name she could do about the answer.

Voices faded in and out, half-heard in the background, Audrey's, Stuyvesant's, other people's.

"I know for a fact that Milicent is leaving. She's put her apartment up for sale."

"I think that's just panic. Milicent *always* panics."

"But she says she saw the lights of the police cars that night, from her window. She says it was almost like see-ing—well—that dreadful thing happen."

The answer could only go two ways: either she was mad or possessed.

"I'm not the only one, you know. I've heard other people say they're not sleeping so well. They can't stop thinking about it."

"I guess that's understandable. If I lived here, yes, I'd think about leaving. But where can you go in New York where there isn't *something* going on?"

Mad or possessed. There were people like that, sure. They shut them up in institutions and gave them shock treatment. Or called in a priest and had them exorcised. She'd have to squeeze in the time somehow, wouldn't she, right at the start of the fall season—Candie, make a note, will you? I need to find a priest. Unless they just came for her first in a plain van with their white coats on, walking purposefully into the boutique and—

Oh, Jesus Christ, how could a thing like this happen to me?

" . . . And this is Tom Havers, darling, a gallant captain of industry—Tasha Fontaine, queen of high fashion."

"This is so nice." A loud corporate boardroom voice, the quick white smile of a successful shark.

"I'm happy to meet you." She wasn't interested in captains of industry. She was interested in only one thing, right now.

Cats.

"High fashion . . . " Tom Havers said.

"I run a boutique."

"Ah! You're public?" His nostrils widened, smelling a takeover.

"No."

"Ah." His eyes moved sideways in search of deeper water.

Audrey drifted, taking Tasha with her.

"It's so hot in here, darling, isn't it? Or perhaps it's just little me."

Cats. They were what the big, frightening question was all about.

And don't leave it any longer.

They were in the biggest space they could manage to find, between a mass of potted ferns and a window overlooking the park, when Tasha took a breath and said, "I've been meaning to ask you something, Audrey, about Christine."

"I expect so." The wide, attentive eyes rested on hers.

"Why would you expect so?" Her tone was almost angry, she heard. She liked things straightforward, hated innuendos.

"Because she fascinates you, darling. Or is that quite the word?"

"No. In fact I'm trying—" she didn't finish.

Audrey waited, then said, "Don't mind little me. I'm always jumping to the wrong conclusions."

The question. Ask the question.

There's no rush, for God's sake.

Oh yes there is. Remember what they said. You must hurry, they told you, before it's too late.

Go for it, then.

But it was frightening, like diving into dark water, breaking the surface and going down, going down deep, leaving the light behind.

Ask the question. Ask it *now.*

"Did Christine ever paint cats?"

Her eyes surprised, Audrey said, "Cats? No. She hated them."

Deep, dark water, the breath held, the silence closing in.

I hate cats, I always have.

The water freezing, its vastness trapping her.

Not mad, then. Possessed.

"Are you all right, darling?"

The voice came from miles away as the mass of ferns moved gently to and fro in the underwater current.

Freezing. It was freezing here.

"What about a nice glass of brandy?" a faint voice came. "I'll join you—let's be devils."

Audrey's hand on her arm, more than just touching it, actually supporting her as she rose through the dark and the silence and reached the surface and burst into the light, breathless, her lungs aching for air.

"A brandy?" she heard herself saying.

Reality was back, the shock of reality, of knowing the answer now.

"I'm sure they'll get one for us," Audrey said, "if I ask nicely. I think you need—"

"No. I'm fine. I'm fine."

Sure. It was okay now, she had the answer. Terribly *not* okay, actually, but it was something she could handle, would have to handle. The thing about Marcia being on the roof had seemed to be the clincher: Christine had told her something she couldn't possibly have known. Sure, it could have been a coincidence, a freak chance in a thousand. But now it had happened again.

What were the odds on that?

"Why did you think," she heard Audrey asking, "that Christine might have painted cats, of all things?"

"I—I'm not sure. It was just a thought."

And there was something else trying to get her attention, something so weird, so way out that she didn't want to give it any room in her mind with so much else going on there. She knew Audrey was still watching her, worried about her, because she must have lost her color or something when the answer had come to her through the deep dark water. You don't tell people they need a brandy, do you, unless they're suddenly looking like they're going to pass out? But she didn't mind about Audrey watching her; the attentive—okay, inquisitive—Englishwoman didn't mean any harm; she was safe with her, as safe as she could ever be.

So she let this new thought come into her mind, in case it would help, offer a ray of light. Though it wasn't a thought, she saw now.

It was a name.

The green fronds of the ferns moved gently to the draft from the ceiling fans as she stood there ready to dive in again, take another dizzying plunge into the dark freezing water, deep into the fathomless reaches of the unknown.

On a breath—"Audrey?"

"I'm right here, darling."

Watching her now with her eyes alerted a little, afraid she might be going to pass out after all, but of course that wasn't going to happen, it'd be too humiliating afterward— they'd all think she'd had too much to drink or something. The social graces . . . 'We must maintain the social graces,' an aunt from New England had told her when she was a kid in her first party dress.

Then suddenly she was asking, "Do you know anyone called Jason Newberry?"

Audrey's eyes changed, had sudden surprise in them. "I did once," she said.

"Who is he?"

"He was one of Christine's boyfriends."

"Was he"—Tasha's hand brushed the air—"at the reception, or—or anywhere I might have met him?"

In a moment, "No, darling. He shot himself last Christmas, because she dropped him."

Audrey's hand grabbed at her—but too late—as the massed green ferns whirled overhead and she went down, down, into the deep, dark silence.

Twelve

Did you get wet?"

"Not really," Tasha laughed as she brushed the drops off her tan safari suit. "I was just crossing the sidewalk." She'd come here in a taxi, because Vince hadn't been available when she'd called.

The summer storm had been building all night, to break with a crash across the city before 8:00, flooding the streets.

"How was the traffic?" Stuyvesant asked, and gestured to a leaf-green leather chair.

"Chaotic! I could have walked this far if it hadn't been for the rain." This place was only two blocks from Temple Mansions.

"We needed it," Stuyvesant said, and pulled another green chair closer and sat down, crossing his legs, his eyes resting lightly on Tasha's, almost without expression. "My assistant was only just able to squeeze you in, so I hope you'll forgive my getting down to things right away."

"I didn't mean to cause any trouble."

"Don't worry, it happens all the time. You're feeling yourself again, I hope?"

He knew she wasn't, or she wouldn't have called him first thing yesterday, the morning after the party. He had still been there when she'd passed out that night.

"I don't think I know," she said, "what myself is, right now."

His faded blue eyes moved over her as they talked, right down to her python shoes and back. She wasn't sure she liked it, but maybe a shrink could tell things about his patients even by the way they dressed, the way they crossed their legs.

"Why don't you just tell me why you're here?" His voice was toneless, just as his eyes were expressionless. He didn't look the kind of person who would go all the way to Europe to admire the Florentine ceilings.

"I think," she said, "I'm losing my reason."

He gave a little nod. "Most of us think that, at some time or other."

Not like this, mister. This is for real.

Stuyvesant got up and went over to his desk, and she noticed he had a slight limp. The desk was paneled in green leather to match the chairs; except for the neutral beige carpet the whole decor was green, a restful color—wasn't that why surgeons wore green gowns? Stuyvesant wanted her to feel restful, not sick to her stomach, frozen with fear.

He picked up a pencil, the green-shaded lamp on his desk bringing a shine to the scalp under his thinning hair, casting the shadow of his nose to one side, making it look broken.

"Tell me how you think of yourself, Tasha. May I call you that?"

"Why not?" He didn't react, but she thought it was an odd way to answer. Maybe she meant, do whatever you want, just pull me out of this thing before it's too late. "Think of myself? I'm terrified."

"That's just telling me how you *feel*. Normally, are you a happy person, active, successful? Or nervous, depressed, a failure?"

"Yeah, happy, active, successful. Normally." She thought she could hear a voice somewhere, and her mind raced to identify it, but couldn't. "Is that your assistant I can hear through the door?"

Stuyvesant put his head on one side, listening. "Yes. Why do you ask?"

Letting a breath out she said, "I've been hearing voices." And this wasn't Christine's. Thank God there was something, then, in this world, that wasn't Christine's.

Stuyvesant was making notes. "And how do you normally get on with other people, Tasha? Do you feel happy about the way you handle them? Or guilty? Are you considerate, or a user?"

She uncrossed her legs and sat up straight in the chair, her hands resting on the padded leather, grateful for its warmth, because her hands were freezing.

"Look, maybe I'd better say it again. I've been hearing *voices.*"

Stuyvesant nodded briefly. "We'll get to that in good time, Tasha. First I need to find out what kind of person you are, normally, and that just means a lot of dull and rather general questions. But otherwise, you see, I can't tell how much you've changed, or try to find out what's changed you."

He waited patiently, watching her across the desk.

Okay. Do it his way. But she was beginning to think she shouldn't have come here. And that, by the way, was *exactly* what she'd been thinking at Hanif Khattak's party— that she shouldn't have come. So how long was this going on for, her finding herself in places where she thought she shouldn't be?

Where was it safe?

"I get on well enough with other people, I guess. I—"

"You guess?"

He waited.

"Okay, I get on well with them. Period." She kept her voice as level as she could. "And I think I'm considerate most of—"

"You think?"

He watched her, with no expression.

"Look, I—" and she left it. She'd come here to work with this guy, so let's just do it. His way, he's the expert. "I'm pretty considerate, and—what was the rest?"

"You're happy about the way you handle people?"

"Usually."

Stuyvesant made another note. "And when aren't you happy about the way you handle people?"

"Like right now."

He nodded again. "It's perfectly all right for you to feel anger toward me. Just let it happen. Now tell me about your sex life. Is it satisfactory? Unsatisfactory?"

"My sex life is just fine."

Stuyvesant's eyes remained on his notepad, but he wasn't making a note. In a moment he asked, "Is it fine because you have a good relationship with a 'significant other,' or because you have agreeable and virile men friends? I assume you're not married, since you don't wear a ring."

Tasha closed her eyes. So this is therapy. In just three minutes we're down to sex. 'Those guys do a lot of good,' Elizabeth had said, 'if you can find one who doesn't want to screw you on the couch as part of the therapy, and charge you for it.'

"Right," Tasha said, and opened her eyes. "I don't wear a ring because I'm not married—you're very observant, Dr. Stuyvesant. And my sex life is satisfactory because my fifteen men friends are so virile that every time we meet we fuck up a storm, even in the lobby at the Waldorf."

She could feel sweat gathering in her armpits, yet her hands still felt frozen. The voice of this creep's assistant still sounded faintly through the door. Maybe she was on the telephone to someone who didn't hear very well. But it was so nice that the voice didn't belong to Christine. Christine hadn't spoken to her since Tasha had asked if she knew who had murdered her. Maybe it had been a shock for her. Floating around in her parallel universe, she'd known she'd died, maybe, but hadn't known she'd been murdered. Could have come as a shock, yeah.

"When you're enjoying relations with a man," she heard Stuyvesant asking, "do you fantasize?"

Tasha didn't answer. She was quite sure now that this had been a big mistake. It was just that when she came to in Hanif Khattak's elegant and civilized room with all those elegant and civilized people pretending to be suddenly engaged in earnest conversation as Audrey helped her to the nearest bathroom, her first thought was that since she'd obviously gone crazy she'd better see that guy who'd just been introduced to her as the "inventor of psychiatry." And here she was, looking at him across his desk and wishing to Christ he'd drop dead.

"Normally," Stuyvesant was asking her, "about how long is the interval between your sexual experiences?"

"Oh, it kind of varies. Sometimes five minutes, sometimes six, if I'm feeling tired."

The gold clock under the glass dome began chiming with a clear, measured note, and when it had finished Stuyvesant asked, "Do you ever masturbate, Tasha?"

"Like crazy. It costs me a fortune in bananas." She got out of the green leather chair and picked up her bag, slinging the strap across her shoulder. "Dr. Stuyvesant, I came here because right now I'm absolutely terrified about what's started happening to me, and I hoped you could help, maybe even listen while I explained the problem." It sounded quite cool, the tone level, and she tried to keep it that way because Audrey Symes and Hanif Khattak were acquainted with this creep and she didn't want to embarrass them if Stuyvesant mentioned her visit: she didn't think he'd necessarily respect the confidentiality rules. But as she went on talking it got more and more difficult to keep her voice calm, because there was something boiling up inside of her and she didn't think she could stop it. "So I'll just go find some friendly shoulder to lean on instead, or if that doesn't help I'll go jump in a lake or get smashed and cut my wrists—"

"I'd like you to sit down again, Tasha. If—"

"And listen to that line of crap?" She realized she was moving toward his desk, didn't want to, but was. "Look, I know the good Dr. Freud tells us that when a kid sticks his finger up his nose he's really acting out the urge to screw his mother but there *are* other things in life than sex and it's time you took an interest in them, so you could actually help the people who come in here instead of salivating all over their love lives." Standing in front of his desk now, right up close, aware of the glass-cube paperweight not far from her right hand, staring at his thinning hair and wondering how deep it would go, the glass-cube paperweight, if she picked it up and buried it in his skull, seeing it break the skin, bringing blood, cracking the bone like an egg-shell—

"It's perfectly okay to be angry with me, Tasha."

"Dr. Stuyvesant, I feel whatever I want to feel, whether it's 'perfectly okay' with you or not—I don't need your fucking permission!"

Her voice echoed sharply from the glass-fronted cabinets behind his desk, and she closed her eyes and just stood there, wondering what had gotten into her, wondering how to get it out, the sweat running down her sides, her chest tight now, making it difficult to get her breath.

Then she was aware that Stuyvesant was pushing his chair back. "So tell me about these voices you've been hearing."

Tasha opened her eyes and mustered a stage laugh. "*Now* he asks me!" She hitched her bag higher and turned and walked to the door, her legs weak, trying to bring her down. "I'll settle your bill on my way out, just as a matter of principle."

"You wouldn't believe," she heard Stuyvesant saying behind her, "how much ground we've covered since you came into this room."

The voice of reason, and it cut through the murk of her consciousness like a ray of light. When she turned round she saw he was at the water dispenser, filling a plastic cup, and she suddenly realized what a terrific thirst she had.

He came across to her with his little limp, looking as if he were smiling, which was as close as he ever came. "I imagine you need this," he said, and held out the cup of water. "We let quite a lot of the fear come out in anger, you see—they're the same thing, as I imagine you know—and it wasn't doing you any good, keeping it bottled up. Then we—"

"You mean you gave me all that crap deliberately, so I'd—"

"Oh, no, don't misunderstand me, I don't play tricks. They were perfectly valid questions I asked you, and a lot of the time, believe me, I discover that some kind of sexual problem is indeed at the root of things." He took her empty cup and dropped it into the bottom of the dispenser and filled another one. "But your reaction discounted that; you're healthily uninhibited on the subject, and I quite enjoyed your little jokes." He was standing in front of her again, holding out the fresh cup of water.

"Thank you," she said, and took it, drinking, not looking at him now, wondering if she should apologize for her outburst, but to hell with it, he was a shrink, he must be used to having people react all over him. And she wasn't absolutely certain he wouldn't have gotten a kick if she'd told him seriously that yeah, she masturbated a lot and it bothered her.

"Voices," Stuyvesant said. "Voices in your head?"

"Yes."

"So tell me about them." He gestured to the couch. "Would you rather sit or lie down comfortably?"

"I think I'll just prowl."

"Good. You still have some adrenaline in your bloodstream from the anger. Do you exercise?"

"I jog, and go to an aerobics club."

He limped across to his desk. "You might want to drop in there for a few minutes, then, when you leave here, to get rid of the remaining adrenaline." He got behind his desk and pulled his chair forward and picked up the glass-cube paperweight and put it into a drawer. "In case you get angry again," he said, and switched on his smile. "Voices in your head, or would you rather begin from the beginning, which isn't there, is it?"

Tasha took a breath, going over to the water dispenser and getting herself some more. "No. It began with a scream."

Stuyvesant listened for more than fifteen minutes without interrupting, turning the pages of his notepad, writing and turning and only sometimes looking up when she hesitated, looking for the right word, the right meaning. By the time she'd finished she was sitting in the deep leather chair again, her breath coming a little fast, as if she'd been jogging.

"So why did you decide to see a psychiatrist," Stuyvesant asked, "if you feel you're possessed?"

"I guess I . . . hoped you could tell me I wasn't."

She waited, in a kind of way praying.

"I see." Stuyvesant made a note. "So let's start by asking, why do you think you're possessed?"

"I explained that."

"I know. But sometimes people contradict themselves, you see, and that's always important. It helps us get to the root of things."

"Okay. It's because Christine told me she hated cats—which was confirmed—and that the man was on the roof with Marcia, which was also confirmed." She hadn't given him Fido Hamilton's name. "And then this guy called me—Jason Newberry. And he's dead."

Stuyvesant didn't reply, went on writing his notes. It made her mad when he wouldn't give her an answer right off the bat. She'd come here to *know* things, and she wanted to know them *fast,* because the gold clock under the glass dome was ticking away and Elizabeth was at the boutique handling everything herself and there was the world of sanity out there being washed nice and bright by the rain, and she had to get back to it before she got stuck in this one, the world of the mad.

She couldn't wait any longer. "I didn't contradict myself, did I? So do you think I should see a priest?"

Stuyvesant looked up with a wintry smile, shaking his head. "No, I don't think you should see a priest."

"So tell me why I'm wrong, about the cats, and Marcia, and that guy who called me."

"There's an easy answer, Tasha, and I'll give it to you for what it's worth. But like most things in life, the easy things aren't worth very much. What we're dealing with here is a delusion, and also a fixation. You've come to believe that Christine is 'talking' to you, and you're fixed on the notion that she's still somewhere around. Now, the memory tends to feed our beliefs, and will even trick us if we're not watching. So when your friend told you that Christine hated cats, you suddenly 'remembered' hearing her voice telling you that very thing, 'proving' the voice you 'heard' was real. And when your other friend said he'd been on the roof with Marcia, you 'remembered' Christine's telling you that too. And when——"

"It doesn't work, Dr. Stuyvesant."

"If you don't call me Clive, how can I call you Tasha?"

"It doesn't work, Clive, because I didn't 'suddenly remember' those things. When I heard Christine tell me about the cats, it left such an impression on me that finally—two nights ago at Hanif's party—I deliberately asked Audrey whether Christine had ever painted cats, thinking she might say, 'Sure, she used to paint them a lot.' But she didn't. She said she hated them. And it was the same thing with

Marcia—I deliberately asked the man if that was who he was on the roof with. And he said yes. So there was no 'sudden remembering.' No tricks."

Stuyvesant spread his dry, pale hands. "As I mentioned, that was the easy answer—for what it was worth."

Tasha got out of the chair again, taking her empty cup and dropping it into the dispenser, turning to face the man at the desk. "So you don't have any answers that are worth more?"

She waited, beyond praying now, silently yelling for help. *Because if this guy couldn't explain these things it would mean there was only one answer that worked. She was, after all, possessed.*

"Oh, yes," Stuyvesant said, and got up too, coming around his desk to stand facing her with his thin pale fingers locked together and his hands held palms down. "Yes, I may have some answers, but—"

"You *may?* Jesus Christ, I need—"

"There could be so many answers, Tasha, and we just have to go on analyzing the material until we get to the root of things."

In the silence the gold clock chimed again.

"Analyzing the material." She realized the words didn't have any actual meaning, and that was frightening, as if she'd suddenly gone deaf.

"That's right." Stuyvesant stood watching her.

"Okay," she nodded. "Sure." She hoped it was the right answer, one he'd accept, so she could get out of here. Then the meaning of the words he'd said came to her in a kind of delayed reflex. "Yeah, we'll analyze the material, right."

He nodded, satisfied, and went with her to the door, his hand lightly touching her shoulder. "The rainstorm's over, by the sound of it, but would you like Martha to call you a taxi?"

"I'll walk. I feel like some fresh air."

"I can understand that." He opened the door for her.

"You can make an appointment, if you wish to see me again. In the meantime, Tasha, I suggest you take a break for a few days, get away from New York and your home environment. Sometimes that's all that's necessary—a relief from stress, overwork, too many responsibilities."

"Sure," she said, "I'll do that."

Take a break, yeah.

Tasha lay in bed watching the shadow play on the ceiling as the leaves stirred down there on the sidewalk between the lamps.

She hadn't meant it this morning when she'd told Stuyvesant she'd take a break, and of course he'd known that. Goof off, right at the start of the busy fall season, yeah, leave it all to Elizabeth again. But that was the man's point, wasn't it? Too many responsibilities, sure. And anyway, a few days wouldn't bring the building down.

"You *need* a break," Elizabeth had said when Tasha had sounded her out this afternoon, "especially since you didn't go to Milan. It was good advice the guy gave you. Take it."

So Candie had hit the travel agents for her and found a flight out tomorrow morning to Tampa, Florida, with two nights at the Ocean Shore Hotel, and an hour ago Tasha had thrown a couple of YSL swimsuits and her snorkel gear into a bag and put it by the front door, and now she lay watching the shadows on the ceiling, waiting for sleep to come and blot everything out.

Nobody watched her from the wall tonight, nobody called Christine.

She hadn't tried again to take the portrait down, wasn't really in the mood for another telephone call from Jason Newberry or anyone else who'd died. She'd asked Steve, one of the cleaning crew, to do it for her, and he'd seemed quite concerned.

"You mean this one, ma'am?"

"Yes."

He went across to the picture, then stopped in his tracks. "Isn't this the young woman who got—"

"Yes, Steve, it is. That's why I want it put in a drawer for a while, where I can't see it."

He looked at her, nodding. "Boy, I can understand that, yeah. Be real depressing. Did you—" but he left it. Did she know the poor young woman, then? But he came here to clean, not to ask personal questions.

Tasha watched him as he lifted his hands to take the portrait down, steeling herself for the sound of the telephone, seeing her face, Christine's, turn and slant as Steve held it between his hands, looking down at it for a moment while she went on waiting for the phone to ring, for a mirror to fall, for Steve to crumple suddenly and hit the carpet, anything like that, limited only by the fevered imagination, by the borderlines of terror.

But nothing happened.

"Where shall I put it, ma'am?"

"What?" The hairs on her arms settled again. "In a drawer somewhere. Okay, in the bottom drawer of the bureau in the sitting room." It had belonged to her grandfather, a beautiful redwood piece that she never disturbed, could find no use for. Anything put in there would be lost forever.

So it was a personal thing. Steve could take the picture down but she couldn't, without something happening to stop her, without the dead reaching out to her just like in the ads, reaching out from the grave. Putting it a bit strong, yeah, spare us the drama.

But that was exactly what happened, wasn't it?

He was one of Christine's boyfriends.

Was he at the reception, or anywhere I might have met him?

No, darling. He shot himself last Christmas, because she dropped him.

This is Jason. Like they knew each other. *Jason New-berry.*

I'm sorry, but you have the wrong number.

No.

So why did Christine get her boyfriend to call? Why hadn't she called herself—*Hey, leave that right where it is, Tasha, it looks good on the wall there, where I can see you.*

But she hadn't voiced her thoughts for a quite a while, now. That didn't mean she wouldn't, of course, at any time. There'd never been any warning.

The shadows played on the ceiling, brushing the silence, and then into the silence a sound came through the open doorway to the sitting room, a small night sound, the creaking of woodwork as it shrank in the cooler air, that was all, but Tasha lifted her head from the pillows, watching the doorway to the sitting room, listening.

The sound came again, and her nerves drew tight—was it coming from the redwood bureau? She went on watching until her neck began aching, but she didn't hear anything more. There was just the silence again for a while, until the telephone began ringing on the bedside table and her body jerked as the shock went through her and she cried out with a primitive wordless sound as her blood ran cold and the ringing of the telephone went on and on and she did nothing to stop it, could do nothing, couldn't move.

This is Jason. Jason Newberry. With the blood from the gunshot splashed over the Christmas tree and the blue smoke curling among the fairy lights.

The telephone went on ringing, but Tasha couldn't move.

Hello, this is Christine. Running for her life for the place where they found her, bright with blood in the floodlights.

Went on ringing, the only sound in the room, in the night, too late for anybody who knew their manners to make a call, went on ringing while she lay there smelling of sweat, smelling of fear, the animal fear of a forest creature

brought suddenly face to face with the predator in the dark
and shocked to stillness, freezing, waiting for death.

Went on ringing.

And finally stopped.

Thirteen

S he thought some guy was following her," Detective Woodcock said, sifting through the reports. "She *thought* he was." He looked across at Behrens, who had his feet on the desk and was dropping more reports onto the floor, where they settled like a snowdrift. "I mean, Bern, don't you *know* when you're being followed?"

The big, round clock on the wall read 1:03 A.M.

"We do, yeah. We're policemen."

Another report sheet drifted onto the floor. They hadn't counted them, but Woody thought there were maybe fifty or sixty, like there'd been fifty or sixty yesterday, and the day before. Bernie had asked to be informed of any incident, right across the city, where a young woman had complained of being followed, or of being accosted, or threatened, or molested in any way, by a strange man. So there'd be another fifty or sixty reports tomorrow. But outside of these, from the complainants who'd called in, there'd be two or three hundred incidents unreported, involving gals who didn't want to make a fuss, or were too scared, or thought they wouldn't get much attention anyway. So what he and Bernie were doing here was looking for the needle in just one little bitty corner of the fucking haystack.

"Descriptions," Behrens said, and picked up another wedge of cold pizza and looked at it and dropped it back into the box. "I asked for descriptions, right?"

"One here, Bernie. Man, late twenties, black hair, bad breath, talked nice, tried to feel her."

"Terrific. And an unusual man, too, didn't weigh anything, wasn't either short or tall, had no clothes on."

Woodcock let the report float downward.

"What I don't like," Behrens said, "is that if we don't run this punk down real soon, there's some young woman walking around right now who doesn't have long to live. Jack's not going to stop at eleven."

"You've said it a thousand times," Woodcock told him, and picked up the next report.

"So I guess I better shut the fuck up."

The silence came in, went on.

"But I know how you feel, Bern."

"No," Behrens said, "you don't."

Woodcock shifted some papers. "Bern?"

"Yeah?"

"It worries me, too. You know? I ain't the fucking Tin Man."

Behrens looked across at him. "Sure. But this case is *mine*. The responsibility is *mine*. And if that motherfucker goes and does it again, the blame is going to be *mine*. See the difference?"

Woodcock picked up another report, didn't look at Behrens.

"Sure, Bern."

He wanted to say more, you bet, he wanted to tell Detective Behrens that he didn't have to see himself as Jesus Christ on his way to Calvary with Case #H9073 engraved on the cross, the whole team was working its guts out around the clock, in here at the desks and the phones and out in the field, and none of them wanted to think some other innocent chick was going to get what Wittendorf got before they could do anything to save her.

The only ray of light, Woody thought, was something Sergeant Lowenstein had said once. "When tensions start up in the team, it means they're getting close to a breakthrough. Don't ask me why, but trust me, it's a historical fact."

So they were getting close to a breakthrough, okay? Well, that was nice. "Another chick here," he called across to Behrens. "Said she thought she was being followed."

"Description?"

" 'Kind of a weird kind of a guy.' "

"So what kind of difference does this kind of make?"

"It's the second one from near Farmer's Market, on Fifty-sixth and Lexington."

Behrens looked at him for a minute with his red-rimmed eyes and then said, "File it."

"Okay."

"And Woody?"

"Yeah?"

"I'm an asshole."

"Yeah."

"I'm glad you agree. I hate it when people don't agree with me."

"I know." Woody got off his gray metal chair and went over to the coffee machine and pulled another cup from the stack and hit the lever. "So what's this about the Fontaine chick getting our priority attention if she calls in?"

"Tasha Fontaine," Behrens said, "is not a chick."

"Whatever you say, Bern." Woody came back to his desk and set the cup of coffee down on the stained, ringed surface. Right, yeah, Orsini said he thought Bern had the hots for Fontaine, which was just Italian for an interest, maybe, in her looks, which you could understand, plus the appeal she made to Bernie's protective instinct, since behind the quick white smile that chick—excuse me—that young lady was scared of something. Woody had only seen her from a distance when she'd stopped by the crime scene that morning, and only briefly yesterday when she'd come through the office to talk to Bern, but it had been unmistakable—Tasha Fontaine was running scared.

"She gets priority attention," Behrens told him, "because she's trying to help us, and Christ knows we need all the help we can get. There's also an element to this case that's kind of weird."

"Like the scream she heard? The one she couldn't have heard?"

"That's part of it. She feels involved with Christine Wittendorf in some way, can't get her out of her mind."

"Join the club," Woody said.

"Yeah, but with her it's on a more personal level, more subjective." Catching the smell of Woody's fresh coffee, he went across and got himself a cup. "And what that is worth to us," he said as he came back from the machine, "is maybe less than that shred of orchid petal we found on the grass, a whole lot less. On the other hand, I believe it's possible that Tasha Fontaine knows how we could catch Jack in his tracks and bring down this case overnight." He watched the iridescent reflection of the light tubes swinging across the surface of his coffee. "But I don't think she knows she knows."

Woody looked at him, and when he spoke, his voice was hushed. "Jeeze, Bern."

"Have I answered your question?"

Fourteen

A t the airport the next morning, Vince Fisher
pulled Tasha's bag out of the trunk of the limo and
set it down at the skycap's counter while she got
her ticket ready.

"I'll wait for you right here, ma'am, but if they move me
on I'll make circuits and come round every few minutes,
so—"

"Don't worry, Vince—"

"But if we've missed the plane, you might need me—"

"If I've missed it, I'll just get on another one. There's no
problem."

"Well I'm really very sorry, ma'am. I hate being late."

He hovered around her, upset, until Tasha managed to
reassure him. He'd been apologizing most of the way to the
airport for being five minutes late at Temple Mansions, and
apparently five minutes was unthinkable to Vince Fisher,
especially when there was a plane to catch. But in any case
Tasha hadn't been able to find the bag she wanted in her
dressing closet—the worn Saks pigskin one she could take
on the beach—and then the elevator had got stuck at one
of the floors above and she'd finally had to run all the way
down the emergency stairs, so Vince had arrived less than

a minute after she'd started waiting for him on the steps outside the building, it was really no big deal. But it was nice to know he valued punctuality.

And what was nicer still was that when she hurried into the terminal and checked the nearest Eastern screen she saw that Flight 907 had also been delayed and she had another twenty minutes to wait after all.

So relax . . .

Yeah. I'm on vacation. And how long had it been since she'd been able to say that? Not since mid-April, when she'd flown out to Nassau with Peter van Riet and found he couldn't start the day without a drink or finish it without another dozen, so she'd packed her bags while he was having a late breakfast and left him a note; *Have fun, Peter, and I hope you win your battle with the booze. I mean that—you're too good a guy to lose. T.*

Marilyn Schwartz was in the gift shop when Tasha wandered over there to look for a magazine—anything without fashions in it, even *People,* at a pinch—so she turned away in time and wandered on toward the gates; Marilyn would want to talk about the dress she'd need for the Shriners' charity ball and that was okay because the one Tasha had her eye on for her was the Scaasi sequin Elizabeth had ordered from Milan—but she was on vacation and she wanted everything to be different, to feel different; in the next three days she had to pull herself out of this waking nightmare and get back to normal.

Last night had been the ringer—no pun intended— because it could have been simply *anybody* on that goddamned telephone, one of her friends in Europe who wasn't au fait with the time zones, or someone who thought she wouldn't be in bed yet, or simply a wrong number. But she'd lain there terrified, with so much adrenaline building up in her system that she'd had to stop herself from throwing the phone across the room when it finally stopped ringing.

Going into the bathroom—she hated using them on a

plane, you felt like a sardine—she touched up her face a little, not surprised as she looked in the mirror that Vince had almost done a double take when he'd seen her waiting for him on the steps—she looked as if she'd spent the last three nights carousing until dawn, and with the wrong people. Unless she could work miracles in the few days ahead she'd have to make an appointment with Angel Face the minute she was back in New York.

Not Angel Face, no. The place she used to go to, on 61st. She needed to leave all those hang-ups behind her now, and yesterday she'd made a start by tossing the flacon of Infiniti into the wastebasket. She'd also tried to find another limo service in the yellow pages, but they all looked alike, and Vince had already impressed her to the point where she felt comfortable with him—not always easy in the close confines of an automobile—and look at it this way; if she changed to some other service wouldn't it be an admission that she still couldn't choose what to do in her life—because of Christine?

Christine was dead.

Will all passengers for Tampa please board Flight 907 at Gate 5? Passengers for Tampa on Flight 907 should now be boarding.

But there were still ten minutes to go and Tasha found somewhere to sit and watch the people, because that too was going to be part of the therapy—just to sit and watch life going by instead of running around New York like a rat in a trap.

And being haunted out of her mind.

A young guy—rather like Fido Hamilton, dark and intense—and his girlfriend were talking and laughing together as they made their way to the gate, carrying tennis rackets, and Tasha wondered what it might be like to take a short trip with Fido, see him a few times first, check him out. Or maybe there'd be some guy already there in Tampa at the Ocean Shore she could spend a little time with; with so much tension building up in her during the past ten days she felt the need of physical outlet with a man. Bill Spain? Charles Fry? Al Padolini? They didn't make a habit of sleeping around, and she might even have to hunt one of them to his lair, which would be rather fun. That shrink had been right—she'd only just arrived at the airport and already she was thinking about having fun!

This is the last call for passengers to board Flight 907, which is leaving in a few minutes now for Tampa, Florida.

Tasha got up and slung her handbag, getting her ticket out as she crossed to the departure gate.

"Hello," the girl said with a smile, "I was thinking we'd have to leave you behind."

"No way," Tasha smiled back, "I need this trip."

She was holding out her ticket when she heard her name being called.

Will Miss Tasha Fontaine please pick up a white paging-phone . . . We have an urgent message for Miss Tasha Fontaine . . . please pick up a white paging-phone.

"Okay," the girl said. "This is your boarding pass."

"That call's for me," Tasha said, not wanting to believe it, having to believe it—Mom okay? Dad okay? She turned quickly away to look for the nearest telephone.

"You'd better have your ticket!" the girl called after her.

"Hold it for me, please!"

"Okay, but I can't hold the plane!"

Tasha bumped into a lost-looking man who was squinting up at the schedules monitor and apologized and saw a white telephone opposite the toilets and picked it up.

"This is Tasha Fontaine."

It couldn't be anything to do with Mom unless there'd been an accident, but Dad had been having these dizzy spells for a month or two and he was in and out of the clinic having tests.

"Yes, Miss Fontaine, you're requested to call your secretary at La—La Boutique, would it be?"

"Yes. Right. Thank you."

Every pay phone was in use at the console and she scanned the row of booths and tried to judge whether anyone looked like finishing their conversation anytime soon, but they were all taking their time, heads tilted and hands on hips and elbows jutting, and she wondered if she'd do better someplace else. Her secretary—what would Candie want? Nothing urgent ever went on at La Botica; they just sold clothes, for Christ's sake.

Relax, yeah, you're on vacation—or you were. Knowing Candie, what would "urgent" mean? She was a cool enough gal, took the breaks as they came, wouldn't blow things out of proportion, so that didn't look very good, did it? But it didn't necessarily mean—

The man in the sharp blue suit was hanging up and turning away and brushing ash off his lapel and Tasha took over the booth in an ambience of cologne and cigarette smoke, holding the still-warm telephone and tapping the number out and listening to the ringing tone.

Elizabeth?

Nothing would ever happen to Elizabeth.

"La Botica, how may I help you?"

"Candie, this is Tasha. "What's—"

"Oh! I'm sorry to hold you up, but there's been some kind of a fire in your apartment, and the security people called for you here and I thought I'd try to catch you at the airport."

"A fire?"

"Yeah, I don't have the impression it was all that big, and they got it out okay, but the sprinkler system went off, so I guess there's a bit of a mess and they thought you'd want to be there."

"Sure." Not Mom, at least, and not Dad. Just a shitty mess to start her grand vacation with—or to end it with, right. "Okay, Candie, tell them I'm on my way. And call the airline and have them fly my baggage back to Kennedy for pickup—it's already on board, and the flight's just leaving."

She was waiting in line for a cab when the Eastern Airlines 727 lifted off and left a dark crescent of exhaust gas across the sky.

"Of course," Emily said, "you have dry bedclothes in the storage closet, but it'll be a day or two before you'll feel like moving back in."

Emily was in charge of the Temple Mansions cleaning crew, black, motherly and concerned.

"We'll do all we can," Steve said, "meantime." He looked around him at the soaked silk wallpaper and the flooded carpets. "Place is going to take a bit of time drying out—that's the worst part."

"Yes," Tasha said, sickened by the damage and the smell of the fire.

They turned as a security man came in through the open doorway.

"What started it?" Tasha asked him.

"I'll show you, miss." He moved past her and she followed him into the bedroom, seeing the blackened area of wall opposite the bed. "The fire department said there was something draped across this lamp shade here, some kind of fabric—you can see the residue—and the lamp was left burning in your absence, and the heat of the bulb set it on fire." He looked at her. "Do you remember draping anything across the lamp shade, Miss Fontaine?"

Water still dripped from one of the sprinklers, splashing musically into the black Chinese bowl on the dressing table.

"Yes," Tasha said in a moment, having to make an effort to keep her voice steady, "it was a scarf. But I know I didn't leave the lamp—" she broke off as a shiver passed through her. "Never mind. That's what must have happened, if they say so."

Fifteen

The telephone began ringing when Tasha was putting some uncrushable shirtwaist dresses into an old suitcase, and because there was sunshine in the windows and the security men had only just left her apartment she only hesitated for a couple of seconds before she answered it.

"Hello?"

"Darling, what a mess you must be in!"

"Oh, hello, Audrey. Yeah, I guess I am. The sprinklers went off." And there was the smell of smoke still in the air; Emily said she'd spray the rooms with freshener once she'd gotten them cleaned up. "How did you know about it?"

"I phoned the boutique to ask if you were free for lunch tomorrow, and they told me what had happened. So look, I've got the guest room ready for you, and you can move in just as soon as you like."

"Well, gee, that would've been great, but I've already made reservations at the Waldorf."

"For how long?"

"Three nights."

"You can stand little Audrey's company for that long, darling, and I want to talk to you anyway. I'm worried about you. And incidentally I'm a Cordon Bleu cook."

Tasha thought that if she'd wanted to stay with anyone in the whole of New York for three nights, it would be with this warm, relaxed Englishwoman. She needed comfort right now, as much as she could get.

"I'm going to say yes," she told Audrey, watching the water dripping into the Chinese bowl. Her pleasant, airy apartment looked like a sinking ship.

"Marvelous! When can I expect you?"

"I'll be at the boutique all day until at least six o'clock, so it won't be before six-thirty or seven."

"Any time is fine. Ask the concierge to let you into my flat—his name's Alfonso. I wasn't sure I could persuade you, of course, but now I'll tell him you'll be coming—and I'm *so* glad. But the thing is, I've got to be at a totally ghastly cocktail party at the Plaza this evening, but as soon as everybody's smashed enough not to miss me I'll be home to whip up a cozy little *diner à deux*—you must be feeling *so* miserable! The guest room is at the end of the passage, turn left, midnight-blue curtains with silver stripes, I think they're why nobody ever wants to come a second time, and I'm going to change them, so meanwhile be a sport and avert the gaze."

A feeling of relief came into Tasha as she said good-bye, but it couldn't quite get rid of the lingering shock she'd felt when she'd come rushing home and seen the flame-blackened wall in the bedroom, and water soaking the carpets and everything. And even that wasn't all: there was more, and worse. Looking around the apartment now before she left, she felt more vulnerable, more accessible to malevolence than ever before in her life, because of the one thought uppermost in her mind as she dropped the suitcase into the hallway and locked the door.

Last night when she'd gone to bed she'd turned off the lamp on the dressing table as usual, and there'd been no reason to switch it on again this morning. So when she'd left for the airport, that lamp, with the crimson scarf draped across the shade, had not been lit.

*   *   *

"I do hope you like gazpacho, darling."

"I love it."

"Oh, marvelous.. Suitable, I thought, for a hot summer's night. Not too much paprika?"

"It's perfect."

Audrey watched her guest across the small, round table for two. There was so much she had to ask her, and she'd have to be so tactful. Rescuing people who were going through the hellish prepartum stages of a divorce—like Sue Sperling last week—was relatively easy: you just let them cry on your shoulder until they were exhausted, then you gave them enough Remy Martin to send them off to sleep. Tasha was a different case: she was frightened to death of something, and might not even be prepared to say what it was.

"Can I help?" Tasha asked as Audrey took their soup bowls away.

"There's nothing to do, my love, so just sit and dream about Tahiti kabobs with sauce choron—do you know it?"

"I don't think so."

"You're not dauntingly vegetarian, are you? I should have asked."

"Anything goes."

"Oh, splendid—and you brought *exactly* the right wine."

"A lucky shot," Tasha said. "Can I look at the pictures, while you're—"

"But please! So few people ask."

They were mostly impressionist, with a couple of Braques and an outlandish Hieronymous Bosch tucked in a corner. Nothing by Christine Wittendorf, but then she wasn't in their league.

"An odd mixture," Audrey said as she came in bearing dishes, "but the impressionists went through the floor last year, so I bought what I could, because they're going through the ceiling next year. But I also enjoy looking at them, which I hope will save my soul."

"I would think your soul's pretty safe," Tasha said.

"Really?" Audrey's large amber eyes rested on hers for a moment. "That's because you don't know my darkest secrets, which St. Peter's going to find totally unacceptable." She eased the pieces off the skewer onto the rice for Tasha without breaking their pattern. "The trick is to take it off the broil as soon as the lobster flakes at the touch of a fork, or you'll overdo the beef." She poured the wine and sat down, her eyes animated in the candlelight. "Sauce choron, actually, is simply your good old béarnaise with a soupçon of tomato to bring up the flavor." A wistful smile came. "I had the choice, you see, when I left Oxford—already turning the scales at a hundred and fifty pounds—of signing on at a health-and-fitness sweatshop for the duration or at the École de Cordon Bleu in Paris. Having decided to go to hell on my own handcart, I must admit that the only time I feel a flash of regret is when I see a body like yours in a dress like that, but with a bit of luck I'll send you waddling out of here in three days' time heading for the nearest video store to buy up all their Jane Fonda tapes." She poured herself a little more sauce. "But do tell me, darling, how did that beastly fire start?"

The sudden question jarred Tasha's nerves, and it was a moment before she could answer.

"Christine started it."

Audrey put down her fork, staring at her. "Did you say *Christine*?"

"Yes."

"Oh, my God . . . I obviously shouldn't have asked, or at least not yet, but I just thought you might want to talk about it." Audrey reached out a soft freckled hand, touching Tasha's lightly across the table. "So what we'll talk about instead is how to cook chicken Napoleon in thirty minutes flat with one ear on the doorbell—the trick is in the brandy. And you need to try the wine, darling; it's the perfect complement, and anyway I'm trying to mellow you out, which I'm sure you've noticed."

They were ensconced in bamboo peacock-tail chairs later in the evening by an open window before anything was mentioned again of the fire in Temple Mansions. Audrey had turned the lights down to a background glow and lit more candles, and the sound of Zamfir's flute came softly from unseen speakers as she poured cognac from a black frosted bottle into balloon glasses and handed one to her guest.

Tasha had been lulled by the food and the wine into a state of pleasant lassitude, but was aware that Audrey's hospitality was doing much the same service—and intentionally—as a psychiatrist administering a sedative, and however ungrateful and cynical this sounded, she knew it to be true.

But, yeah, she certainly did want to talk about the fire in her apartment, and it was going to be easier now, with her nerves relaxed.

"You're very good to me, Audrey."

"No, darling, I'm just trying to be good *for* you."

"That, too." Tasha swirled her cognac around the glass, watching it cling. "And I'd like to tell you what's been happening to me, and why I passed out at Hanif's party and things like that, but it's very much to do with Christine, and she was a friend of yours and she's also dead, and not to be spoken ill of. So there's a problem, you see."

Audrey shook her head. "Not really. I don't think there's much you can tell me about Christine that would come as a surprise."

"Okay, but stop me, anyway, if I say anything that . . . seems out of order." She looked at Audrey in the soft light of the candles. "Was she a close friend?"

Audrey laughed gently. "Close enough to fight with. You couldn't have Christine as a friend without sometimes having her as an enemy. Didn't you find that?"

"I didn't have time. I—"

"Oh, yes, I remember. You told me you hadn't known her for long."

"Make it ten minutes."

"Oh." Audrey waited.

Tasha told her about the taxi in the rain.

"Yes," Audrey said, "that was Christine. Talk to her for ten minutes in a taxi, and she left you with an impression that was hard to forget."

"Right. I often thought about her; she'd just come into my mind. All that vivacity! I think I dreamed about her, once. But after she died, it wasn't hard to forget her anymore. It was impossible."

"Ah." Audrey waited again.

Traffic rolled below the window, six floors down, and somewhere a drunk was singing.

"I heard her scream," Tasha said, "when she died. It wasn't far away, where it happened, and the windows were open, like this." She was aware that Audrey had become very still, the glass of cognac dangling from her hand and sending a jewel of refracted light across the floor. "That scream went right down into my guts, like a knife going in. Like the knife that was killing her out there." She was surprised, hearing herself say that; she didn't normally go in for melodrama. Maybe it was the cognac talking, yeah, but that was *exactly* what had happened, so let's up and say so—right? "And it all started from there. From the scream."

The flute piped softly from the shadows.

"All?" Audrey asked.

"It would take time," Tasha said, "to tell you."

"I usually can't sleep until at least three in the morning."

Tasha took a breath. "Then I'll give it a go." As the story came out, some of it disjointed, some of it badly put, Tasha lost the fear that she might easily blow her new friendship with this woman by sounding too wild, too weird, even crazy, might even be asked to leave in the morning. Audrey was giving no sign of irritation as the eerie recital went on, simply splashed a little more cognac into their glasses now and then and sat back again to go on listening, framed by the peacock-tail chair.

"So you see," Tasha said finally, "I think she started it."

"The fire?"

"Yes."

Audrey said in a moment, "I see." But of course she didn't. This sounded like a case for counseling, surely. "You must be under quite a lot of stress, running La Botica. I believe the competition's pretty fierce, isn't it?"

The Zamfir tape had run itself out, and there was silence now except for the murmur of late traffic. Tasha deliberately let it go on, not answering, until at last Audrey stirred in her chair.

"I'm being a touch less than sensitive, am I?"

"I'm not sure what you mean." Tasha felt drained now, as if she'd sat through the whole of Wagner's *Ring* again, and come out punch-drunk. Because she really believed—she *knew*—that Christine had started that fire. Nobody would have gone into her bedroom after she left for the airport—the cleaners came through every other day, and this was one of the days they didn't show. Nobody *could* have gone into her apartment this morning, without the security guards' knowledge. *Nobody.*

Except Christine.

"I mean," she heard Audrey saying, "I'm simply jumping to the obvious conclusion, putting it all down to stress of work and saying you've just been imagining things."

"Remember the cats?" Tasha said. "Remember Marcia? Remember Jason Newberry?"

"How right you are." Audrey leaned forward, the bamboo chair creaking. "But it's not necessarily . . . as you think it is. You said you were going to see Clive Stuyvesant. Did you?"

"Yeah. Because when crazy things start happening, the first thing we think is that we're crazy. Just like you think I'm crazy right now."

"Not really, darling." Audrey got out of the deep bamboo chair and dropped a cushion on the floor and settled on it, leaning her back to the wall below the window and looking up at Tasha with her face in shadow. "But for the record, what did Clive say?"

"He thinks I'm crazy, too."

"Are you going to see him again?"

"I don't know. I don't know how far this thing's liable to take me, where I'm going to finish up."

Audrey felt a sudden piercing of the heart. Suppose this very nice and very normal-looking young woman was, in point of fact, going slowly 'round the bend, for whatever reason? It happened all the time. Stress overload, burnout, a rogue gene as a birthright, you name it, anyone, these days, could go clean out of their minds at nine o'clock any next morning and surprise the hell out of everyone else.

"You won't finish up darling, anywhere unpleasant. You've got little Audrey by your side." Her hand brushed their air.—"Of course, you must have lots of friends, I don't mean—"

"No one close. I've always been too busy to need them."

But that had changed, quite suddenly, like everything else had changed. She was sitting here as part of a cozy little scene in the candlelight with someone who was offering her friendship, and they would normally be talking about the Milan show and the future of the impressionists on the world market and whether Di was going to get married again after the divorce—things like that, sane, ordinary things. But they weren't. They were talking about a murder victim setting her apartment on fire. She wasn't really a part of this cozy little scene at all; she was somewhere out there in the cold, in the dark, nursing the seeds of insanity while they grew inside of her like a monstrous child.

"Perhaps it might help," she heard Audrey saying, "if you knew a little more about Christine."

"I don't *want* to know any more about Christine!" Tasha's voice was suddenly shrill and she was on her feet and the liquor had splashed from her glass across the coffee table. "I'm *trying* to run away from her, for God's sake! I was running away from her when she started the fire, to bring me back!"

In the silence Audrey asked quietly, "Is that really what you think happened?"

"What?" Tasha swung round, stared down at her. "Of course." Her voice, too, was quiet now. "I'm sorry, I—"

"Not to worry." Audrey got up and found a paper napkin from a drawer and mopped at the spilled liquor, picking up the bottle and starting to pour some more into Tasha's glass.

"No—no more, please. I've had too much already— that's obvious."

"Of course it isn't. Flying off the handle now and then is good for us all. I suspect you don't do it nearly enough."

"I've never needed to," Tasha said. She put her glass down and dropped back into the chair. "Not till now."

Audrey settled on her cushion again on the floor, and said in a moment, "What makes you think anyone was trying to stop your leaving New York?"

"They said it was a scarf I'd draped across a lamp that started the fire. It was Christine's. And when I left there, the lamp wasn't lit."

"Christine's?"

"Yes." Tasha looked away. "I took it from the house in Sutton Place, for a—I don't know—a memento. She said it was okay."

The silence drew out. "Christine said?"

"She talks to me—haven't I tried to tell you?"

Watching the small, tortured face of Tasha Fontaine in the candlelight, Audrey again had the feeling that she could be watching someone slowly losing her reason, and realized with a shock of despair that here was something she didn't know how to deal with, here was somebody, at last, she wouldn't be able to rescue.

But she'd have to try, and try like hell. "Let me suggest something, Tasha. When you learned, the next day, who had screamed in the night, and why she had, you must have felt an enormous compassion. You found yourself involved, just as you've told me. But you've overcooked it, old thing. You've let your imagination run wild, and now you're in too deep and you can't pull out again. And even though you're trying to run away from it all, there's still that compassion, that sense of *identity* with Christine, going on inside you." She took a sip of cognac, hoping to God she was getting this right, because if Tasha were going to let her talk about Christine it might make things even worse, if it didn't do the job she wanted it to do. "We all felt much the same as you did, because of the appalling way she died. But you've let it get out of control, because, I suppose, you actually *heard* it happening. That must have been terrible for you. It must have left an impression very tough to deal with. So what we need to do is root out that compassion you still feel for her, wipe out the impression, because now it's inappropriate. It hasn't been long—ten days, is it?—but it's over now. It's over, and it's time for you to move on—without Christine."

Tasha sat with her head back against the cushions of the big bamboo chair, watching the last of the lights going out in the windows across the city as late workers finished their shift.

"I'd like to," she said wearily, "but I don't know how."

"Perhaps I do. You remember I once said you were lucky in having known Christine, but not for long?"

"Yes."

"Shall I tell you why?"

"Okay."

"She was a monster."

Somewhere a candle had burned out, and a gray tendril of smoke came threading from the shadows, twisting as it met the movement of air from the open window.

"She couldn't have been," Tasha said sharply, surprised at her own voice, at the sudden surge of resentment.

Watching her, Audrey was warned. Tasha was already *defending* Christine, before she'd really started. This was going to be more difficult than she'd thought.

"She used people, darling. She played with them like toys. And some of them she broke, and not by accident. She broke Jason Newberry. I was there."

Audrey waited. To someone with this amount of compassion still in her for Christine, this amount of sympathy, these revelations were going to be tough to take. But this was the way it had to be done; you couldn't fight Christine with kid gloves on.

Tasha had closed her eyes, could see the glow of the city's lights against her lids. She didn't want to answer, to say anything at all because it would take her deeper still, bring her closer to the woman—the ghost, the ghoul— who'd been weaving her web around her for so long now. But maybe she'd have to go closer still before she could start pulling out. Maybe if she knew more about Christine she could find her weakness, and work on it, *force* her to go back into her own world and leave this one alone, and everybody in it. But it wasn't easy; she felt, and quite strongly, that she was betraying the dead.

"But there were so many people," she told Audrey, "at the funeral, and at the reception. So many people crying."

"They were the ones she didn't break."

"I refuse to believe—"

"The ones she broke weren't there, you see. Even if they'd been invited, they wouldn't have come. She made a lot of enemies. Everybody loved her—at first. She even made an impression on you that night in the taxi, in just those few minutes. She was like that with everybody. She scintillated. She dazzled. And sometimes she'd allow you to become a friend, if she liked you enough. And then, after a while, she'd get bored, and drop you flat, and you went down hard." She was aware that her voice had an edge on it now, but didn't try to soften it. "She did it to me."

Tasha opened her eyes. One by one the candles were going out, and the shadows were closing in around them. She didn't mean to speak, but suddenly she was saying heatedly, "I just don't *believe* this! I had lunch with Fido Hamilton, and he told me Christine had a lot of style and managed all her affairs so well that nobody got hurt."

"Fido Hamilton," Audrey said in a moment, "probably knew her better than anyone else. They had quite a relationship going. But that doesn't mean he wasn't taken in."

"Did she love him?"

"Before you can love anyone, darling, you've got to be able to love yourself, and she couldn't do that. But I'm quite sure he thought she loved him—she would have told him so. It was one of the ways she acquired power. He's rather smitten, by the way. Did you know?"

"Smitten?"

"By you."

"Fido? We hardly know each other."

"It can't be anything new to have a man fall for you at first sight." Audrey leaned forward and spoke with sudden urgency. "The thing is, the fact that Fido Hamilton was forgiving in the extreme doesn't alter anything, Tasha. For the rest of us, Christine was bad news. It so happens that I was one of the many people she tried to break, and although it didn't quite come off, it hurt me, and for that I was ashamed. I didn't like myself for letting her take me in— and that was another of her accomplishments: she didn't like herself, and she managed to project that into other people. Christine was a bitch, darling, a first-class dyed-in-the-wool bitch, and if you won't let yourself believe it then you'll lose your only chance. Once you can see her for what she was, you can stop grieving and get her out of your mind. Out of your life."

Tasha moved suddenly, restless. "She didn't do me any

harm. When I took—when I *stole* her scarf that time, she said it was okay, she understood I just needed a keepsake. I don't want to hear any more—"

"She didn't harm you when she set your flat on fire, as you believe?"

"I don't know"—Tasha was on her feet again, spreading her hands out—"I don't know why she did that, I mean she might just have been—"

"You said she was trying to stop you from leaving New York—"

"So I could be wrong, okay?" She stared down at Audrey, wondering why she was defending Christine like this. Jesus Christ, that was a hell of a mess she'd made in her apartment, wasn't it? With the carpet flooded and the davenport settee and all the chairs soaked through and the whole place stinking of smoke? But something was stopping the anger coming out. "Maybe she just needs me in New York! Maybe I'm the only one who can help her! Maybe—"

"Help her in what way?"

"To nail the guy who killed her—couldn't it be that?"

Audrey froze. This whole scenario that Tasha was working out was so logical that it had the tone of cunning one associated with the mad. It even revealed a knowledge of Christine's character that Tasha couldn't possibly possess, after that one brief meeting. For the first time since Audrey was a kid who didn't dare look under the bed she felt a chill along her nerves as she was made to face the uncanny.

"She was vengeful," she said, "certainly."

"And you say she used people. So she could be using me right now to avenge herself, to get this guy caught and sent to death row. Doesn't that make sense?"

Audrey got off the floor, feeling restless herself now, putting her glass on the tray and Tasha's with it, giving her hands something to do while she thought out the answer, because it needed great care. Give just a hint that she believed anything Tasha was saying, and it could send her overboard.

"Sometimes," she said at last, "we think something makes sense, and later realize it was complete and absolute bullshit. You want me to give it to you straight up, darling?"

"Sure."

"Then I already think this whole thing you're making up is complete and absolute bullshit. You—"

"Maybe it's that you hate her so much because of what she did to you that makes—"

"I don't *hate* her, for God's sake! She's *dead.*"

"But that time when she hurt you—"

"I was livid, of course, for a while, but after a stand-up screaming match, we called it quits and were friends again."

She slapped my face, and knocked me flying . . . It was quite a shock.

Tasha froze, felt her head begin slowly spinning, and had to make a conscious effort to steady herself. It was a long time since she'd heard that voice, more like an echo than the voice itself, coming into her mind through fathomless night, suddenly here, suddenly gone, to leave an unearthly silence.

She didn't know how long it was before she heard herself asking Audrey, "You had a row with Christine, did you say?"

"A screaming match, darling, which is rather noisier."

"I see." Tasha watched her in the lowering light as the flame of another candle flickered and went out. "Was that when you slapped her face and knocked her flying?"

The smoke drew out from the darkened wick and lay on the air, its acrid scent reminding of another day's death. When Audrey spoke it was in a whisper.

"We were alone when that happened, and neither of us would ever have told anyone. So how could you know?"

"I know because you're wrong. She *did* tell someone."

"Who?"

"She told me."

"When?"

"Just now." She watched the color draining from Audrey's face for a long moment, then picked up the frosted black bottle and poured herself another shot, lifting the glass. "So your 'complete and absolute bullshit' theory doesn't work, you see. Long live Christine!"

Sixteen

Everybody was having a good time at the Wollman Rink in Central Park, and the man was watching them.

He had been coming here every week since he got back to New York—not every week regularly, but whenever he could take a bit of time off to watch the skaters. They looked so graceful, and some of the young guys were extremely clever, leaping into the air sometimes and spinning 'round and landing again facing the right way, and doing other things like that, showing off. There were a few falls, of course, and the man had noticed that in general the people who brought their own roller skates were very good, while the ones who rented them often went sprawling, because they were beginners. But they took it in good part and just laughed and got up and went wobbling off again—laughed or screamed, depending on whether it was a guy or a girl, because it was only the girls that screamed, of course.

It reminded him of the way they'd screamed, some of them—those who weren't too busy running to find enough breath—and now he was hearing their screams again and feeling the sound go through him like a beam of hot red light, reaching down to his groin and setting it on fire. He liked that.

It was humid after the rainstorm; the air seemed to cling to his face. But at this time of the day when that dreadful sun went down at last behind the buildings the city seemed cooler, even though it wasn't, or not very much.

He played with the lipstick while he watched the skaters. It was in his pocket, between his fingers.

Sometimes the scene he was watching kind of dissolved in front of him, and he wasn't here anymore, but somewhere else—usually the same place, the terrible, horrible place. He always tried hard to stop it happening, but couldn't always succeed. It wasn't anything new, of course; it had been happening for years. But he hated it. It was like the feeling you'd have if you were trapped in a burning house and trying to get out, coughing in the thick black smoke, or inside a car that had gone into the river and the water was getting higher and higher and your head was under the roof now, that kind of feeling. It was horrible.

Another girl went sprawling over there, sliding along the surface of the rink in her little white shorts with her arms and legs flying out, not screaming but laughing—he always hoped they'd scream, but this one didn't, and he was disappointed. The Wollman Rink was about the only place in Manhattan where you could hear women screaming in public, and that was why he came, really; he liked hearing them scream, even though it was only because they'd taken a spill on their roller skates. They made almost the same kind of sound as the other ones, though not *quite* the same, of course, there was what you might call an added dimension to the other kind, because of what was happening to them.

A kid came round with some popcorn, but he didn't buy any. He never indulged in things like that. Then everything was dissolving again and he called out in his head, *No, no, no!* But he couldn't stop it.

These are for you, he said.

He never called her "Mom."

He held out the bouquet of orchids.

You stole them!

I didn't!

Of course you stole them, you little bastard, you got no money!

They're for you! I got them for you!

But the tears were coming because of her face, her eyes, and he didn't seem to have the strength to hold the orchids out to her any longer and when she screamed at him again he began wetting himself, as usual.

You stole them—I know you did. You're a fucking little thief!

And she snatched the orchids away from him and threw them on the ground and swung her bony red fist at him hard enough to send him spinning against the wall; then she grabbed his torn Dodgers T-shirt and dragged him squealing to the top of the cellar steps and pushed him all the way down and slammed the door and locked it with the big rusty key and left him there. He couldn't think of anything for a long time; there was just the dark and the pain in his knees and his elbows and the smell of the stuff down here, all the rotten stuff she threw down here, until at last he felt something nibbling at his foot and made a grab for it and felt the soft, warm fur like a bag of something-alive with its long, scaly tail hanging over his fingers until he threw it away from him as hard as he could and it squealed and went on squealing until it hit the wall with a soft flat thump and the squealing stopped.

Nobody would come for him, he knew, until next morning, so he got the cardboard boxes and made a home for himself like he always did and crawled inside and pulled the flaps shut so he'd be safe from the rats while he slept; and then in the morning he watched for the first light to come creeping across the patch of sky he could see through the window bars, until the huge gold heads of the sunflowers outside were beginning to glow, and another day began, with his stomach so empty it felt like claws inside.

You stand too close and they'll eat you up.

He'd been younger when she'd told him that. He'd been standing right underneath one of the huge sunflowers, looking up at it, thinking it looked almost like a person with its dark round face and its burning gold hair, and that was what she'd said to him, so from that time onward when he'd lain in the cellar watching the light come he'd been glad the bars were across the window, so the sunflowers couldn't reach in and eat him up.

A lot of people were laughing suddenly and he looked across the rows of seats and saw that a red long-haired dog had gotten into the rink, perhaps to look for its master, and the skaters were swerving and weaving trying to avoid it and some of them were going down and the dog was yelping and wagging its tail with excitement and the people in the stands thought it was all very funny.

He didn't think it was funny. Dogs shouldn't be allowed to get into the rink. He twiddled the lipstick in his fingers, inside his pants pocket. It was in a case, a fancy Tiffany silver case with her initials on it, CCW.

He'd watched her using it for the last time, touching the soft pink tip to her mouth, like she was kissing it.

CCW.

He'd never known her middle name.

Why didn't you get an abortion, for Christ sake?

He caught his breath as everything changed again. He hadn't been ready for it. He was never ready for it—it came like a blow from the dark.

I wanted to, but my Dad wouldn't let me! He said I'd got to finish what I started!

Listening at the kitchen door, shivering at the door.

His name was Pete, the man she lived with. He had a red face and a thick body with bare arms; his arms were always bare and had coarse black hair on them and tattoos, a woman with big breasts and a kind of helmet on, and three red snakes twisted together. He didn't like what he always called "your fuckin' brat." Pete wasn't his father. He'd never known who his father was; he was never mentioned. Pete was a big man, and had a wide black belt with a brass buckle.

You could'a fuckin' drowned it, couldn't you?

I tried, in the bathtub! How many times have I got to tell you? I fuckin' tried!

He was in the way, of course. Pete couldn't stand the sight of him when he was home, bouncing and grunting on the bed with her most of the time with a bottle rolling on the floor, and when he was away in his big roaring truck she couldn't stand the sight of him either because she couldn't leave him on his own while she slipped out to see her "clients" in case he set the place on fire, because he had a liking for matches and hid them away when he could, and of course she found them. Then one day she thought of the cellar.

A girl screamed, and he looked up and saw who it was; the one with the long brown hair, the pretty one he'd noticed before.

He didn't like pretty girls.

She picked herself up and started off again, her short navy-blue skirt swinging as she moved her legs. She was a beginner, and she'd rented her skates, he could tell: they were a red-painted pair. He'd been watching her for a while now, on and off.

He rubbed the lipstick in his pocket, felt how hard it was. He always took something, wasn't discriminating provided it was something personal, intimate if possible, depending on how much time he had, not money or keys but a shoe or a pair of panties or a comb or a packet of condoms from her bag—or, in this case a lipstick, something she'd kissed.

He hadn't ever been kissed.

"I don't think so."

They should never say that.

Two of them were skating together, a young man with his arm round a girl, in love, he was sure, and he wanted to stand up and yell at them, yell and yell and make them listen.

WHAT IS LOVE? WHAT DOES IT FEEL LIKE?

Yell and yell.

TELL ME HOW IT FEELS!

Yell at them, but the man in uniform would come hurrying between the rows of seats and tell him he must leave, he was causing a disturbance.

He would never know what it was, what it meant, what it felt like. He was sure of that. It was too late now.

But he knew what the other thing was.

He'd done it with the rats.

Pete had kept cans of diesel oil in the shed, and one day he'd got an empty coffee tin from the garbage and brought some of the oil down to the cellar and got the matches off the narrow ledge, where she never looked, and the next time she'd shut him down there for the night he hadn't crawled inside his cardboard-box home for a long time, but waited and watched in the faint starlight from the window for the small bright beady eyes to show themselves, coming closer, with the sound of the little sharp feet across the sheets of cardboard on the floor, the eyes bright now and looking up at him, wondering if it was safe to try a nibble at the soft boy-flesh, closer and closer and—*now!*

Holding it with the old brown gardening glove he'd found in the shed, because they'd bite your fingers if you weren't careful, but with the glove on he could hold it safe enough, squirming and squealing while he poured the diesel oil carefully over it so as not to spill any, and got the matches and struck one and lit the rat and let it go, a ball of flame now, running around and around in the dark, squealing and squealing as the frying-smell came and then the sizzling noise and the ball of flame started bumping against the wall, moving slower now, much slower, finishing up in a corner with no more squealing, just the sizzling smell and the last of the flames dying away.

He didn't know what love was, but he knew the other thing.

They glided gracefully together, the young man and his girl down there on the rink, turning their heads to smile at each other, and he wanted to stand up and yell at them.

I KNOW THE OTHER THING!

Gliding together, his arm round her waist, a perfect picture of young love.

Yell and yell.

THERE'S SOMETHING YOU DON'T KNOW! IT'S THE OTHER THING! I KNOW THE OTHER THING, AND YOU DON'T!

Shaking, he sat shaking, didn't stand up of course, mustn't yell at people, they'd be so surprised, wouldn't they be surprised? But it had made him feel superior, yelling at them in his mind. He knew what to do with rats, and they didn't. With rats and pretty girls who said, "I don't think so."

Then there was the night when he put some diesel oil in an empty can and got some string and grabbed a rat and hung it up by its tail and lit the oil underneath it and listened for a while to the squealing as the rat struggled and spun on the string with its fur on fire and the delicious barbecue smell beginning, and when the squealing was finished with and the rat looked roasty black on the outside he cut it down and waited till it was cool enough to peel, and ate it, with the warm juice running down his chin, and in the morning when he woke he didn't have that clawing in his stomach, because he wasn't hungry now.

Then one night of course he went too far and set the cellar on fire, all the cardboard boxes and the stuff she threw down there, and he screamed and screamed like a rat in a trap and a neighbor heard him through the cellar window and saw the smoke, and when the police came they put him in a shelter for abused kids because he'd been alone in the house and they found the bruises on him, all over him, everywhere, and that was the year when he first went to school and began hating the other kids there, because there were no more rats to hate and he had to hate something or he couldn't know who he was. It was part of him now.

Suddenly the big lights came on around the rink, and the colors of the skaters were bright now as they made their way so gracefully 'round and 'round, and he found himself looking for one of them in particular again because he'd lost her, the girl with the long brown hair and the navy-blue skirt that swung when she moved her legs.

He didn't want to lose this one. The lipstick was hard in his pocket and he squeezed and rubbed it, feeling glad he'd chosen it as a memento last time, something very special, something she'd kissed, if you wanted to see it like that. It was the first time he'd taken—oh *there* she was!

Gliding around on her own with her long hair flowing out behind. He didn't want to lose this one, like the one he'd lost outside Farmer's Market.

But we must be very careful, mustn't we? Very careful indeed. After all, he'd already *selected* the next one, and there were going to be orchids for her and everything like all the other times; it was much better like that, more rewarding, giving him the feeling he was in control, the feeling that he was God, at least for one person, the God who would be with her in the last hours of her life, the last minutes, the last seconds as she screamed, as she screamed down there, one of her roller skates coming off because the strap had broken, laughing now as she picked herself up, not screaming anymore, but he would make her scream again in a little while, wouldn't he, sometime tonight, because the fire was in his groin and there wouldn't be time for the orchids and all that, he wanted to watch her hands come up with her fingers spread out to protect herself as the knife flashed in the light and her eyes grew wide like they always did and she screamed, just once, never more than once, not because the strap of her skate had broken but because the blade was across her throat to stop the *silly fucking noise she was making, squealing like a silly fucking rat,* they made him sick, these girls who said they didn't think so, they didn't *think* so, what was he, a leper or something, a pariah dog, *how dare they,* the long red blade going slash, slash, slash with a smoothness and a lack of noise you would hardly believe if you were there.

Running with sweat, he was running with sweat at the thought, and there was one thing that mustn't happen now, *he mustn't lose her,* he mustn't let this one get away, because God was going to make her scream again tonight, just one last time.

Seventeen

Thiis is Theodora," Fido said.

"Hello. I'm Tasha Fontaine."

Theodora didn't say anything, simply looked at her, more than that, studied her face, looking from one eye to the other in turn. Tasha found it disconcerting.

The whole place reeked of pot.

"Fido knows someone," Audrey had told Tasha last night, "who works in a little club in the Village. She conducts séances."

Theodora was still studying her face, and Tasha half-turned away.

"When will you be free, Theo?" Fido asked her. His arm slipped around Tasha's waist, maybe to reassure her. She was totally out of her depth in this kind of place and it must be showing. She wondered for a moment if this woman Theodora was dumb, then suddenly realized the obvious: she was stoned out of her mind.

"Jesus Christ!" she had told Audrey last night, "you want me to go to a *séance*?"

"Not really, darling. I just thought we'd both pop along there for a little fun. Fido's always there, and I know he's hoping to see you again."

"Did you tell him we'd go?"

"But of course not! I don't *commit* people to things. Let's simply forget I mentioned it."

Tasha had caught the note of irritation—it was quite out of character. There'd been a subtle change in Audrey since she'd convinced her that Christine sometimes "came through" to her. It seemed to be something even Audrey couldn't deal with.

"But a *séance* . . . " Tasha had said. She knew very well they wouldn't just be "popping along there," if they went at all.

"Well, darling, I just thought that if you really believe Christine talks to you sometimes, this person might be able to persuade her to—I don't know—tell you more about what's really going on. Her name's Theodora somebody."

"Free?" Theodora asked Fido, turning to look at him. "Oh. In about an hour." She was studying his face too, Tasha noticed. Maybe this was the way a medium always looked at people, seeing in them more than others did. For the first time, Tasha thought it could have been a good idea of Audrey's to come here; she was ready to try anything that worked, anything at all, however weird.

"We're in line, then," Fido nodded, "so don't forget us, Theo." He led Tasha gently away to his table, and once again she felt the strength in him, could almost feel it even when he wasn't touching her. Audrey followed them.

"Is there anybody here, darling," she asked Fido, "I might conceivably know?" She looked around her; most of the people were sitting at small bare-wood tables with candles on them stuck into bottles, not moving around very much, not even talking; a lot of them had a glazed look in their eyes as they drew the smoke in deep. The sound of New Age music floated down from the ceiling, which was lined with sagging canvas that showed patches of soot above the tables where the candle smoke went up.

"There might be," Fido told her. "Quite a few painters come here."

Tasha assumed that Audrey would drift away if there were anybody she knew, so as to leave her alone with Fido. She didn't want that to happen; she wasn't here for romance. "Would you like to smoke?" he was asking her.

"No. Christ," she said to Audrey, "if they raid this place and my name gets into the papers—"

"Not to worry," Fido said. "That man over there with the two lesbians is a police lieutenant, a cross-dresser, and he's not the only cop that comes here. La Botica is perfectly safe."

"If it weren't," Audrey said to Tasha, "I wouldn't be here either. I, too, have a reputation to lose."

"Of course. I wasn't thinking—"

"No offense, darling." Audrey touched her hand across the table.

"Drinks, then?" Fido asked.

Audrey waited. Tasha asked, "What's everyone else having?"

"Aud?"

"Oh, vodka tonic, dear boy. And thank you."

"I'm having the same. Tasha?"

She didn't really want a drink, she wanted to get to the action, because it frightened her. They were going to raise a ghost, weren't they? Christine's? But there was an hour to put in, so she said, "I'd like a brandy and Canada Dry on the rocks." She didn't imagine there was anybody at all in here who wasn't either half-smashed or half-stoned, and if she just asked for Perrier with a twist she'd be like the man who could see in the country of the blind.

"Don't misjudge them," Fido said as he waved for a waitress. He'd obviously been watching Tasha's face. "Most of these people have come here to wind down the tension after a hard day's work. Quite a few are from Mad Ave and Wall Street. Have you ever seen the floor of the stock exchange when the market's really moving?"

"I—I'm just interested," Tasha said. "It's another world for me."

"You're safe with us, darling." Audrey was watching her too, and Tasha felt she was under a microscope, the same feeling she'd had with Clive Stuyvesant. Everybody watched her, these days.

Christ, that sounded like paranoia. Was she going to have that to deal with, too? A well-documented, classic mental aberration?

Elizabeth had watched her too this afternoon, looking so cool in the apple-green silk paisley she'd treated herself to in Milan, even cooler than usual, watching her quietly as they'd gone over the guest list for the soiree La Botica was putting on next week to introduce some of the fall creations; Tasha had asked twice whether Barbara Heatherton had been invited, and Elizabeth had had to tell her twice that Barbara Heatherton would be in Paris until September.

"Oh, God, that's right. I don't seem to be concentrating all that well, do I?" It was okay to say that; she and Elizabeth understood each other, never dodged issues. And this was an issue. Face it.

"Are you going to see Dr. Stevenson again?" Elizabeth asked.

"Stuyvesant? I'm not sure. He's such a fucking know-it-all."

"Isn't that their job?"

"Okay, but it's the way they do it that counts. He makes me feel like I'm in fifth grade and still bed-wetting."

Elizabeth adjusted her green suede belt, keeping her eyes lowered, and Tasha thought how incredibly poised she looked, poised, elegant, and centered. Sometimes Elizabeth made her feel like a middle-aged matron, and just at the moment she was making her feel like some kind of zombie from out of the woods pretending to run a boutique in New York City. And what would Clive Stuyvesant say about that? He made her feel like a fifth-grader, her junior partner made her feel like a zombie, what did other people make her feel like? Did she have a list? Identity crisis, right?

Put it down on the chart: tendency to paranoia, plus an identity problem, this is beginning to be such fun, when are we coming to the multiple-personality bit, where everything really shakes itself to pieces?

"Don't feel," Elizabeth said, looking up, "that if it takes a little time for you to get over this—this thing about Christine Wittendorf, the business will suffer. You're indispensable, of course, but I'd manage to keep things running smoothly, at least for a while."

And the thought that had flashed through Tasha's mind hadn't been charitable. Was Elizabeth looking for more control? Finally, if everything went wrong, total control?

But all she'd said was something like it was a real comfort to know that La Botica would remain in good hands if she needed a little time off.

"There's Bryan Lough," she heard Audrey saying, "sitting over there with his girlfriend—what's her name? I knew I'd see someone sooner or later. Excuse me, darlings, while I say hello."

Fido helped her with her chair, which Tasha thought didn't happen too often in this place, and when he sat down again he put a hand on hers, just letting it rest there. "Bryan Lough," he said, "has probably spent somewhere on the high side of three million dollars with Audrey in the last few months, mostly on Picasso. How are you feeling?"

"Feeling?"

"You must be a bit uneasy." His dark eyes watched her, and she thought she saw kindness in them, sympathy. "I don't imagine you make a habit of going to séances in the Village."

"It was Audrey's idea."

"But you thought it was a good one."

"I guess." She liked the feel of his hand on hers, its gentle strength. It took some of the fear away, the fear of what might happen when Theodora started raising the dead. Because that was what she was going to do, right?

Suppose Christine knocked the table over or set fire to the place or something? *Christine,* Audrey had said, *was a monster.*

"Most of Audrey's ideas are good," Fido nodded, not taking his eyes off her. "In any case, I profit handsomely. I wanted to see you again, and here you are."

"I—it's nice for me, too. But right now I'm in a state of panic, as you rightly divine, so—"

"It's to do with the Marcia thing?"

"What? Yeah." She was surprised he remembered.

"Audrey tells me you get messages from Christine. Ones like that."

"Yes."

"Well, then, Theodora's just the person we need. She's very good, you know. The real thing. You'll see." His hand gave hers a gentle squeeze, or she imagined it, wanted it. "You'll feel so relieved when she's got it all sorted out for you. Then you can come home with me, and I'll show you some of the moons of Jupiter."

"The moons—?"

"From my roof garden. Jupiter has twelve moons, and you can see four of them with an ordinary pair of field glasses, even above the city lights."

"It's a really cute line."

"I hoped you'd think so."

"What is her name?" Theodora asked.

She had an accent, Tasha noticed, but couldn't place it. "Christine."

The room was very small, with dark red curtains draped everywhere, covering the walls; dust clung in their creases. A thick black candle was burning in a bowl, throwing their shadows across the table. Audrey and Fido were sitting on each side of the medium; Tasha was opposite, facing her, and quite close—the table too was very small, and round, with a dark red cloth over it, stained and threadbare.

"I need her full name," Theodora said.

She had some kind of robe on, and the facets of her jet beads winked in the light. She was smoking, squinting as she watched Tasha from under her hooded lids. Her eyes were filled with shadows.

Tasha took a breath and wished she hadn't, wished she could just get up and leave this room with its tawdry pseudo-dramatic ambience behind her and breathe some fresh air outside. *It's another world for me,* she'd told Fido a while ago when they were waiting for Theodora. She'd meant this place, but also more than that. A couple of weeks ago she hadn't even known these people who were sitting with her now at the small shabby table in this small, shabby room. They'd been strangers. Yet tonight, instead of taking Elizabeth to The Checkered Cloth and going over their plans for the dress show, she was trapped in a stinking den of weirdos, desperate for help.

Trapped? Sure. By Christine. Whatever she did these days was because of Christine.

"Wittendorf," she told the medium. "I don't know her middle name."

Theodora watched her through the smoke from her cigarette. The jet beads flashed softly in the candlelight, and Tasha realized the woman was shaking very slightly the whole time, with some kind of palsy.

"Wittendorf? Christine Wittendorf?"

Tasha nodded. "Yes."

"The woman who was murdered?"

"Yes."

The shadowed eyes enfolded Tasha like clouds. "Why do you want me to summon the spirit of such a one?"

"To see if there's anything she wants to tell me."

"What are you to her? What is she to you?"

The tone was sharp suddenly, accusing, and Tasha felt a rush of anger, wanted to tell this woman it was none of her fucking business. But that wouldn't be true, would it? This was very much the business of the night.

When her anger died away she said, "She's spoken to me sometimes. I think she's trying to get through."

Theodora drew in smoke one last time and crushed the butt of her cigarette into the tin ashtray on the table. "Why should she try to get through to you?"

"I don't know. I'm hoping you'll tell me."

The black eyes widened. "Hoping *I* will tell you?"

Tasha thought about this, then said, "I mean that *she'll* tell me, through you."

You had to get things right with Theodora. She felt Fido stirring beside her, clearing his throat. Did he know this kind of stuff? Had he sat in on seances before? Was this really his idea, not Audrey's? Was he a weirdo, too, with his moons of Jupiter and everything?

She shouldn't have come here. And, yeah, she'd felt exactly the same thing when she'd been in Clive Stuyvesant's consulting room. There shouldn't be any place in her life for psychiatrists or weirdos. She was a normal human being, for God's sake.

Wasn't she?

"You realize," Theodora was saying, "that you are asking me to attempt communion with a spirit in torment?"

Tasha thought she placed the accent now: it was German, or maybe Dutch. "I guess," she said in a moment. "But maybe you—we—can help her in some way, to lessen the torment."

The dark clouds enfolded her from across the little table. "It can be very dangerous—don't you realize?"

"For whom?"

"For you."

"Why?"

"She may prefer to be left in peace. She—"

"Look, she can't be in peace and in torment, too, right? I mean, what are we talking about here?"

The silence came down like a curtain. Tasha had started to get mad again, had let it show this time. But—Jesus Christ, was she expected to believe in all this shit, or wouldn't she be better off just getting out of here, so she could try and feel normal again in the normal world outside?

She felt sweat gathering on her forehead, and smoothed it away with her fingertips. The air in here was getting to her—for "air," read cigarette smoke and pot and this woman's unwashed body, because you sure couldn't picture Madame Theodora under a shower. If they didn't get down to business pretty soon now she'd pass out for the want of something to breathe.

"I am the judge of what happens here," she heard the woman saying. "Do you understand?"

"Sure. Whatever you say." But there was anger again in her tone, and Theodora caught it.

"You may believe you feel anger toward me. It's not anger. It's fear. They are the same thing. And you are right to feel fear. Some spirits don't wish to be disturbed, as I've tried to explain to you. Most of the people who come to me wish to contact the spirit of a relative or a friend. Was Christine Wittendorf your friend?"

"No."

"Then why do you seek to disturb her?"

"I have to get closer to her."

And that sounded strange, because only last night Audrey had told her, talking about Christine's death, "It's over, and it's time for you to move on—without Christine." And she'd told Audrey, "I'd like to, but I don't know how." But maybe this was how. Get closer still to her, know thine enemy, and take the fight from there.

"Why do you have to get closer to her?" Theodora asked.

"I need to know why she's riding me like this."

"What exactly does that mean?"

"She's possessing me."

The shadowed eyes opened wider. "You don't know what you're talking about. Possession is a terrible thing."

"Oh for the love of God, don't you think I *know* that?"

Tasha hit the table with the flat of her hand and felt the sting. "I'm not here for cheap thrills, okay? I'm a New York businesswoman, I run a very successful business and it takes quite a bit of intelligence and a whole lot of guts, and it's my whole life out there, and I'm not in the habit of sitting in at séances and stuff like that to pass the time—frankly, I prefer a good movie if I can find one. But since Christine Wittendorf was killed, she's been possessing me, and *yes* it's a terrible thing and I need your help, but if you won't give it to me that's perfectly okay; I'll keep on going it alone. Now, do *you* understand?"

The eyes of Theodora watched her from across the table, just three feet away, less, and the facets of the jet necklace shimmered in the light as the trembling of her body set it pulsing.

"Have you seen a psychiatrist?"

"Yes."

"What did he say?"

"Nothing constructive. I shouldn't have gone there."

"Why not?"

"Because I hoped there was a chance I'm just crazy." She felt her eyes wet suddenly, and tossed her head back, furious with herself. "But I'm not. I'm possessed. And that's why I came to you."

The silence settled in, filling the turgid air, soaking into the walls. As Tasha waited, she decided on one thing: if the next thing this woman said wasn't helpful, even simply cooperative, she would get out of this place right now and never come back.

In a moment Theodora said without expression, "If I seek to raise the spirit of Christine Wittendorf, will you accept the risk it entails?"

"Yes."

"The danger to yourself could be very great. The danger to your mind, and to your soul. I am compelled to warn you of this."

"I consider myself duly warned."

From beside her she heard Audrey take in a breath, and Tasha turned to her. "Look, I think you should go. Both of you. This is between me and—and Christine."

"I'll stay," Fido said quietly.

"Look, she might set fire to this whole place, or God knows what."

"I'm staying, too," Audrey said and touched her hand. "Unless you insist."

"You heard the gypsy's warning." She flashed a look at Theodora. "That's just a phrase, okay?"

"I understand. But if anyone wishes to leave, they must leave now."

Nobody moved.

"Very well," Theodora said, and Tasha felt a sudden rush of terror, and had to deal with it, sitting at the table with her fingers gripping its edge for something to hold on to. She had come here to confront the dead, and if the idea was suddenly frightening because she'd reached the brink there was nothing she could do. It was too late now to run.

"Do you have something of hers?" she heard Theodora ask.

"What? No."

"Nothing?"

"No." Just the ashes of a crimson scarf.

"A memory, then. A memory of her."

"She was sitting with me in a taxi one night, in the rain."

"Very well." Theodora's eyes dwelled on hers for a moment longer and then suddenly she looked down, laying her hands on the thin cotton cloth with the fingers spread open wide, the wan light of the candle touching on a huge garnet ring and etching the creases in the wrinkled skin, tracing the veins. "No one will speak, please. No one will move."

The black eyes became folded away within the painted

flesh of the lids, and Theodora's bosom began swelling and subsiding under her robe as she tilted her head back and began making a sound not unlike humming, a vibration that went on for so long that Tasha began thinking it must be something else, maybe an electrical appliance somewhere.

Then the sound stopped, and she felt her nerves collapse in the silence, and when the humming began again it took her with it, as if her psyche had become tuned in to the vibration. Theodora was perfectly still now; the slight palsy had left her. She sat with her fingers still spread on the tablecloth, her head tilted back and her eyes closed, the sound coming out of her as if from somewhere else, and endlessly, a cello string drawn taut and vibrating in the wind.

Then it stopped again.

"Christine, there is someone who wishes to speak to you. Her name is Tasha Fontaine. Have the grace to give me a sign that you are here with us, and are not displeased that I disturb your peace."

Just silence now, no humming, and Tasha closed her eyes, felt them, more accurately, being closed. Now that she was sightless, Audrey and Fido ceased to exist; it was almost as if she had seen them vanish.

So I'm alone here with this woman, this total stranger, who takes money for raising the dead, for communicating with spirits, but you can't have it both ways, can you, I mean anyone who can do a thing like that, tapping into some kind of other-world plane of existence, would have to be a saint or an angel or someone truly spiritual, ethereal, not someone who goes home with the money in her purse and locks the door of her apartment and feeds the cat and turns on the TV and watches whatever shit they're serving up on whatever channel, someone who—

"Christine . . . I ask you again to reveal your presence here, and to consider granting the wish of this woman,

Tasha Fontaine, that you speak with her through my spiritual agency . . . "

From behind her closed lids, Tasha could see nothing but flecks of colored nerve-light floating like miniature fireworks across the dark. She heard nothing until suddenly a laugh came from somewhere, muted by the walls—or did she imagine it? Or was it Christine laughing, way out there in the other-world? Was this the sign of her presence Theodora had asked her for, and had she heard it too? And was this the message—that they were wasting their time, sitting here like a couple of clowns?

"Christine . . . We know that you left this earthly plane in torment, and we seek to relieve that torment if we can. . . . But we need a sign that you are here among us, Christine . . . we need to hear your voice."

Theodora sounded farther away this time, but Tasha didn't open her eyes to see what was happening; she didn't even try—she knew it was quite beyond her strength even to lift her eyelids. Very quietly, without anything seeming to have changed, she'd lost control of herself, of her body, and as the terror moved in again with the force of a dark, rolling wave she tried to call out, to tell Theodora she didn't want to talk to Christine, didn't want any sign of her presence here because this wasn't normal, this was insane, *the danger to yourself could be very great . . . the danger to your mind, and to your soul . . . I am compelled to warn you of this . . .*

Then stop everything, for God's sake. Don't let her—

"Christine, I will ask you once more—"

No! Keep her away from me! I don't want—

But the black wave of terror rose again and crashed over her, and she went down . . . down . . .

"If you are with us, Christine, I ask—"

No! Oh God, oh Jesus Christ, don't let her—

You shouldn't have said that, he told her as he pulled open the door of the car and she saw the knife, the blade bright as he held it up for her to see, but she jerked across the seat and hit the opposite door open and pitched out and began running, running for her life.

You shouldn't have said that!

His feet pounding after her across the grass as she ran hard, she could run, she could run, she was fast, but she heard him behind her now, nearer, closing the gap, *You bitch, you fucking bitch, you shouldn't have said that, you understand me, you bitch?*

Went on running as hard as she could through the rain, *Oh my God, dear God help me* as one of her shoes flew off and she plunged headlong into the dark mass of the trees and heard him behind her, right behind her now, *he's a madman, he's a maniac,* the bright blade of the knife still in her mind as she ran, ran, ran as fast as she could with only one shoe and no time to kick the other one off and run barefoot, *run, run, run*—

You bitch, I'll kill you for that!

Oh, my God, please—please—

Twisted her foot and pitched down across the grass and looked up and saw the long bright blade in his hand as he stood towering over her for one endless moment, the death-bringer, garbed in black against the city's lights, before he brought the knife down, down, down and she screamed, screamed once in the hideous night before steel split flesh and ravished it and the scream went on, tearing into the silence as an arm was flung around her shoulders and someone called her name and she struggled but they held her tight and went on calling to her through the veils of awakening until she opened her eyes and the door burst inward and faces were staring down.

"What's going on?"

"Nothing, she's okay, she had a fright—"

"Jesus, I thought she was being—"

"Everything's fine," Fido's voice now, "we'll take care of her, she doesn't want a crowd of people in here—"

"Well, hey, she was raising the dead—"

"Go on out, Robbie, and take everyone with you. Do it for me."

Feet shuffled and the door was banged shut and Audrey was saying, "Everything's fine, darling. Don't worry, everything's fine."

Eighteen

Fido adjusted the tripod, bringing the field glasses down a little because Tasha was shorter, and sighted again.

"There we are." He stood away.

"I don't see them," she said.

"But you can see Jupiter?"

"The big star? Yes."

"Planet. The moons themselves are very small, though. Look for the small points of light strung out in a straight line, two on the right side and—"

"Oh, yeah, I've got them now. They're actually moons?"

"Satellites, if you prefer. Our moon's a satellite."

Tasha backed away from the tripod. "Is there life on them?"

"No. Would you like to see the galaxy in Andromeda?"

Tasha folded her arms. "Not really."

"Are you cold up here?"

"Cold?" The roof—the whole building—had been absorbing the sun's heat all day, and it was only just bearable even under the open sky, not long before midnight.

"Still upset," Fido nodded, and took the field glasses off the tripod and began collapsing it. "I wish you'd have a drink. It'd help relax you."

"I'm relaxed." She wanted to stay totally sober, so she could handle whatever came at her next. Or try. And she needed to think clearly.

Call Detective Behrens?

I think I have a clue for you, Bernie. I was at a séance tonight, and went through exactly what Christine Wittendorf went through when she was killed. It wasn't a dream. I wasn't dreaming about her. I *was* her. And here's the clue: it began with a carjacking. This guy forced his way into her car with a knife in his hand, and she got out the other side and ran into the trees, but he caught up. All she could do was scream, in the end. So does that give you anything useful, Bernie?

Bernie?

Sitting there in his bright-lit late-night office with the phone against his ear, his crumpled-paper face tilted as he listened, saying nothing until he'd worked out the best way of telling her nicely that no, it didn't give him anything useful, she was just cuckoo, that was all, and what she needed was a good night's sleep.

Yeah, but there was this little problem. Was she ever going to be able to sleep again, after what happened tonight? *Because that wasn't a dream.* Sure, she hadn't been conscious either; she'd gone into some kind of altered state, but it wasn't sleep. She'd been too alert the whole time, like you are under hypnosis—you know exactly what's going on, though you realize you're in an altered state. She'd been there, been hypnotized once.

She shivered again, keeping her arms folded across her chest. So here was the thing—she'd wanted to get closer to Christine tonight, and Christine had known that, through Theodora, but she hadn't said anything or done anything through the medium herself, she'd locked directly into Tasha's mind and let her know what had happened that night when she was killed. She had let Tasha *become* her, for those last minutes of her life. Dear God, how much closer than *that* could she get to Christine?

But there was more, and this was why the shivering still went on, wouldn't stop.

Tonight Tasha herself had voiced the scream that had wakened her two weeks ago from sleep, halfway across town.

Reality had shifted. Space and time had collapsed, and the living and the dead had become one.

"Are you okay?"

Fido's voice.

"Sure," she said. "Just a little upset, still, like you say."

"I can imagine."

He stood there with the tripod in his hand, looking like a photographer at a wedding. They didn't take pictures at funerals. Could you photograph ghosts? She'd heard about that. It would be real cute to have a picture taken of Christine, wouldn't it, a new one, with all the ectoplasm around her and everything, to put on the bedside table?

Don't let me have thoughts like that. Don't let me go crazy.

Shivering in the warmth of the summer night.

A light went on in a window across the street, and she said—to sound normal, to be amusing company—"So when you're bored with the amateur astronomy bit, you can always find more earthly entertainment, right?"

She thought immediately that it had sounded pretty corny, and wished she hadn't said it; either you're normal or you're not, you can't force it. But Fido looked across at the window, grinned, and said, "Yeah, sometimes I switch channels. You want to stay up here for a while and lie down, look at the stars? Or whatever?"

"Sure. I'd like that."

He padded over to the covered doorway with the tripod, and Tasha looked around her. There was a big striped beach mattress here on the roof with some cushions piled on it and a bottle of something and two glasses standing on a white-painted ironwork stool, like an ad for the Côte d'Azur. This was where Marcia had come. Marcia *et alia*. Christine had seen them here. She was watching now, must be, was still interested in Fido. 'Fido Hamilton,' Audrey had told her, 'probably knew her better than anyone else. They had quite a relationship going.'

Was it okay to be watched by your partner's dead girl-friend while you were having sex with him?

Where had reality gone?

"There'll be a moon later," she heard Fido saying as he came back from putting the tripod away.

"That's nice." She saw he was waiting for her to lie down on the mattress first, so that was what she did. "You must miss her," she said, but it sounded irrelevant and she didn't quite know why she'd said it. Maybe because he'd been really blown away by Christine's death when Tasha had first met him at the reception, and she didn't want him to think she took it for granted right now that he wanted to have sex with her, while he was still grieving. She didn't feel able to take anything for granted after what had happened tonight, anything at all, including reality.

"I miss her like hell," Fido said, "yes."

Catching his tone, Tasha said, "But you don't want to talk about her."

"Or think about her, right now. Any more than you do, I imagine, after what happened at the club."

"Right."

She hadn't told Fido or anyone else what had really happened; she'd just said she'd drifted off and had a night-mare. But they'd known it must have been pretty bad, by the way she'd screamed.

"Do any of your neighbors come up to the roof in summer?" she asked Fido.

"Oh, no. This is my own private preserve; it comes with the apartment. I used to do it as a kid in Vermont; I had three sisters, and we lived in a house with a partly flat roof, and that was my escape from them when it got too much— they knew where I was, but they couldn't stand heights. So I guess it's a childhood hangover. And sleeping under the open sky is nice in summer." He put his hand over hers. "But we could go below, if you'd rather."

"I like it here." She turned her hand over and interlaced her fingers with his, feeling their strength, needing it. "People grow things," she said, "on these roofs." She could see quite a few low sheds and a trellised garden patch and even a small conservatory on the roof of the next building. "I suppose that's a childhood hangover, too."

"I guess."

His face was close to hers and she turned her head and they kissed, and she knew now that he wasn't going to let his grief over Christine get in the way of his life's continuum. Should she tell him that Christine was watching them tonight? Better not; it would be a real turnoff.

Make a joke of it, yeah, keep it in control, tame the fear and the anger and stay sane, stay normal. The other way is death—death to the senses, death to identity, bring on the clowns in the white coats.

His kisses were becoming urgent, but she slowed the pace for a while, pulling away but keeping her hands on him. "Why did you want to see me again, Fido?"

In the faint light she caught his look of surprise. He was a sophsticate and it had been a naïve question, a schoolgirl's. But she wanted to know.

"Surely," he said, "you don't need telling."

"Tell me anyway."

He was lying half across her and she left things like that, could feel his hardness but didn't touch him there.

"You're a beautiful woman," he said, "and I guess the male in me is stirred by the fact that you're kind of lost at the moment. So I feel protective."

"Lost?"

"In your life. With this—possession thing." He tried to dismiss it lightly with his tone, but didn't manage. It concerned him.

"I thought," she said, "you might find me attractive because I look like Christine."

"But you don't."

"I don't?" She sat up a little, leaning on one arm and looking down at him.

"You're the same type, but that's all."

"I'm the same type, but I don't look like her?"

"You might in a photograph, maybe, but not in life. There's such a difference. The personality contributes so much to the appearance—otherwise no one could ever paint a portrait; it would just be a face."

"I saw people doing double takes at the reception. I thought that was why."

He gave a little shrug. "Like I just said, you're a beautiful woman. Beautiful women get double takes. Where have you been all your life?"

"Nowhere like here."

Fido looked around him. "You mean on a—"

"No. Forget I said it." She lay down again, bringing him with her, watching his dark face against the faint light of the sky, feeling his strength flooding all over her now and remembering in a flash of played-back conversation something he'd said when they'd been at lunch in the Italian restaurant. "I went along to see the detective in charge of the case, the next day. He would've sent for me anyway, I knew that. It's one of the first things they do, talk to the victim's relatives, friends, especially boyfriends."

So why had that popped into her mind?

He was awfully jealous, although he never let it show.

Tasha shut her eyes as a cold wave passed through her. She didn't want to hear that voice any more, didn't want to be reminded that Christine must be with her all the time now, watching her, listening—Jesus Christ, didn't they have anything better to do when they died, couldn't they look after their own goddamned business up there or wher-ever it was?

Haunting is for real.

Sure, there are so many stories.

Ghosts are for real.

Yeah, ghost stories too.

But this wasn't just a haunting going on. That always happened in one place. This was everywhere: wherever Tasha was, that was where it happened. This wasn't just a haunting, something you could send in to the *National Enquirer*—hey, I just saw Elvis again, reflected in a beer can at the ball game, and you know, he kinda winked at me?

This is possession. Wherever I go, she is. Whatever I say, she listens. And sometimes she tells me things when the mood moves her, nothing ever important like the name of the man who killed her, just trivial things—*but hold it right there,* was it trivial this time?

'Relatives, friends, boyfriends, especially boyfriends.'

And, very especially, jealous boyfriends.

"Are you okay?"

"What? Yeah. Why?"

"I just wondered."

"What was I doing?"

"You just went very quiet, like you'd gone someplace else."

"I—I was just thinking how nice it is up here under the open sky, like you said."

Did you kill Christine?

Is that why she won't tell me?

Or doesn't she know, didn't she see, was it too dark, were you masked?

Did he kill you?

Lying here talking to the dead, yeah. Talking maybe to a murderer? Or just going slowly out of my mind? Is this what it's going to be like from here on out, reality? Not much better than a snake pit? Do some of those people finally give up and get on the telephone and ask for someone to come and fetch them, they're ready to go, because they can't take it any more? Wouldn't it be more comfortable in a nice private ambulance with kindly looking guys in white coats holding my hand, and then the quiet, civilized conversation with the principal in the shaded room? Better than this kind of reality?

Should she tell him, yes, I'd prefer to go below now, and by the way, may I use your phone, it's just a local call?

Get this over with first, though, okay? The poor guy's suffering, with his dick nigh busting out of his pants, put him out of his misery—or maybe just play it straight like everything's normal, could even be fun, a good way to relax—the best, right?

Sure. Give it a shot.

"You're so incredibly strong, Fido," she whispered.

"I work out."

"I don't mean just that. There's a strength that comes out of you, in waves. It's like being near the ocean." She began helping him with her clothes, and with his. "You've brought something to wear, right?"

"Of course." He had the packet, was opening it with his strong, sure fingers, had gotten his act down pat with so much practice.

She'd kicked her shoes off, but her panties had gotten stuck at the knees and she tugged at them again, not feeling anything even now, just wanting to get it over as a gesture of courtesy to an aroused male who had, after all, been kind to her, giving her the self-portrait and sharing lunch with her and trying to be helpful with the Theodora thing, panties right off now so here we go, enjoy it, for God's sake enjoy every minute of it, think of it like a vacation from the snake pit.

But she felt nothing, even as she let his hands attempt

to tease her into what should have been arousal. Lying under the night sky with a handsome guy whom she liked, feeling him ready and raring to come into her, she herself felt nothing, and this hadn't ever happened to her before, this was something *else* that had never happened to her before.

Before Christine.

So it was pretty clear what was going on, wasn't it?

As Fido lowered his body against hers and she felt him entering her the sky darkened without warning and the air thrummed with power and she used it, pushing upward with her hands and hurling him off her, hearing him crash against the ironwork table and send the bottle and the glasses flying as he cried out in shock.

Nineteen

I 'd like the chicken pot pie."

"Okay, that comes with soup or salad."

She stood with one leg crooked, writing on her pad. What would she write? CPP, probably; they all had their shorthand, these girls, because they didn't have the time to write everything out in full, you could well understand that.

"The soup's matzo ball or black bean tonight."

"I'll have the salad," he said. He wondered if her bottom was sore after falling down on the rink like that this evening; she was a beginner, he'd noticed, using rented red-painted skates. He'd followed her to the coffee shop, Mickey's Diner. He didn't intend to let *this* one go.

"Vinaigrette, blue cheese, French, Italian, or honey-mustard?"

She looked down at him now, away from her pad. She had almost-green eyes, and had put up her long brown hair under her Mickey's cap. She was even prettier than she'd looked at the Wollman Rink, and this affected him, because he didn't like pretty girls, and he was beginning to think about what he would do to her later if she said the wrong thing.

"The honey-mustard sounds nice," he said. Salad would take him longer to eat than soup, and it would make him look busy, like an ordinary customer, while she was getting him the chicken pot pie; it would save him having to just sit here watching her.

"Something to drink?" she asked him.

"Coffee."

"Ya goddit," she said, and gave a quick sunny smile. The name tab on her red cotton top read JENNY.

"Thank you, Jenny," he said. It felt good, using her name; it brought an intimacy into their relationship.

He had to sit doing nothing, of course, until the salad came, and there wasn't much he could do about that, although he could have asked for some rolls if he'd thought. He pretended to take an interest in the big stand-up card that had colored photographs of the desserts on it. At the top there was a bright yellow sunflower like the one on Jenny's cotton top, and he watched his mother's legs going in, being sucked in, as the sunflower ate her up.

You stand too close, she'd told him in the little backyard, *and they'll eat you up.*

But they hadn't, after all. One of them had eaten her up instead, like a huge sticky-jawed *Dionaea muscipula.* That was what had happened in his dreams, night after night for years and years, and he knew it had become the kind of truth that exists in life even though nobody sees it actually happening.

"Here you go," Jenny said, and put down his plate of salad.

"It looks very nice." He didn't lift his head, but pretended to take an interest in the salad. It was just a note of caution that had flashed through his mind: it wouldn't be wise to let her see too much of his face, his eyes, in case something went wrong and she was able to describe him afterward to the police. But even as this occurred to him, he dismissed it with a snort of breath that was actually audible, though not to Jenny, because she'd gone away to see to another customer. Of *course* she wouldn't be able to describe him afterward.

None of them ever had.

None of them.

He stuck his fork into his salad. It was very nice—as nice as it looked—but he was getting the feeling 'down there' again because he was thinking of the others, all the others, twelve of them, a round dozen, you might say, and the thrill was coming back like a soft-footed grinning animal that he loved and hated, padding toward him out of the dark.

That was how he thought of it, had thought of it from the beginning, as an animal he had to feed—tossing it an eye, a finger, a nipple torn away in the frenzy, even as he would have liked to kill it too, the animal, so he wouldn't have to feed it anymore. Because he knew it was all wrong and he shouldn't be doing it. Every time there was a trial reported in the paper he looked for that particular phrase, that question: *Did you know what you were doing was wrong?* He knew the answer was very important.

His fork stabbed at the salad, splitting open a little red tomato and sending the juice all over the table, the heat in his groin growing.

Keep calm, now, keep cool. This won't do at all. It's much too early, we're going to have a lovely time again, such a lovely time, and we mustn't hurry, must we, and spoil everything, no.

While it was happening of course he hadn't known that what he was doing was wrong, because of all the slashing and the slashing and the delirious joy and the wildness of it with the blood coming so fast from everywhere, there couldn't be any right or wrong with a thing like that, it was just a kind of explosion you couldn't hope to stop *and didn't want to stop, didn't want to stop* until it was over and the soft-footed grinning animal went padding off into the dark with blood dripping from something in its mouth, satisfied, sated.

Tonight it would happen again. Tonight it would be Jenny. What would he throw for the grinning animal to catch in its jaws? One of her pretty almost-green eyes? One of her breasts? Or perhaps—

"Didn't you like the salad?"

Thought stopped and he caught, held his breath.

"It was very nice," he said when he could, and looked up at her, into her pretty almost-green eyes. "I'm always a slow eater, though." He said it with a rueful little laugh.

"You want me to put this back under the heat?"

"No. No, thank you, Jenny. I'll finish my salad up eventually, you'll see."

"Okay." She set down the chicken pot pie and gave him her quick smile and went off, her walk kind of jerky, he thought, for someone who liked to skate. He wondered if she could run very fast, if she had to. He didn't think so.

None of them had ever run faster than he could.

None of them.

He picked up his knife and stabbed it into the crust of the chicken pot pie, sawing into the pastry with the serrated edge of the blade and revealing a soft morsel of chicken, or perhaps it was the head of a mushroom—there would be mushrooms in here, it had said on the menu. Whatever it was—and it was fun in a way not knowing yet—it was round and shiny under the light. He went on exploring with his bright, sharp knife.

Rita hadn't run very fast at all.

Rita had been the first, yet he remembered her more clearly than all the others.

She hadn't run very fast at all, no, in fact she'd stumbled, more than once, and then just given up, sobbing and blubbering and waving her hands around in that stupid way as she tried to stop what he was doing, what his knife was doing to her as it *slashed* and *slashed* until the blood came up in fountains and she stopped waving her hands around and the stupid blubbering became a gurgling noise and he had to smash his foot down on her throat to make it stop because it was so disgusting.

"What's your name?" he had asked her, amazed at his courage as they stood waiting for the bus to come.

"Rita."

But she'd hesitated, and then hadn't been able to think how to get out of telling him, without sounding rude. But what was so big about telling him her name? You saw girls' names on their license plates all over the place—they *wanted* people to know who they were. But then of course that was a dangerous practice, true, because total strangers could pretend they'd met them somewhere before, put them at their ease and catch them off guard when they started doing what they wanted to do as soon as they got the chance. He'd always been tempted to roll his window down when he stopped beside a car at the lights, if it had a girl's name on the plate, and warn her about that—"You realize it's dangerous, these days, to let everybody know your name?" But of course they wouldn't have taken any notice.

"That's a pretty name," he'd said, standing quite near her. "Rita."

"Thank you."

But she'd said it half-turned away from him, her head up as she'd stared along the street. It was the last bus they were waiting for, and the night had turned cold, with a wind off the ocean.

She didn't know, of course, what was really going on.

He'd seen her before, several times. Sitting on a park bench eating a sandwich, the first time, taking her lunch break from the tax accountant's office across the street. Then at the checkout at Supersave, when he'd been only three people behind her in the line. Then at the bus stop here, last week, watching her from a distance. And every time he saw her it had gotten more and more clear to him that *this was the one.*

There had never been any others.

From the time when they'd taken him out of the cellar and put him into a shelter and then a school, for all those years and years, he'd never talked to a girl. Not really *talked.* Or held a girl's hand. Or felt her smoothness, smelled her hair or walked beside her, step, step, step together like they belonged.

It had been a dream, of course, it could never come true. The woman who'd thrown him down the cellar steps and the man who'd strapped his hide—that was what he'd called it, *I'm going to strap your hide*—had gone out of his life a long time ago, and then there'd been the teachers and the other kids and the woman from the protection society and the thin man who'd shown him how to throw the newspapers so they'd land just right—there'd been all those people, but he was never able to talk to them, any of them, because they wouldn't listen.

There was something about him that scared them off.

He'd be talking to someone, wanting to tell them about the rats he'd roasted in the cellar and the way her legs had gone sucking into the sunflower and things like that, and they'd get that funny look in their eyes and walk away.

Walk away while he was talking.

You've got to forget it, one of the teachers had said. *You've got to get all that stuff out of your mind.*

And the man in the psychological place where they gave him tests with ink blots and pictures of cows and airplanes and nude bodies, the man there had told him the same thing; he'd got to walk away from all that, he mustn't keep on dwelling.

That was a funny word to use. *Dwelling.* He'd thought it had something to do with living in houses, or places.

In the end, of course, he'd stopped talking to people. Oh, yes, please and thank you and can I go to the bathroom and things like that, but not really talking. So there he was again, back in the cellar. That was what it felt like, being alone again. He'd wake, nights, when there was moonlight, and see the bars across the window. In the morning they were gone, but he knew they were really there all the time.

So it would always be like that, he'd realized, unless one day there could be somebody who would listen. It would have to be a girl because they were ever so much more sensitive and would have the time for him, since they weren't chasing after footballs or smashing things up or roaring around on bikes or shooting guns off and stuff. That was when the idea was born, as you might say, that one day he would meet a girl who would listen, and he wouldn't mention anything about the rats, of course, or the sun-flower; that had been completely wrong, no wonder they'd walked away from him all the time. He was old enough now to know that for the rest of his life he'd have to keep all that stuff buried inside of him. But that was okay. He could talk to himself about it whenever he wanted, while he talked to other people about the things they saw in the newspapers and the movies they'd seen, quite acceptable things like that.

"Did you see about the mineworkers' strike?" he asked Rita.

And he waited, holding his breath. This was the big moment when the whole of his life was going to change, because he'd begun talking to a girl.

"The what?" She half-turned to him but didn't actually meet his eyes, kind of looked into space, listening.

"The mineworkers' strike."

He was astonished at his own courage, because she wasn't making it easy for him, asking him to repeat what he'd said. But then, she didn't realize what was happening. She didn't know—how could she?—that she was the first girl he'd ever talked to like this, would be the first girl he would get to know, really get to know, somebody he could walk beside, step, step, step together like they belonged.

He went on waiting, shivering inside of himself with the anticipation.

"No," she said.

And she turned away again, to look for the bus.

He stood there watching her. The nearest street lamp had gone out, and her face was in shadow, the only part of her face he could see, just her cheek and the tip of her nose. But he knew what she looked like, from seeing her before. She was the prettiest girl he'd ever set eyes on, and that was why he wanted so much to make her his friend. She wouldn't only be the first. She would be the only one, ever.

Rita.

He shivered with the sound of her name in his head, with the thought of who she really was, the person who would listen to him, who would never let him be alone again, who would learn to love him, just like he loved her.

And here she was, standing so near him in the shadows.

He shook with love for her.

A car went past, and she turned her head a little to watch it, perhaps hoping it might stop and offer her a lift, as he could quite gather. He wasn't used to talking to people, she could tell, and it kind of worried her. He could understand that.

"They're striking first thing," he said, "in the morning. The mineworkers."

He could see more of her face now, because it was half-turned to watch the car going away in the distance, leaving the smell of exhaust gas on the air. Then she moved her head a little more and looked straight at him with her light blue eyes, and he caught his breath and had to stand there trying to appear natural while all the time he was shaking inside and couldn't breathe, felt like he was going to choke, because those were the eyes that would one day be full of love for him, and he didn't know what to do with himself, it was like fireworks going off suddenly in his chest. He had to turn away and cough.

"Excuse me," he said.

"Are you a mineworker?" she asked him. She sounded puzzled, maybe because it had been an odd way for him to start a conversation, he could quite see that now, he should have thought of something better.

"No," he said, "I'm with a food company."

That was clever, he thought, even as it came to him, because what he actually did was skin and gut fish at a seafood-processing factory all day for six dollars an hour, and he didn't want her to know that, because she wouldn't be able to fall in love with him. It was quite possible, he thought suddenly, that she could smell the fish on his shoes, because they were the ones he worked in, the only ones he possessed except for a pair of old sneakers with leaky soles that he couldn't use for work because of all the water splashing around the floor. That would be terrible, he thought, if she could smell fish on him.

"Oh," she said.

"What do you do?" he asked her.

"I'm a graphic artist."

She turned away again, watching for the bus, giving him the impression she hadn't really wanted to tell him, she didn't want him to know anything more about her. Yet *she* had asked him if he was a mineworker, hadn't she, so there was no reason now for giving him the cold shoulder.

He wasn't getting anywhere, and he'd got to be quick about it now because he might not be able to sit next to her on the bus and anyway it might not be a good idea to try sitting next to her in case he smelled of fish and then she wouldn't be able to feel any love for him, so he asked her the *big question,* sooner than he'd meant.

"Would you like to see a movie with me one night?"

He could hear the words going on and on like echoes as he stood there waiting, with his breath held, could see the words lit up and enormous across the sky, WOULD YOU LIKE TO SEE A MOVIE WITH ME ONE NIGHT? Everything depended now on what she would say in reply, *everything* depended on that, his whole future, his whole life.

The lights of the bus were showing in the distance along the street as it passed the hardware store and he saw them from the corner of his eye and felt the choking sensation again because the bus was coming and time was running out and Rita hadn't answered him yet.

Then she turned her head in his direction, not looking right at him, just turning her head a little bit, like she didn't think he was worth looking in the eyes a second time.

"I don't think so," she said.

The night was very quiet.

In the quietness he heard those words, too, echoing and echoing—but they couldn't be what she'd really said, he hadn't heard her right. He couldn't lose her now, because he needed her, and if she turned him down it wouldn't be very fair, would it, not fair at all, it would be very cruel, IT WOULD BE VERY CRUEL, he could see those words, too, lit up across the sky, bright and enormous.

"What?" he asked her, wanting to know, demanding to know, his hands clenched in his pockets and his teeth tight together.

"I don't think so," she said again without even turning her head this time, and next morning the paper said the body of a woman in her early twenties had been found in an alleyway near a bus stop in the northwest part of town, and her name was being withheld until relatives were informed.

But he had known her name.

Rita.

She'd been the first, yet he remembered her more clearly than all the others, which was only natural—you could quite understand that.

"Still working on it?"

Jenny. Not Rita. Jenny.

"Yes," he said, "I'm afraid I eat rather slow." He gave a rueful little laugh.

"Take your time," she said, "we don't close till ten."

When she'd gone he thought about what she'd said, and the way she'd sounded surprised when she asked him if he was still working on it. He'd hardly eaten any of his chicken pot pie; he'd been thinking of Rita while he'd prodded his knife into the lumps of chicken and the mushrooms, slitting them with the point and watching them come open. He wasn't hungry—that was the real truth—but he couldn't sit here forever poking around, it would look suspicious, like he was waiting for the place to close.

He'd have to get rid of this stuff somehow, make it look like he'd eaten it up.

When it was 9:45, he put some money down on the check, leaving exactly 12 percent for Jenny, not to seem too mean or too generous, not wanting to arouse even the slightest suspicion, because the time was getting close now and he couldn't afford to make a slip, that wouldn't do at all.

Because he knew what she'd say.

He knew what she'd say when he asked her. It wouldn't be any different this time, with this one. They'd all said the same thing, in different ways, *I don't think so,* or *I guess not,* or *maybe some other time,* it all meant the same thing, *it meant no,* didn't it, *it meant they didn't want to have anything to do with him,* they weren't going to fall in love with him and hold his hand and walk beside him, step, step, step like they belonged.

One day, though, it might happen. You couldn't deny there was a chance. One day a girl would say, *sure, I'd like that,* or *hey, that'd be real nice,* and he would take her to a movie or maybe a modest little dinner at some place like this, and they'd do it again and finally he'd have somebody he could love, somebody who would love him, and the whole world would change, become quite different, and he'd be a real person among real people again, and know what love was like.

He wanted that to happen, wanted it so bad that sometimes he made his hands bleed just thinking about it, found he'd been clenching his fists so tight his nails had dug in and broken the skin.

Oh God, he'd think, his head tossing on the hot pillow, oh Christ, he'd think, rocking along in the subway, oh God, oh Christ, I want to know what love is like. That isn't much to ask.

One day, maybe. But not today. He could feel it wouldn't happen today, tonight. He always knew.

He knew what Jenny would say.

She was coming this way now, tucking her pencil behind her ear, her eyes busy on his table to see what the situation was.

"So, you about ready for some dessert?"

She picked up the dirty plate. There wasn't much left in the pie dish now, only a few bits and some crust.

"No dessert," he said, and thought he'd sounded a bit short, but the truth was he had difficulty talking just right at these particular times, it was always the same. "Thank you," he said, pushing the words out on his breath. In his pocket his fingers rubbed and rubbed at the Tiffany lipstick case, rubbed and rubbed.

"Coffee?"

"No coffee."

Jenny picked up the check and the money. "Thank you," she said with a quick smile. "Come back and see—"

"Jenny?"

"Yeah?"

She stood waiting. Her almost-green eyes had a look of slight surprise in them.

"I saw you on the rink," he said, "earlier."

Rubbing at the Tiffany lipstick in his pocket, harder and

harder, concentrating on it in secret while he reached the moment when he would say what he would say. Then suddenly it was said, and louder than he'd meant; came out in a rush.

"Would you go skating with me?"

The hand in his pocket was still. Everything was still. He watched her eyes, watched the change coming into them as she thought about what he'd just said. He swallowed, heard himself swallow, didn't look away, mustn't look away from her eyes. There was something in them now that he'd seen before, in the eyes of those others, a look he knew well, of sudden caution, almost fear. It was there tonight in these eyes, Jenny's, because—as he knew—of what she was see-ing in his own.

Waiting, he was waiting, wanting to know, would she go skating with him?

"Right now," she said, looking down at him with her almost-green, almost-frightened eyes, "I'm seeing a guy. But hey, thanks for asking, okay?"

"Oh, for God's sake," Mary-Lou said, "look at this!"

She was checking under all the tables as usual for things customers might have dropped, while Jenny cashed up at the counter. The cooks had already gone home.

"What?" Jenny called across the room. 7.23 + 3.29 + 12.20.

"Someone threw all their food down the wall!"

Jenny looked up from the calculator. "You mean they threw up?" They couldn't have: everybody would have heard.

"No," Mary-Lou called. "They *poured* it down the wall!" She started for a mop and bucket. "Now why would anyone want to do that, for God's sake? If they don't like anything, they can tell us, can't they?"

"I can't think why," Jenny said. It was Table 9, where the

guy in the white shirt had been sitting a while ago, the guy who'd asked her to go skating with him. "You need some help?"

"I can handle it," Mary-Lou said.

Jenny was still cashing up when Mary-Lou slung her shoulder bag and headed for the passage to the rear of the building.

"Y'okay there, Jen?"

"Sure. See you tomorrow." 2.56 + 9.87 + 3.12.

"I'll be late, remember?"

"What? Oh, yeah. No problem." Mary-Lou had to go see her dad in the hospital. "Hope he's okay."

"Gee, I dunno," Mary-Lou called from the passage. "G'night, Jenny."

A door slammed.

It was 10:45 when Jenny checked the burners in the galley and left the main lights on and locked up and set the alarm and slammed the door at the rear of the building, the keys to her old-model Caprice in her hand.

The night was calm and warm, with a few stars showing above the warehouse opposite the restaurant. Her shoes grated across the loose asphalt as she walked toward the car. She'd almost reached it when she thought she heard another sound from behind her, and spun around.

Twenty

Detective **Bernard Behrens** was deep in a drugged sleep at home in his apartment at 11:13 the same night when the telephone finally roused him and he rolled over and picked it up.

"Behrens."

"Orsini. This just came in—a young woman was the victim of a knife attack in the parking lot of a restaurant on West Fifty-fifth ten or fifteen minutes before eleven o'clock tonight. The knife was found at the scene."

"She dead?"

"No. She's in a coma."

"They didn't get the guy?"

"No. He got clear."

"Where's the victim?"

"St. Clare's."

"Get there. Call Woodcock."

Behrens hit the door of the closet with his shoulder as he windmilled into his clothes. He'd been in a drugged sleep minutes back—not because he was on anything—the drug was nineteen hours at the precinct and in the field without a break and he'd finally come on home and fallen down on the mattress, been there since 7:00 this evening, a dead duck, breaking a fucking lace as he bent over his shoes and did without, getting out of the place less than five minutes after the phone had jerked him awake, *the knife was found,* was that so, *the knife was found at the scene,* Hail Mary, kick the Buick awake and gun it across town to the hospital.

"When d'you expect her to come out of it?"

"We can't say."

"I mean," Behrens said, "gimme the ball-park, are we talking about a couple of hours or a day or a week? You know what the injuries are."

"If I also knew this patient's medical history over the last ten or fifteen years, I could probably give you a better idea, Detective." The young intern adjusted his white coat, straightened his stethoscope. "I'm a doctor, not a clairvoyant."

Behrens looked at the man, his face wooden. "Does the name Christine Wittendorf mean anything to you?"

"I saw the news awhile back."

"Okay, when this lady comes out of her coma, she might be able to describe Wittendorf's killer for us. You know?"

The intern looked at the rumpled clothes and the sleepless eyes and the two-day stubble and across at the face of the woman in the bed and down at his chart and back at the detective again.

"I'd say we have a chance of at least a partial return of consciousness within two or three days, but that's not much more than a semi-informed guess. Her condition could change dramatically either way. It's possible she may never recover consciousness at all—that's a massive cranial injury she has there. What we're hoping right now is that she'll actually survive it. Or hadn't you thought of that?"

"We think of a lot of things, Doc." Behrens watched the

guy walking away, his head tossing half a degree one side, half a degree the other. Then he looked at Orsini. "Okay, we keep surveillance on her, twenty-four hours a day. You call Woodcock?"

"Yeah. He went right on over to the crime scene."

"Let's get there."

On their way down to street level Orsini asked, "Is this case breaking, Bernie?"

"If she doesn't die on us."

The knife lay on the swing-up table in the police van, inside a transparent plastic bag. They stood looking down at it: Behrens, Woodcock, Orsini, and the off-duty cop. In this light the bag looked dirty, but wasn't; they all looked like that in low light. The knife looked clean, the blade gleaming under the plastic film. It was a butcher's blade, hollow-ground, black handle, copper-riveted.

"He never got a chance to use it?" Behrens asked the off-duty cop.

"No."

"Must make you feel pretty good."

"Just lucky. What are they saying up there?"

"She could be talking to us in two or three days."

"If—" Orsini started off, but got a look to kill from Behrens.

"So what happened?" Behrens asked the cop.

"I was walking across there between the warehouse and the restaurant, going toward my car, and I heard a scream, started running." He was a young guy, Behrens thought, still had some excitement in his tone, thinking maybe he'd saved a life here. And maybe he had. "The guy was attacking her, and—"

"With the knife?"

"I didn't see the knife right away. He was just kind of trying to get her onto the ground. She was coming right back at him, beating him with her fists, and I'd started hollering at him by now, told him I was police—you know—and then she went down and he took off, while—"

"You didn't have your gun?"

"No. Off-duty I kind of—"

"They're handy, kid, in uniform or out." *Holy shit, he could have brought Jack down, Jack the Knife, saved more lives, made history with just one shot, bang and you're dead, Jack, the case is closed, holy Christ.* "Go on."

"So I . . . you know, did what I could for the victim. I mean, I couldn't leave her there and go chasing—"

"You did the right thing, sure, the only thing." Kid needed reassuring, he'd sounded kind of slow, the last thing he'd been saying, it was coming to him now, Jesus, he should have been carrying his weapon, he could have picked that guy off and—"When did you see the knife?" Behrens asked him.

"Soon as I got the ambulance here I started looking around for anything I could see, or find. It had landed halfway under one of the concrete blocks—"

"You didn't touch the handle—"

"Hell no, hey, I'm not a rookie—"

"Call it a dumb question. See anything of his face?"

"I guess it was just a blur, in that light."

"Description?"

"Twenty-five to thirty-five, five-ten, one-fifty, light-colored hair cut short, white shirt, dark pants, and shoes."

"Ran hard."

"Yeah, he was fast."

"Fit guy."

"Right."

When Behrens had finished he gave a nod and turned to talk to the driver, wanted the knife sent along to Forensic, soonest; then he told Orsini to stay here and supervise the operations at the scene. Then he went down the step from the van with Woodcock following.

As they walked across to the Buick, they heard the off-duty cop.

"Sir? I'll be armed at all times, from here on out."

"There you go," Behrens called back.

Mary-Lou cracked the door open and squinted at them over the chain as they showed their badges.

"Hate to get you up this late," Behrens told her when they'd broken the news.

"That's okay." She went on trying to tidy her hair. They were sitting on the blue flower-patterned settee, Mary-Lou in the middle, her bathrobe pulled around her, no belt. "Two or three *days*?"

"Time goes quick, Mary-Lou—call you Mary-Lou?"

"Sure."

"How did she seem to you, at the restaurant tonight?"

"Seem? I—"

"She upset about anything? Nervous? Quiet?"

"I guess she was about like normal, you know? Actually it was her day off, but she came in to take over from the manager around half-past eight—he gets tired a lot, it's diabetes."

Woodcock heard a spring twang under his butt and shifted his feet. The case was breaking, he kept saying in his head, the case is going to go down, Jesus, we're real close to that motherfucker now.

"Didn't say she thought she might've been followed?" Behrens was asking. "To the restaurant?"

"No, she said nothing like that. She was real, like, normal, you know? She's always the same. She's real nice to get along with." Her voice caught as she said, "Gee, I wish this hadn't happened."

"Sure. But she was lucky, Mary-Lou. Could have been a whole lot worse. How many customers went through Mickey's tonight? From eight-thirty on?"

"Maybe thirty or forty."

"Any of them seem like they were acting strange?"

"I guess not." She pulled her robe tighter around her. "We get a—you know—a quiet kind of crowd at Mickey's."

"Jenny say anything—"

"Somebody spilled some food down the wall, now I come to remember."

"Spilled it? By accident?"

"I guess not. He must've done it deliberately."

"You didn't see it happen?"

"No."

"What did he look like?"

"I don't know. It didn't happen in my section. I just found it there afterward."

"That happen often?"

"I guess not. Why should anybody throw their food down the wall?"

"I don't know, Mary-Lou. Anybody get fresh with Jenny tonight? You see anything? She complain?"

"I guess not. But it happens—she's real pretty."

"But it didn't happen tonight?"

"She never said nothing. I never saw nothing."

"Mickey's has a liquor license?"

"Yeah."

"Anybody get drunk tonight? Noisy?

"Gee, no. That doesn't happen much. We're not—you know—a bar."

"Sure." He asked another dozen or so questions, then this one: "Jenny say anything about getting some flowers sent to her today, or recently? Maybe orchids?"

"She never said nothing." With a little laugh: "People don't send us guys orchids!" She pulled her robe tighter again, and Woodcock thought, hey, this is some chick, I just noticed, look at that leg, and what the fuck am I doing thinking things like that when the case is breaking?

Behrens searched around in his head for the next question, felt like trying to catch a hen in an empty barn, he was losing too much sleep, when H9073 finally went down he'd hit the sack for longer than Rip van Winkle, you listening?

Couldn't catch the hen. "I guess that's it for now, Mary-Lou. If I think of anything else I'll call you, okay? And if *you* think of anything, you call me. Anything at all—you get that?—doesn't matter how silly it might sound. Anything." At the door, he said, "Anybody keep a firearm at Mickey's?"

"Not that I know." She looked scared. "Mean we should?"

"Depends how you feel about it after tonight, but if you decide it's a good idea, make sure you go to a firing range and train with it, and keep it where *nobody* can reach it."

"I'll talk to Frank. He's the manager."

"Sure." Behrens opened the door.

"Is there any use me going along and being with Jenny tonight?"

Behrens shook his head. "Get some sleep and call St. Clare's tomorrow, see how things are going."

In the parking lot Woodcock said, "Bernie? That coulda been the murder weapon we were looking at tonight in the van. Right?"

"Yeah."

"Jeeze. We're *that* close."

"Yeah."

By daylight in the morning there were going to be fifty uniforms knocking on doors and asking people if they saw a guy hanging around near Mickey's last night, maybe somebody strange to the area, and if so what did he look like, he get out of a car, what car, things like that, a couple of hundred things, while the overnight Forensics and photographers and dirt-sifters and beachcombers covered the crime scene inch by inch and took all their treasures back to the labs and poured them out of the plastic bags under the hundred-watt bulbs and put some of them under the electron microscope and did all the other stuff, so when the day finally came and the prosecutor looked at the detective in the box and said are you *certain* this blood spot found at the crime scene came from the defendant's body the witness could answer, yes, sir, we're certain—we checked the DNA.

But they'd covered the crime scene eleven times before in Los Angeles and Chicago and Boston and New York and they'd done it again twelve days ago in Central Park and nothing had come of it, Jack the Knife was still on the streets, and Jenny Olivia Kuratczyk, twenty-four, waitress, was lying up there in the intensive-care unit with nothing to tell them, nothing to say, could go on lying there until there was a dramatic change, like the man said, and she wouldn't even get to say good-bye.

And Jack still around, itching, burning to try again, desperate for the fix, the orgasm, more desperate now because Jenny hadn't done it for him, there'd been no fancy knife-work, no bloodletting, no thrill.

If it had been Jack last night, and not some other guy, there was that, too, wasn't there, they could pick him up and bring him in and it didn't have to be Jack, be a different case, a new one, not this one, not H9073. They'd be no closer tonight than they'd ever been—it would just mean there was another sicko in town with a knife.

Behrens gunned the motor of his Buick. "Yeah," he told Woody through the driver's window, "we're that close. Thing is, though, how close is close? Could be a thousand miles."

Twenty-one

J ogging south along the Central Park Mall, Tasha slowed again, listening for the sound of footsteps behind her.

But she still heard nothing.

There was a slight mist this morning, an hour after first light; it lay in pale swathes between the trees, the aftermath of the rain shower that had fallen during the early hours, beating on the roofs for a few minutes, loud enough to waken her, then ceasing suddenly and leaving silence and the smell of wet leaves coming through the open windows.

She slowed again, just a little bit, and went on listening.

Paranoid. Yeah, okay, an extreme case of paranoia, but it was nobody's goddamn business. Fear was fear was fear, and she had to deal with it, do everything she could to stop it bringing her down. It was a one-man game—right, sexist—a one-person game, and nobody else could help, not Audrey, not Clive Stuyvesant, not Fido, not even Bernie Behrens. She was in this on her own, so leave it to Superwoman.

Thop, thop, thop . . . the blue-striped Nikes absorbing the shock, the misty air cool against her face as she jogged through the trees, Superwoman, yeah, with fear coming out of her with every breath, she could smell it—go anywhere near a dog right now and he'd have his teeth in her.

Hanif was over there, cutting across the grass to the East Drive, Hanif Khattak in his little white shorts. He saw her and waved, and she waved back. She hadn't thanked him yet, would have to do it today—the morning after she'd passed out at his party he'd sent flowers, with a note saying he hoped she was "fully herself again," which she thought was really sweet—her host, after all, was hardly responsible for the fact that she was going slowly out of her mind; there was a limit to hospitality, even Hanif Khattak's.

He'd overtaken her yesterday, jogging past the band-shell on his way home and calling out to her cheerily—"I think I left the coffee on!"—feeling he should apologize, she assumed, for not slowing down to keep pace for a neighborly chat, even though he must know it was the primordial offense in the serious jogger's world. She liked courteous men, sensitive men with manners like Hanif, and Fido Hamilton.

Poor Fido!

It was perfectly okay, he'd told her as he'd driven her back to Temple Mansions last night in his crimson Porsche; his only concern was this "thing" that seemed to be getting at her all the time, the "Christine thing," and he was really sorry Theo hadn't been of any help at the séance earlier. He'd sounded almost angry about it, angry with Christine. If there were anything he could do, Tasha must call him right away—for just somebody to talk to, a shoulder to weep on, whatever.

It hadn't been quite the romantic idyll he'd expected, with Saturn—or was it Jupiter?—riding high above the city while they made tempestuous love on the beach mattress, Monte Carlo style. He had actually suffered bruises when she'd hurled him away from her and was limping when he'd seen her up the steps of Temple Mansions. He'd also been in shock, as she had, and neither of them had wanted to talk about that frightening access of force that had come into her when she'd flung him against the little iron table.

"I'm sorry," she'd told him, "I thought—I suddenly thought she wouldn't have wanted you to—you know—be with anyone again so soon. I mean Christine."

His eyes had been very dark, darker than usual, as he'd stared at her in the faint luminosity from the night sky; then he'd given an exaggerated Frenchman's shrug. "You could be right," he'd said quietly, and they'd started picking up the broken glass where the bottle had crashed from the table.

Tasha didn't want to think about—was trying to forget—the sensation of sudden fierce power that had been in her suddenly in the instant when she'd hurled Fido aside like that. He was a big guy, and she could never have done it alone—or have had the urge to do it.

Get it out of your mind, yeah, don't give it room. What we don't think about can't have any power over us, right? That was last night and today is today, with the world beginning all over again, complete with its new concerns.

One of which was the man somewhere behind her.

Thop, thop, thop . . . her rubber soles slapping the asphalt, a curled leaf, dying early in the year, spinning slowly past her face through the misty air.

She'd first noticed him a couple of mornings back; at this hour there weren't too many people in the park and she knew all the joggers by sight. He wasn't wearing a tracksuit or shorts or anything, just a pair of tan slacks and a white T-shirt, a young guy with a short haircut and sunglasses, the kind with the mirrored lenses.

So he was a new kid on the block, that was all. She wouldn't have noticed him if she weren't clinically paranoid, or—okay, gimme a break—if she hadn't been trained by now to look twice at anything strange, to prepare for any new shock that might explode in her face before she saw it coming.

With compliments from Christine.

So on the second morning she'd slowed her pace along the mall and waited for this new guy to come up behind her and overtake her, like Hanif had done, like other people had done, the fleeter of foot, the more ambitious. But that hadn't happened: this guy had slowed too, and when Tasha peeled off through the trees toward Temple Mansions he'd been back there at the same distance, not looking her way but jogging steadily, head down.

So, wasn't that okay?

Maybe. But these days she wasn't sure that anything was okay, anything at all. There'd been a warp in her personal universe, a shift in the space-time continuum, and it had left little gaps where Christine had shown through from her own world, wherever that was. So Tasha wasn't sure that anything going on was really okay, and she had to check it out. Give it to Tasha, yeah, she'll check it out.

Excuse me, sir, but why are you jogging behind me and not wearing the regulation gear? And why did you slow your pace yesterday morning when I slowed mine? And the same thing just now?

Well, gee, lady, I didn't actually notice you, and quite frankly it's none of your goddamn business what I choose to wear, so will you go look for some other guy to pick on?

I'm not picking on anybody, I'm just frightened, that's all, terribly frightened of everything, because of Christine.

Thop, thop, thop . . . running scared through the misty morn.

So few people around at this hour. Remember that woman who got herself gang-raped and left for dead in Central Park that time? Been an investment banker or something? It hadn't happened at night, in the dark; they'd gone for her in the early morning, just like now. It could happen anytime; the thin, trembling surface of big-city civilization was like the surface of the ocean near the shore where people were swimming—at any second a fin could break through and the jaws open in the depths beneath and the blood come crimsoning.

Glancing across her shoulder, Tasha saw the man with the mirrored lenses still loping through the trees, facing in her direction again but looking down all the time, *all* the time, *but people don't jog like that, they look up sometimes, look around them, right?*

He wasn't doing that.

She turned again and headed for Fifth Avenue and home, speeding up now, wanting to be nearer the traffic, people, safety. It would be nice, sure, not to think this way, not to be scared, but she daren't turn her back on things and forget them, not at this stage, because it wasn't only Christine she had to contend with.

There's something maybe you should know, Bernie Behrens had told her at the police precinct. *The man who killed Christine has killed before. He's a serial.*

Oh my God . . . How many?

Eleven. As far as we know. If it had been just Christine, it would've been bad enough. Worse, there were others. Worse still, he could do it again. And again.

And as Tasha was leaving, Bernie had said, *Anytime you need me, you'll get instant attention. If I'm not here there'll be somebody else on the team—there's five of us, plus the supervisor, okay? Count yourself one of the family.*

Did he say that to everybody?

Why had he said it to her?

Was she in danger?

If she were in danger, how close did he think it was?

Going through the lobby she caught a heading on the front page of a paper on Lewis's desk: KNIFE ATTACK THWARTED—WOMAN IN COMA. There'd been something about it on the radio, too, while she was drinking her coffee this morning.

A *knife* attack.

Worse still, he could do it again. And again.

*   *   *

Twenty-five minutes later, after she'd got out of her track-suit and showered and slipped into a cool aquamarine linen dress by Geoffrey Beene, Tasha went to a window as usual to watch for the roof of Vince's limo to come sliding to a stop below the building at exactly 8:45. It was then, as she glanced upward across the park, that she saw the sunlight sparkling on a pair of mirrored lenses among the trees.

Twenty-two

Get me St. Clare's," Behrens said into the phone. Woodcock looked at him from across the desk, and Behrens knew why.

The detective watching Jenny Kuratczyk in the intensive-care unit would call this desk the instant she came out of the coma. There was no need to ask the hospital for information. It was just that they'd got nothing else to do on this bright and sunny morning.

There was a new guy assigned to the Kuratczyk case—Detective Wallens, younger than Behrens, smarter—Behrens thought—but lacking in experience, not always knowing when he should listen instead of look, smell instead of listen, dream instead of smelling. Dreaming was important, dropping into a semi-doze and letting the vibes come to you, just letting them come, then tuning in.

"This is Nurse Walken, may I help you?"

"Behrens, Homicide. Is Jenny Kuratczyk still under?" He thought he sounded brusque. Neither he nor Woodcock had gone back to the sack after they'd left the crime scene before midnight; it was now 8:50.

"There's been no change, Detective. Do you wish to speak to your—"

"No. Thank you." He hung up.

"Bernie?"

He looked across at Woodcock. "Yeah?"

"They put a name to those prints and we go down. Right?"

"Yeah, but don't get excited. I can't stand to see anybody's eyes shining this hour of the morning."

"But that's all we need, Bern."

"Yeah. But bring the lids down, for Christ sake, I can't stand the glare."

It was true, of course. The prints on the handle of that knife had been flashed to the NCIC before 2:00 A.M. for a nationwide check, but they'd had to get in line because a computer was on the fritz somewhere, which was why Detective Woodcock here had been sitting with his ass in an uproar for the past six hours. But sure, it was true, if they found a match for those prints they'd have a name and a face and a last-seen record and the Wittendorf case could go down within the day once they'd flashed the mug shots on the TV screen in the Crime Stop program and the telephones started ringing.

ARREST MADE IN SERIAL KILLER CASE.

Yeah, nice. Headlines. But there was this little problem with the M.O., the method of operation. There had been no orchids sent to Jenny Kuratczyk yesterday. He and Woody had met her folks at the hospital, the man white and shaking, the woman quiet with shock as they waited for their child to come out of the coma, or not come out. Jenny had lived with them in their apartment since her divorce a year ago, they said, didn't have a steady boyfriend, didn't date too much, they couldn't think of anybody in this whole wide world who'd wish to do her harm, the woman quietly shaking her head all the time, clutching her handbag like she needed to clutch onto whatever kind of reality was around, her child hurt bad and unconscious and they said this man was trying to kill her, what next, in God's name, whatever next?

Behrens looked at the dregs in his cup for a while, the way a Gypsy looks at tea leaves, then went across for a refill. The M.O., yeah, was the problem. No orchids. The only way it could be Jack was if he hadn't picked out his next victim yet, couldn't find the right face, the right type, and had gone wild because of the waiting, had needed to kill again, with no time for the usual frills.

Behrens didn't think it was Jack this time. Just don't tell Woody, break his heart. They wanted this case to go down so bad it hurt. After almost two weeks they had the whole of the city on their backs, from their own supervisor through the captain and the chief of police to the mayor, who'd personally called Behrens yesterday and said look, a guy couldn't just go after a girl in the middle of Manhattan and leave all that mess behind without also leaving enough evidence to put him behind bars inside of twenty-four hours, this was a shocking case, the victim had been a well-known artist, and the increasing delay in making an arrest was leaving the NYPD looking like it couldn't handle its job—are you there, Detective, are you there?—because Behrens had just sat on his ass at his end of the line picking at his nails while the mayor went on giving him proof beyond any possible doubt that this fine city had a civic leader who at best was mentally retarded and at worst had a brain no bigger than a grasshopper's balls.

Behrens took a sip off the top of his coffee and found it too hot and put down the cup and shut his eyes and waited for some vibrations to drift his way, but couldn't feel any; all he could see was the face of Tasha Fontaine—as he often did when he let the pressure off and gave his sixth sense a bit more room—maybe because she was getting closer to Jack the Knife than they were, closer all the time. He knew this, could feel it on his skin, could sense it in the air like a sudden cold draft, could hear it in his head like a whisper from the dark, *the scream is the key.*

Yeah, Tasha Fontaine was getting closer all the time to Jack the Knife. Or he was getting closer to her. Behrens was able to know this not because of any particular logic or reasoning, but because of the life he'd led and the death he'd seen in the past twenty years that had given him his exhaustive hands-on education in the field of human outrage.

When the telephone on the desk began ringing, Woodcock reached for it and gave his name.

"Oh, hi! Yeah, he's right here." He passed the phone across the desk. "Fontaine."

Behrens took in a breath. "This is Bernie," he said. "Is everything okay?"

"I'm calling from the limo," he heard her voice, tightness in the tone. "I don't want to waste your time, Bernie, but there was a man watching me in the park this morning when I was jogging. And watching Temple Mansions after I got back there."

"You're on your way to where, right now?"

"La Botica."

"Okay. When you get there, have your driver go across the sidewalk with you, see you into the building. I'll be along there in a few minutes. I don't think there's anything you need worry about, but I'll check and make sure."

Tasha put the handset back on its rest and looked through the smoked window at the storefronts along Fifth Avenue. "Did you see the paper this morning?" she asked Vince.

He cocked his head. "Excuse me, miss?"

She asked him again, and his light gray eyes flicked upward to watch her briefly in the mirror. "No, I didn't have time. What happened?"

"There was an attempted knife attack on a woman last night, just over on West Fifty-fifth."

"A *knife* attack?"

"Right."

He'd got the connection. Vince was easier to talk to,

Tasha thought, now that she'd brought him out a little by encouraging conversation; he'd been so reserved when he'd first started driving her.

"Do they think it was the same man, miss?"

"They made no comment."

"What can the police do anyway? I mean, last year we had forty-eight cabdrivers murdered, and there was only a handful of arrests. Things are getting out of hand in this city."

"Forty-*eight?*"

"That's right. Just cabdrivers. I don't know the grand total, everybody included—I drove a cab myself once, that's why I was interested." He swung the limo south onto Seventh. "Straight to the boutique as usual is it, miss?"

"Yes. Did you hear what I was telling Detective Behrens just now on the phone?"

"No, miss."

But he would say that anyway: he had the formal manners of a butler.

"I was telling him there was some guy watching me this morning, in Central Park."

Vince's head leaned to one side a little. "There are some men," he said, "never get tired of watching the ladies."

Tasha left it. She didn't want to sound paranoid, hoped she hadn't sounded paranoid to Bernie on the phone.

"Vince," she said as the limo swung west onto Forty-ninth, "do you have a minute when you drop me off?"

She saw his head move to check the time on the dashboard. "No problem," he said. "The traffic was good to us this morning."

"I'd just like you to see me into the building, that's all. A friend of mine had her bag snatched yesterday, coming out of a restaurant."

"That's terrible," Vince said. "Sure, I'll be glad to walk you across."

He left the limo's motor running as he escorted Tasha

into the store, his peaked cap set straight on his head and his steps sounding important.

"You'd make a handsome bodyguard," she told him with a smile, and he ducked his head like a schoolboy. Maybe she'd been too familiar this time, but the hell with it—surely it must have pleased him.

"Same time this evening, Miss Fontaine?"

"As far as I know right now. If not, I'll call you and find a cab."

He nodded and turned away, and she called after him as he reached the door. "Thank you, Vince!"

He half-turned and touched the peak of his cap and went on out.

"Is he your driver?" Elizabeth asked as she came from the back of the salon.

"Yeah."

"He looked cute."

"Yeah, he's nice. Kind of old-fashioned."

"Did you sleep well?" Elizabeth's eyes were attentive.

"Pretty well. I'm okay." Tasha slung her bag across the back of a gold baroque chair. "I'm okay. There was a guy watching me in the park when I was jogging awhile back, that's all."

"So what else is new?"

"Maybe it was just that, yeah." Vince had said the same thing.

"Sheila de Witt called," Elizabeth said, "to ask if we could give her a private preview of the Tuesday show. I said I'd have to ask you."

"What do you think?" Even as she said it, Tasha was aware that it wasn't in the least characteristic: when people—usually Elizabeth—asked her for a decision she gave them one, right or wrong; she didn't just return the ball.

Elizabeth lifted a slim shoulder and dropped it. "If we do it for Sheila de Witt, we'd have to do it for everybody—because they'd certainly get to know."

"And there wouldn't be a show."

"Not really."

Tasha had to think about it, didn't want to. They were in the downstairs salon, with the early sunlight filtering through the white silk blinds.

"Okay," Tasha said at last, "so that's what we tell her—if we do it for her, we'd have to do it for everybody."

"Just say no?"

"Right."

The glass door was banged back suddenly and the mailman came in and dropped the bundle for La Botica onto the reception desk and gave them the usual routine in his hearty old-timer's voice: "Hi, ladies! Be good today, okay?" And went on out, having put them in their place like a good Christian chauvinist, he got on Tasha's nerves.

Everything got on her nerves, because of the man in the park.

"The only thing is," Elizabeth said, "that last season Sheila de Witt spent better than a quarter of a million dollars with us, and this fall she's going to marry Grant J. Westheimer, and I *do* mean the oilman."

"She also paints her nails gold, and for that alone I'd get a kick out of turning her down. Sheila de Witt doesn't happen to be the only—"

She broke off, and felt the blood leaving her face as she stared past Elizabeth's shoulder to the sunlit street.

"You okay?" she heard Elizabeth asking.

"No."

Because the man getting out of the car and coming across the sidewalk toward La Botica was wearing tan slacks and a white T-shirt and mirrored sunglasses, and as Tasha watched him pulling the elegant glass door open she knew she wasn't safe anymore, could never be safe, whatever she did, wherever she ran, wherever she hid.

* * *

"This is Pete Scabrock," Detective Behrens said. He'd followed the man in. "Can we go someplace more private?"

Tasha led them into the storeroom at the rear of the salon, feeling the adrenaline still on the rush as she shut the door and looked at the man again, now without his sunglasses. He had the eyes of a predator as he returned her gaze, a male looking at female prey.

"See this guy again," Behrens said, "you'll know who he is." He gave a nod and the man favored Tasha with a token smile—just a quick compression of the lips—and left them. Behrens took three photographs from his coat and held them out for Tasha to look at. "This is another guy you'll see around. Charlie Vines. They're both detectives. They'll work in shifts, okay?"

Tasha leaned her back against the end of a clothes rack, her legs weak now as the reaction set in, the fright coming out in anger. "He looked like he couldn't wait to fuck me, Bernie, or didn't you notice?"

Behrens swung his tired face to watch her, his eyes patient. "Cops are studs—didn't you know that? It goes with the territory. But I'm sorry it surprised you—really. He's a very good cop. Now look at the mug shots carefully and commit this other guy's face to memory."

When Tasha gave them back to him she asked, "Am I under protective custody, or what?"

"Protective surveillance. I'm sorry about that too. I—"

"You could have warned me, for God's sake."

"Maybe I should have, yeah. But I didn't want you worried. I didn't expect you'd be keeping such a sharp eye out—but that's good, that's very good."

"So I'm in danger, right?"

"You're exposed," Behrens said, his shoulders sagging as he stood there watching her, nothing but kindness in his eyes, kindness and resignation. "Serials—serial killers—tend to attack the same type of victim. We think we know who killed Christine Wittendorf, as I told you. And you're his type of victim. You also live very close to the scene of his last attack. And with serials, lightning sometimes strikes twice in the same place." He looked away, his baggy eyes taking in the dresses along the rack, the silks, taffetas, satins, sequins, as if he were looking at something—a way of life—he didn't understand. Then his head swung back to look at Tasha. "And then there's this weird *connection* you seem to have with Christine Wittendorf."

After a moment Tasha said crisply, "So how long have I got? When does the show start?"

Behrens heard the fear, admired the courage. "It starts when I fail to stop the curtain going up. And I'm not going to do that."

Tasha leaned away from the clothes rack, folding her arms, warming herself with them as best she could. "Is there anything else you should be telling me, Bernie?"

He thought about that, took his time, picking at his worn, ragged nails, studying them, unwilling to bring a note of fantasy into this whole thing but feeling it might be important. Because the scream was the key. "I've got simply no idea what it adds up to," he said when he was ready, "if it adds up to anything at all. But maybe you ought to know this. That scream you say you heard, the night when Christine was killed. Only you heard it—nobody else."

Tasha watched his eyes, thought they looked apologetic, as if he hadn't wanted to tell her this. "But they must have," she said.

"You'd think so, yeah, but we checked it out. I had a policewoman scream her head off in the park, right at the crime scene, while I was standing on the steps of Temple Mansions with one of my colleagues, watches synchronized. And we didn't hear a thing. And there weren't any calls from the East Side, where you live, reporting it. But we got a half-dozen calls from the other side of the park, nearer the Wittendorf crime scene, came in within minutes, woman heard screaming." He took a step closer to Tasha, hands dug into his coat pockets. "The night Christine was killed, there were no calls reported at all, even from the West Side of the park near the scene. None. From anywhere. So if Christine Wittendorf screamed that night, it was only to you."

A siren started up somewhere out there among the streets, its sound pressing faintly through doors and windows into the buildings of the city, bringing the tidings of drama, of alarm.

"Whatever," Tasha heard herself saying.

An odd word, she thought, but accurate, a verbal shrug, expressing precisely what was in her mind. Whatever you say, Bernie. Whatever works for you. If it happened that way, okay. A dying woman screamed for help that night, but only to me. Only to me, in the whole of Manhattan, the whole of New York City. Okay. Whatever. I'm tired now, see, tired of being haunted, tired of being hunted, tired and terribly scared, because there's nothing you can do, Bernie, though I know you want to save me. There's nothing anyone can do, because at the back of all this there's Christine. And this is the way she wants things for me, so that's the way it's going to be.

You remember I once said you were lucky in having known Christine, but not for long?

Yes.

Shall I tell you why?

Okay.

She was a monster.

See, Bernie, that's why there's nothing you can do. Christine was a monster, and still is. And this is her show.

He was turning away, maybe puzzled by her one word, "Whatever," but getting the message that she accepted what he'd just told her, didn't want to talk about it. He stood for a moment to look at a dress on a mannequin, ready for display in the salon, one that Tasha had left Elizabeth to choose, to decide on, because decisions came hard these days with the world sliding out of focus all the time. It was a Valentino, a sheer silk vermilion sheath bursting into a soft explosion of ruffles swirling around the legs, new in from Milan, a breathtaker.

"How much?" Bernie asked her.

"That one? Thirty-five thousand."

He turned his crumpled-tissue face to her. "And you have to mean dollars, right? This one dress?"

"Yeah."

"Well, sure, hey, it's real pretty. Like to buy it for you, but right now I guess I'm clean out of cash."

Tasha came close to him, smelling coffee, staleness, fatigue. "I'll take the thought for the deed."

He nodded gently, smiling a little. "You gotta deal."

Tasha went with him to the door of the salon, and as he pulled it open he turned to her and said, "Just one other thing. I talked to the doorman at Temple Mansions a while ago—Lewis, is it?"

"Yes."

"Right. I told him if anyone sends orchids there for you, he has to call me, right away. So I'm telling you too, in case he forgets, because this is very, very important. You get orchids, *call* me, okay?"

Twenty-three

I t **was stifling** in the little greenhouse on top of the roof, and the sweat was trickling on him as he stunned the fly with the flyswatter and watched it spinning in circles on the trestle table for a little while before he picked up the tweezers and dropped it into the green, gaping mouth of the *Dionaea muscipula* and saw the jaws close slowly on it as he waited for the buzzing to stop.

It made him almost happy again, but not quite.

He had stayed awake all night long, tossing and turning on the warm mattress, not even a sheet over him, the night was so humid. Tossing and turning, flaying himself in disgust for doing what he had done earlier, it had been *stupid, stupid, stupid,* it could put him in prison, a thing like that, *in prison for the rest of his life,* and he wouldn't ever be able to stand that, because of the bars in the cellar window and her throwing him down the steps and the smell of the roasted rats and everything.

He couldn't think what had gotten into him, following that girl out of Farmer's Market and then *this,* the look on Jenny's face when she'd heard him coming up behind her, like she was surprised, well she *should* have been surprised, the little *bitch,* because he hadn't ever done it this way before, on the spur of the moment as you might say, it was the weather, perhaps, this awful heat and of course the humidity, the sweat trickling from under his arms as he swatted another fly and watched it spinning on the table, silly fly, there was nothing it could do, so why all the fuss, he would like to know?

He'd always been so careful before, with all the planning and everything, buying the flowers and using the florist's box, taking great care, taking the greatest care, enjoying it, that was very true, *enjoying* every minute. And now look at the mess he was in!

VICTIM STILL IN COMA.

It was like a reprieve when he'd seen that in the paper. But she could come to at any time, couldn't she, and tell them what he looked like, *describe him exactly* so they could make what they called an artist's impression—and *then* where would he be?

The little jaws gaped, like the beak of a young bird in the nest, then he dropped the fly in, still buzzing, silly fly, and the jaws closed s-l-o-w-l-y with their thin, delicate spines coming together like bars across a window as he stood with the warmth coming into him "down there."

And another thing. *He'd lost the knife!*

They'd have his fingerprints now. *After all those times—eleven times—*all of them done safely, the screaming and then the blood flying and he was away, away over the hills before the sirens started, *after all those times* he'd done this *stupid* thing, let it get the better of him, behaving with no more control than your typical rapist, your happy-go-lucky Boston Strangler, a stupid psychopath.

It mustn't happen like that again.

He'd already chosen the next one, days ago, made his *choice*. He should have started making his plans for the great occasion, finding the right florist and timing the whole affair by the clock, minute by minute, *enjoying* it as he always did, *savoring* it like these little green jaws with the quivering going on inside them, the delicious quivering, *that* was how it should be done, THIS IS HOW IT SHOULD BE DONE, slowly and carefully and in safety, leaving nothing to chance.

He'd been disgusted with himself the rest of last night and all through the day, *disgusted.* But now that was going to change.

NOW THIS IS GOING TO CHANGE.

And soon. As soon as he could make it, in case that silly little roller-skating *bitch* woke up and gave him away.

SOON.

As soon as the next chance came. He knew who she was and where to find her, and all that was left was the final planning, step-by-step, the stalking, you might call it, yes, the *stalking,* that was a nice word, like *creeping,* he enjoyed words like that, enjoyed saying them, thinking about them.

One of the wings came off this time, but no matter; the silly thing wouldn't need it anymore, spinning around and around and *up* we come and *down* between the sticky little jaws and *oh . . . oh . . . oh . . .* just *watch* them close around that silly buzzing body . . . and hear the buzzing *stop.*

As soon as the next chance came, then.

Maybe tomorrow.

Twenty-four

Tasha and Elizabeth were checking the dresses for the preview tonight when the phone rang and the intercom buzzed and Tasha took the call.

It was Audrey.

"I know you're working, darling, but I just wanted to find out how you were."

"I'm fine."

"You don't sound fine."

"We're choosing the stuff for the show tonight, so maybe I'm just a little distrait."

She watched the model making another turn, the ruffles of the silk Valentino swirling around her legs.

"Then I won't keep you, darling. Come over tonight for a little something, so that at least I'll know you're being fed."

"I—I'm not sure what my plans are, Audrey. But I really appreciate the call."

Tasha nodded to the model and exchanged a look with Elizabeth. They could sell this one a dozen times tonight, but it was an exclusive: hence the price tag.

She knew, actually, what her plans were for tonight, because she'd just made the decision. It was going to take some courage, but it would have to be done.

"If you change your mind," Audrey was saying, "phone me, darling. I do so want to look after you."

"I'm fine. Really. Maybe tomorrow."

When she put the phone down, Elizabeth asked, "The emerald Scaasi?"

"What? Yeah. Let's see it again."

But Tasha couldn't concentrate as the model came back, her feet splayed like a ballet dancer's, her cool smile playing professionally on her mouth.

"It goes in?" Elizabeth asked.

"Goes in?" Tasha pretended to give it thought as the model stood waiting. "What's the ticket?"

"Twenty-four thousand."

"Okay. Sure. It goes in. It's a stunner." Then she remembered that all these dresses had been Elizabeth's personal choice in Milan. "They all are."

"Thank you." But Elizabeth's eyes were concerned as she glanced away. Tasha wasn't concentrating, and she should be. The show tonight would gross half a million for La Botica over the next few weeks and get them coverage in *W,* guaranteed.

When the last dress had been chosen, Tasha bit the bullet. The model had gone back to the storeroom, and Elizabeth was standing close. With her voice low Tasha said, "This is really your show tonight—you know that?"

"My show?"

"It's the payoff for all your work in Milan."

Elizabeth looked at her steadily. "What's coming, Tasha?"

"I—I want you to handle it, that's all. Lap up the congratulations and everything."

In a moment. "How are you feeling?"

Tasha had never learned to be right upfront with Elizabeth. "Okay, yeah, I need a break. Badly."

Elizabeth went on watching her. "Can I do anything?"

"Sure. Take over the show."

"Nothing to it. If that's what you want."

"I need to see someone tonight. Someone who might—you know—straighten me out."

The model had come back into the salon, was waiting to help them ready the show.

"All right," Elizabeth said. "I hope they succeed."

Watching Elizabeth and the model across the salon, Tasha had a sudden, frightening sense of being somewhere else, distanced from them; she was here physically but there was a kind of abyss between them, keeping her back from the world she'd known—the one they were living in, the normal one—and across the abyss she watched them with the yearning eyes of an outcast, feeling that whatever she did now she could never be back there with them again.

Theodora stroked her ginger cat.

It was enormous, taking up the whole of her lap as she sat there in the chair watching Tasha. The chair was enormous, too.

"Yes," Theodora said at last, "from what you tell me, this sounds like a case of possession."

Even though Tasha had suspected it, hearing it spoken aloud came as a shock.

"Okay," she said. She was getting good at finding exactly the right word for what she meant. Whatever. Okay. Okay, then I'm possessed. It doesn't sound like something you can stop happening, be like trying to ward off a ghost, your hand would just go through it.

She'd called Theodora at the club in the Village during her lunch break today and fixed up to see her in private tonight, at her home. Tasha had made up her mind that since Christine was at the back of all that was happening to her, she would have to fight her off, and that could only be done through someone like Theodora, a psychic who could open up the channels. Or try. It had worked last time: she'd been there with Christine at the gates of the dead, had seen them opening for her.

But now she had demands to make, if she could contact Christine again, just one more time. *Get out of my life. Keep to your own world, and leave me the fuck alone.*

Theodora stroked her cat. "You'll need to get rid of your anger," she said, "if we're to establish contact. Or you'll just drive her away."

Tasha let out a breath. But it figured, right? Telepathy was a psychic phenomenon. "That won't be easy," she said. "She's breaking up my life. She could even get me killed."

"From what you have told me," Theo said, "yes, that's possible."

"Then what can I do about it?" Tasha sprang out of her chair.

"You can start by sitting down again."

"When I'm ready." Tasha moved around, brushing against the huge potted fern—everything was big in this room, including Theodora—and confronting herself suddenly in a mirror and freezing, her breath blocked in her throat while her brain tried desperately to rationalize: she'd come here to ask this woman to raise the dead, and she'd done just that, and here was Christine in the mirror. Or somebody who looked like her, name of Tasha Fontaine, yeah.

"I want to know *why*!" Tasha turned to stare down at Theodora. "Why me? Why does she want to possess *me*?"

A faint rattling sound began, and Tasha jerked her head in its direction, ready to defend herself, to attack if necessary.

"Excuse me a moment," Theodora said, and heaved herself out of her chair, carrying the ginger cat like an enormous muff. "The sauerkraut sounds like it's on too high." She went through the archway into the kitchen.

Tasha stood in the middle of the cluttered room, letting her eyes close so she couldn't see anything, because she didn't belong in rooms like this one, talking to people like Theodora. Okay, so what the hell was she doing here?

Taking a last stand. Making a last throw. You got a better metaphor, let's have it.

Sweat trickling on her face and she found a Kleenex, mopping. She'd never in her life been this angry, known this amount of rage. Her eyes throbbed with it; she could feel the veins at her temples, her mouth dry as a husk. But it wouldn't get her anywhere. This was going to be the last shot and it had to make a hit.

Hands were on her arms suddenly and she screamed, whirling, staring into the calm, shapeless face of Theodora, who reached out and held her again gently, letting her eyes dwell on Tasha's, letting them be all that Tasha could see, or need to see, as the soft wave of something that felt like silence flowed from the woman's hands and washed through Tasha's nerves, quenching the fire in them and bringing cool, bringing relief.

Then Theodora was sitting in her chair, facing her—Tasha wasn't aware of having sat down again. The rage had gone; she felt drained.

"Maybe," Theodora said, "because you were handy."

"What?"

"You asked me a minute ago, 'why me?' It could be because you were handy, the only one around at the time. You were sleeping when it happened, you told me, and her scream woke you. Is that right?"

"Yes."

"Can you remember what you were dreaming?"

"Yes, very well."

"Do you want to tell me about it? And unclench your hands—don't let's get silly again."

Tasha relaxed, found she'd been clenched all over, not just her hands. "I was dreaming about Christine. We were—"

"Oh, indeed . . . Oh, indeed . . ."

Tasha waited as long as she could. "So does that—I mean—"

"See," Theodora said quietly, "we go places in our dreams. We go where we dream about, and we meet the people we're dreaming about. You didn't know that?"

"I guess it's not—you know—my field."

"The cosmic order is not your field?" Theodora looked away, stroking her huge ginger cat, looked back. "It's your home. And since we reside in multiple universes, our dreams are just as real as what we choose to call reality, because we need to make the unmanifest manifest and give the ego its job to do." Her massive shoulders lifted and fell again. "Sometimes, of course, we just run time backward in our dreams and play it again. Where were you when you dreamed that time about Christine?"

"In a taxi, in the rain."

"Ring any bells?"

"Sure. That was the only time I ever met her—"

"In what you call 'real' life? This one?"

"Yes."

"So, as I say, in the dream state we sometimes ask Sam to play it again. But it doesn't really matter where you were, in your dream that night. All that matters is that you were with Christine, the *only* one with Christine, the *only* one she could call out to for help."

The big cat watched Tasha with its round amber stare.

That scream you say you heard, Bernie Behrens had told her this morning, *the night Christine was killed. Only you heard it. Nobody else.*

She felt her hands tightening again, relaxed them.

"That's good." Theodora nodded.

"Okay, so there was the dream connection. Okay." Tasha was having to learn things fast in this new weird world Christine had got her trapped in. "So why did I dream we were in the taxi, in the rain? Why didn't I dream I was in the park with her?"

Theodora stroked her cat, watching the pale violet veins on the back of her hand, the marmalade stripes of fur. "But you did." She brought her eyes up. "Didn't you?"

And Tasha heard the scream again, her own, heard the scream as the man stood towering over her with the long bright knife coming down . . . down . . . "But that was at the séance," she said, the sweat springing on her face again. And this woman had known, even though Tasha had never told her, had just walked out of the club in the Village without telling anyone at all what she'd experienced. "That was just a few nights back."

"There isn't any time, you see, out there. There's only now. Everything happens now, and any given event only comes into our consciousness when we give it our attention. Try the image of a piano, to picture the dream state—the whole keyboard is there in front of us, but we only play one note at a time, and in no particular order—sometimes past, sometimes future. You mean you've never experienced something and said, 'Gee, I dreamed about this last night'?"

"I guess." But Tasha didn't want any of this other-world bullshit, she just wanted to live a normal life, sell some dresses, go on vacation, do normal things. "I guess."

"Unclench your hands."

"I want out." Tasha said it low, leaning against the chair back and shutting her eyes, feeling the sweat creeping on her face again, on her neck. "I want out, Theodora. I'm losing it—can't you see that? You can see everything. I'm losing my mind. So can't we start? Make a start? Get in touch with her again, tell her I want out, she has to let me go?"

The rattling began again, but fainter this time; Theodora turned her large head and looked toward the kitchen, turned her head back. The odor of boiled cabbage was in the room, rancid, clinging.

"I can't do that."

Tasha looked at her. "Why not?"

"I'm not qualified."

"You need a degree or something? Look, you did it before, at the—"

"There would be no point," Theodora said, "in just making contact again. She has you in her possession, don't you understand? Do you think she'll let you go just because you ask her to?" Her eyes came up. "No way."

Tasha watched her, the woman stroking the cat. "What does she want from me?"

Theodora turned her head away, her eyes looking out into a space of her own making, their focus lost in it. After a while she said, half to herself, "I believe she needs you to do something for her."

"Do what?"

"That I cannot say. But it's very dangerous. She has no concern for your safety in this."

In a moment Tasha asked, "It's to do with the man who murdered her?"

"I don't know."

"She wants me to find him somehow, or—"

"I do not *know.*"

"Then ask her!"

"There would be no *point.* It would only make her angry, like you. You would pass your anger onto her."

"Then . . ."

Then what? This was it? The end of the line and the train gone, leaving her with this mad haunted world to go on living in for the rest of her life? And after that, where would she be? Trapped in that other-world with Christine? With a monster?

She got out of the chair so fast that she sent it rocking on the thin, stained rug.

"Where are you going?" she heard Theodora ask.

Tasha looked down at her. "I don't know." In a whisper. "Where is there for me to go?"

In a moment Theodora said, "I can see nowhere safe for you to go—in this city."

Tasha stared down at her. "So it's simple, then. I'll get out. Get out of New York."

The big cat screamed and flew off Theodora's lap, leaping for the heavy red drapes and clawing its way to the top, crouching there and staring down, its fur raised from its body, a low howl keening from its throat.

Tasha stood frozen, feeling the air in the stuffy room cold against her skin as the low, thrumming sound went on in the throat of the cat, filling the silence with rage.

Theodora turned her head and looked up, watching the cat for a while, not calling to it, doing nothing, just watching. Then she looked down at Tasha.

"If you can."

"If I can?"

"You tried to leave New York once before, you told me. But she stopped you."

"Yes." The word sounded crisp, controlled. She knew what to do now. "But she won't stop me again."

From the top of the drapes the cat's throat thrummed with menace, and Tasha stared up at it, matching rage with rage. "Stop that fucking *noise*! It doesn't scare me!"

"It isn't the cat," Theodora said.

Tasha whirled on her. "*Of course it isn't the cat!* It's that *bitch*!"

The woman watched her from the depths of her enormous chair, her eyes turned upward, looking out at Tasha from just beneath their lids. "Yes," she said, "that is the voice of Christine. So be warned: you won't find it easy to leave this city."

"I'm not looking for an easy way out. Just a way out. And so help me God I'm going to take it."

In a moment Theodora said, "Very well. And now that I know you're determined, I can tell you this: it's your only chance."

* * *

In the limousine Tasha said quietly, reflectively, "My life's not going too well, Vince."

Her driver's gray eyes flicked to the mirror, concern in them. "I'm sorry to hear that, miss."

"Thank you."

She didn't know what had made her say such a thing; it was so personal, and Vince was still rather formal with her, as of course he should be, she supposed. But he was someone to talk to; it was better than silence, disallowing her mind to run round and round in a frightening circle, *It's very dangerous. . . . She has no concern for your safety in this,* as they drove sedately back to Temple Mansions in the limo through streets that were quieter now, coming to a gentle halt at the lights and moving on again when they changed, everything so normal, so comfortable.

"You've had problems in your life, I expect," she said to Vince. "Things going wrong."

He allowed himself a short laugh. "Just like everybody else." The lights changed, and he started across the intersection. "If there's anything I can do, Miss Fontaine, you've only got to ask."

"Just be there when I call," Tasha said. "I don't want to use the Seville for a while. This city's so dangerous."

"Give me as much notice as you can, miss, that's all I ask."

"Of course I will." She took a moment to center herself, to look for the courage this was going to need, because of the way the ginger cat had howled. Then, when she was ready, she said, "Vince?"

His eyes came into the mirror. "Miss?"

"I need to get away for a while, out of New York. Just for a day or two. Would you drive me?"

She waited. On a plane she'd be alone, but in the limo she'd have Vince along, her new bodyguard.

He was hesitating. "I was planning to do a bit of work on the car, but it can wait. Where exactly would we be going?"

"Just out of the city. Somewhere north, of course. Let's say Connecticut."

"For a day or two."

"Yes."

Watching her in the mirror he said, "I don't normally do long runs, Miss Fontaine, but this is important to you, isn't it?"

"Yes, Vince. It's very important to me."

She watched him shrug an inch deeper into his blue serge jacket as he made his decision. "When would we leave, miss?"

She closed her eyes and let the breath go out of her. "As soon as I can put a few things together. Later tonight. I'll call you."

Twenty-five

The gardenias," he said.

"These?" The young woman slid open the glass door of the display case, and cold air drifted out.

"No. These, in the corner." They were still almost in bud, and fresher. But some people, he knew, preferred the matured blooms because their perfume was stronger. He could quite understand that.

This was the only florist he knew that was open this late in the evening, nearly eight o'clock.

"Is it starting?" the young woman asked, glancing across at the windows.

"Just starting." He brushed his shoulders, where the first few raindrops had fallen as he'd crossed the sidewalk. "It's going to be so *refreshing* when it gets going, isn't it?"

"I can't wait—and I didn't even bring an umbrella!" She carried the spray of gardenias tenderly across to the counter. "For the box," she asked him, "would you prefer white, pink, or gold?"

"Such a wonderful choice! The gold. Irresistible."

"We have a big demand," she nodded, "for the gold." She took down a flat, opened it and slotted the tabs, reaching for green tissue paper and lining the box with quick, deft fingers. "I don't think I've seen you in here before," she said with a bright smile.

"No." She was pretty, he thought, quite a pretty girl. Maybe one day he might come in here again, and get to know her, and ask her out.

"For somebody special?" she asked, smiling again.

"Very. Very special. Can I take a card?"

"A message card? Help yourself." She laid the gardenias into the box, taking great care not to bruise them.

Mother, Sister, Wife, Daughter, Sweetheart, True Friend. No, none of those. "Do you have any blank ones?"

"On the lower shelf." She glanced across him again, the smile still simmering prettily. "You're new in this part of town?"

"What did you say?"

"I said—" she looked at him directly, the smile leaving her face as if he'd slapped it away by the tone of his voice, the look in his eyes. "Nothing," she said, and swallowed.

Through the open doorway, the tapping of the rain grew louder as it hit the yellow-striped awning overhead.

"Here it comes," he said.

The young woman nodded, didn't look at him. She tied the bow on the gold box and took his Visa card and called the number through, watching the street, the raindrops.

"That looks very nice," he said as he turned away from the counter, "really very nice," tucking the box under his arm to keep it dry when he crossed the sidewalk. "I'll look forward to coming here again."

She nodded quickly, glancing away, looking scared about something, well it served her right, it just served her right, asking him questions, taking such an *interest*, "You're new in this part of town?" What *next*, one would like to ask?

Questions were so dangerous.

* * *

Half an hour later the sky was black overhead, and tremors shook the city as lightning stabbed the skyline to the east over the ocean. The raindrops were heavy now in the streets, and between the buildings and across the vacant lots, cats scuttled for shelter.

Twenty-six

Detective Behrens checked the corner post of the
new house to make sure it was square with the
floor, using the 3-4-5 rule. He could have used a
set square, but he enjoyed the magic of the geometry: you
measured three inches up the post and four inches along
the floor—or the other way 'round, it didn't make any
difference—and then you measured diagonally, and if you
didn't come up with an exact five inches then you had a
parallelogram on its way, not a square.

Rain beat at the windowsill outside, dropping straight
from the sky; there wasn't a breath of wind tonight.

He got four and fifteen-sixteenths, and tilted the post a
degree and remeasured, got it square.

Fiddling while Rome burns.

Bullshit. This was therapy, and what could he do if he
went back to the precinct? Sit at his fucking desk and wait
for something to break? If something broke, they'd call him.

This is therapy, right; when everything is swinging
'round your head like a fucking carousel gone crazy then
you have to calm down, back off, and get your house in
order.

Behrens has spoken.

He fixed a crosspiece to keep the post at right angles until the glue set and then stood back, a small but uncomfortable electric shock shooting through his nerves as the telephone started ringing.

He went over to it.

"Behrens."

"This is Gebhart, sir." Gebhart was the detail on the evening shift at St. Clare's Hospital. "Jenny Kuratczyk just died."

Behrens didn't say anything, stood listening to the rain, a trace of Elmer's Household Glue trying to stick his fingers together.

"Sir?"

"She never came out of the coma? Never said anything?"

"No."

"Okay," Behrens told him slowly, "get back to the precinct."

He stood listening to the rain. Across town, then, the face of Jack the Knife was fading from the brain of Jenny Kuratczyk, the face they wanted, the description, the source for the artist's impression. If it was Jack the Knife who'd attacked her. Killed her, yeah.

Happy guy now, afford to laugh, got a lucky break.

Behrens picked up the phone again.

Woodcock answered.

"What the hell are you doing there?" Behrens asked him.

"Hey, I—you know—I picked up on some sleep, so—"

"How much?"

"Gee, Bernie, I dunno."

Lightning flashed behind the Chrysler Building, leaving its dark, pointed image on Behrens' retinas.

"Gebhart call in?" he asked.

"Yeah. Shit."

"I'm coming over. And I want your ass out of there by the time I arrive. Five minutes' fucking sleep isn't enough."

"Bern?"

"What?"

"I wanna be here."

"Why?"

"I gotta feeling."

The raindrops hit the windowsill like a soft rattle of shot.

"Jesus Christ," Behrens said and hung up.

He never argued against people's feelings, because no matter what they said, that was where the truth was. That was where the angels flew.

Twenty-seven

He opened the gold box carefully, peeling the Scotch tape away from the cellophane and lifting the lid off.

The perfume of the three gardenias was already noticeable, even though they were still almost buds. They would smell wonderful, simply wonderful, in a day or two.

He put them in water, in a short cut-glass vase—his best one—and set it on the bedside table. He would smell gardenias in his dreams!

There was a soft warm rushing through his body that he was quite aware of as he moved about the apartment. He'd felt it before, when he was getting things ready. It was the slow, careful preparation that caused it, the hour-by-hour setting of the scene, as you might say. The feeling was so exciting that he couldn't think how he could have lost control like that when he'd seen the girl in Farmer's Market that time and tried to follow her, and when he'd followed Jenny to the restaurant. It hadn't given him this feeling at all; there was just the hot animal urge rising and then the chase, before he knew what was happening, before he could stop himself, and he was so *ashamed* of himself for letting it happen.

He wasn't an animal.

And look at it this way: he'd also denied himself this very slow, very special *pleasure* he'd always enjoyed before, the other times, buying the flowers and bringing them home and unwrapping them, handling them carefully like the young woman in the florist's shop had done, the pretty young woman—stupid *bitch, bitch, bitch* with her stupid questions, *you're new in this part of town?* Trying to *find out* about him, you could be sure!

But she didn't matter now. Everything was going so smoothly that it would be a pity to let such little things worry him. And besides, he was safe again now.

ATTACK VICTIM IN COMA DIES.

Safe again! But it had been a close shave, and he must be very careful in the future, because there were so many girls out there across the town, across the whole country, and he didn't want to lose them, not one of them—he wanted them to go on patiently waiting their turn.

In a moment he went upstairs to the little greenhouse, taking the gold box with him and putting it down on the shelf, finding the pruning scissors with their green plastic handles and moving along the narrow orchid bed, slowly, s-l-o-w-l-y, the rush of warmth in his body pooling the blood in his groin as he cast his mind ahead to *what was going to happen* so soon now, *so very soon!*

Seeing the terror come into her eyes and the blood leaving her face and then the screaming and the running away the trying to run away the silly *bitch bitch bitch* because he was faster much faster faster faster and then the sharp bright knife and the *slash slash slash* and the feel of her softness under the knife and the smell of her blood *as her blood came springing out in little jets and fountains as he slashed slashed slashed* and the night exploded with the joy of it all, the joy of revenge, *the blood springing out of her as her eyes stared in terror at nothing and no one, going now, going now, gone.*

He stopped moving and waited until the feeling passed, had to wipe the sweat away from his face, this wouldn't do, he mustn't anticipate, well not *too* much, not as much as *that,* or it would all be over before he'd started!

In a minute he took a big breath and went on looking again for the ones he wanted, the best of all the orchids he'd grown for her, the biggest and most showy, *for somebody special?* she'd asked him, the stupid *bitch,* of course they're for somebody special, though she's not my Mother, Sister, Wife, or Daughter, none of those, oh no.

She's the woman who'll be in the park.

Not there yet. But she will be soon.

She'll be there very soon.

The big pruning scissors went snip, snip, snip, as he found the blooms he wanted and cut their stems, taking them along to the shelf and laying them gently into the elegant gold box, settling them firmly so they'd stay just like that with their little freckled faces smiling upward through the transparent panel. Then he tied the ribbon again into a bow.

And how are my pretty little monsters in there behind the green canvas screen? He had to go visit with them, just for a jiffy, gazing down into their green sticky mouths as they gaped up at him, almost as if they were singing to him, *Don't be long now, don't be long!* He could almost hear their tiny voices.

But time was going by and he had to leave them, taking the gold box downstairs and fishing the blank florist's card out of its little envelope and tearing it into small pieces, putting a match to them and watching them shrivel into ash. Then he took a pen from the escritoire and held the little envelope steady, the fingers of his right hand weak with the hot rush of excitement that was still surging through his body as he wrote down the name of the recipient.

MISS TASHA FONTAINE.

Twenty-eight

At 9:30 in the evening the doorbell rang in Temple Mansions, and Lewis eased himself off his chair behind the desk and shuffled across the lobby to the door, his arthritis acting up again because of the rain.

At the top of the steps outside was a florist's box, and as he picked it up he peered along the street, but couldn't see any vehicle. It was a late delivery—you could certainly say that; maybe the driver had found the box still in his van after closing and thought to hell with it, I'll have my supper first.

The telephone was ringing as Lewis swung the door shut and went back to his desk, putting the florist's box down while he answered the call. The scent of the rain had drifted into the lobby, lacing the air with its freshness.

"This is Lewis," he said into the phone.

"I don't feel so good."

The voice was faint, had quiet alarm in it.

"Is that you, Mrs. Bessemer?"

"Yes. I can't reach my pills, Lewis. I know how busy you are, but—"

"Don't you worry, Mrs. Bessemer, I'll be right up. Now, don't you worry."

He hung up and shuffled across to the elevator. He would only do this for Mrs. Bessemer, leaving his post and all; there were one or two people in the Mansions who tried to presume on his time with one request or another, but Mrs. Bessemer had never done that until a week ago—just once—and now tonight. She was a sweet little soul, and not back from the hospital very long, and at her age she was having a hard time getting on her feet again. If anything happened because she couldn't reach her pills, he'd never forgive himself.

As the elevator took the doorman to Mrs. Bessemer's apartment, #51, Tasha, two floors below, was closing the zipper around the only bag she'd decided to take—a light overnighter was all she'd need. She'd called Vince a half hour ago and he said he'd be here.

The phone started ringing as she carried her bag to the door, and she stopped to listen to the answering machine in case the call was important.

It was Vince himself, and she hurried across the sitting room to pick up.

"I'm ever so sorry, Miss Fontaine, but there's a bit of trouble with the car. I'm really—"

"You mean you'll be late?"

She heard him let out a breath of vexation. "There's a chance I can fix it, but I can't be sure, so it'd be best you didn't count on me. You know how much I hate letting you down, miss."

"Gee, I was hoping . . . But don't worry." Tasha's hand had tightened on the phone and she closed her eyes for a moment. So she wouldn't be leaving town with her "bodyguard" after all . . . "No problem," she said in a moment, "I'll take the Seville."

"I feel really bad, Miss Fontaine—"

"Vince, suppose I give you some more time?" Now that

she'd bitten the bullet and decided to leave town, she was anxious to be on her way, but if there were a chance of having Vince along she wanted to take it.

She waited, willing him to work something out.

"Look, miss, there's a chance, yeah, like I say—I'm not far away—but if I can't get things going you'll have wasted your time. It'd be safer if you didn't count on me—and I'm really very—"

"Okay," Tasha said. "The Seville hasn't had a run for a while." She wanted to pressure him, make him get the car going somehow, but it occurred to her that the limo might not really be the problem. Vince was such a formal guy, and he might have gotten cold feet at the last minute about driving out so far and sharing her company for so long, putting up at the same motel and everything. "Don't feel bad, Vince," she said finally. "These things happen."

And then as she put the phone down she nearly lurched as the truth hit her. Vince hadn't gotten cold feet. The limo *was* the problem. It had really broken down, just like the elevator had broken down when she'd been leaving for the airport that time.

This was Christine—again.

Tasha stood very still, the anger rising into her throat. *If she wanted to get out of town then that was what she was going to do, okay? And there was nothing anybody could do to stop her.*

Nobody.

Not even Christine.

The voice of Theodora was suddenly in her mind. *Very well. And now that I know you are determined, I can tell you this. It's your only chance.*

So there was no question.

It was a few minutes later when Tasha walked out of the elevator in the lobby and came face to face with Hanif

Khattak, raindrops sparkling on the shoulders of his trench coat.

"Tasha!" he said in surprise, "you're going out? But it's pouring!"

"Just as far as the parking garage." She felt for the release on her umbrella as Hanif trotted to the door and opened it for her. Lewis didn't seem to be around.

"I'll carry your bag there," Hanif said.

"Absolutely not—I'm a big, strong girl! And I haven't thanked you for the flowers yet—it was really sweet of you—I feel so guilty!"

"As long as you're better, my dear. And you look"—searching quickly—"full of life again!"

All this while Tasha was pushing her umbrella open at the top of the steps, anxious to move on.

"I won't keep you," Hanif said, "if you insist." He stood back with that beguiling little bow, his smile gleaming. "Bon voyage!"

"Thank you!"

Rain hit the taut silk of her umbrella with little popping sounds as Tasha hurried along the sidewalk; the downpour wasn't as heavy as it had looked from the top of the steps, and she'd put on a serviceable pair of brogues; the garage was less than a block away.

She heard a car pulling out from the curb higher up, and looked back, but all she could see was its taillight vanishing into a side street. The detective, right? The "detail." He could have given her a ride to the garage, but maybe they weren't allowed to approach the—the what? What name would they have for her in the official records? The protectee? The exposed party? Potential victim? What, exactly? What name did they have for somebody they were trying to keep from being butchered alive?

Then suddenly she remembered something, and stopped dead on the streaming sidewalk with her breath blocked in her throat.

At the séance with Theodora when she'd come out of that nightmare screaming her head off, she'd believed that what she'd just experienced were Christine's last few minutes on earth as she'd run headlong through the rain with her assailant after her, his breath grunting as he closed the gap and raised the long bright knife for an endless instant with its blade shimmering against the dark leaves overhead.

Christine had wanted her to know how it had been on that hideous night, had allowed Tasha to assume her own identity for those final moments, had allowed her to *be* there, to *be* Christine.

Standing dead still on the sidewalk, Tasha knew now that she was wrong.

There isn't any time, you see, out there, Theodora had told her last night. *There's only now. Everything happens now, and any given event only comes into our consciousness when we give it our attention. Sometimes it's in the past, sometimes in the future.*

What she'd experienced, then, had been her own future, not Christine's past. Because what she'd just remembered was that in her dream projection at the séance she'd been running *through the rain.*

And there hadn't been any rain the night Christine was killed.

But there was rain tonight, drumming on her umbrella, streaming past her shoes.

There isn't any time, you see, out there.

Sure. Yeah. So what I saw was a preview, right?

Standing there with her breath coming back slowly, painfully.

Oh Christ . . . I'm so frightened tonight. So very frightened.

At 9:36, a few minutes after Tasha had left the building, Lewis was back at his post in the lobby after going up to help Mrs. Bessemer. The gold florist's box was still on his desk where he'd left it, and he held it under the green-shaded lamp, admiring the ruffles of curled, flecked blooms under the cellophane and then looking at the address label.

He picked up the telephone and dialed Apartment #31, aware of the trace of cologne that Mr. Khattak always left in the lobby when he passed through. Not strictly cologne, he thought, maybe some kind of Asian concoction—sandalwood, say—the gentleman being like he was from Pakistan. It wasn't at all unpleasant.

Lewis waited for the tenth ring, as usual, before he gave up and put down the phone—something trying to get his attention as he set the florist's box at the end of his desk to wait for Miss Tasha; he'd be here when she came back tonight. Something, yes, trying to jog his memory, something to do with orchids. What was it, now?

At 9:38 by the round-faced clock on the wall the direct-line telephone rang on Detective Behrens's desk and he picked it up.

"Behrens."

"Oh, yeah, this is Lewis, the doorman at Temple Mansions."

"Okay?"

Canted at an angle on his tubular metal chair, Detective Woodcock looked at Behrens across the desk and saw his eyes and tilted the chair straight, one hand going onto the desk, palm down, his head held forward as he listened.

"There's a box of orchids been delivered here, and you asked me to let you—"

"When?"

"Oh, it'd be about ten minutes ago. Somebody—"

"Who are they for?"

As he heard the man's tone, Woodcock pressed the palm of his hand hard down on the desk and was on his feet.

"The name on the label is Miss Tasha Fon—"

"Where is she right now?"

"I think she must have gone out, because she didn't answer her phone when I—"

"*Lewis.* Get your security people. Tell them to expect the police there inside of ten minutes. They'll have my orders to go into Miss Fontaine's apartment the minute they get there—*have the keys ready, Lewis.* Anyone sees her, they're to put her under *immediate* police protection."

Behrens dropped the phone and grabbed his mobile phone and punched buttons and started talking as he and Woodcock broke for the staircase, the quickest way down and out of the building.

"You drive," Behrens said as they reached the Buick.

"Get a patrol—"

"*No.*"

As Woodcock burned rubber onto the street from the parking lot he glanced across at his passenger. "Belt, Bernie."

"What? Oh, for Christ—" He dragged the seat belt across and hit the slot, opening up the phone again, hunched into the seat. "Vine. You hear me, Vine? Come in, for Christ sake. *Vine!*"

Sitting at the wheel of his unmarked Camry maybe fifty yards from the exit ramp of the parking garage near Temple Mansions, Detective Charlie Vine rolled the volume control higher on the handset and recognized Behrens's voice.

"Hear you, Bernie."

The rain drummed on the hood, drops bouncing off.

"What's your location?"

"I'm standing off the parking garage. She left the building five, six minutes back, carrying a valise. She—"

"*On foot?*"

"Yeah. I'm assuming she's on her way to get her car.

Seville, metallic blue, I already checked it out. I got the plate."

"You're *assuming*? For Christ—"

"Hold it, Bernie—she just came in sight around the corner. Yeah, she's heading for the garage right now—and here's something new; there's a limo just pulled up alongside and the driver's getting out, opening an umbrella for Fontaine." Vine turned the ignition key and got the wipers going to clear the raindrops. "Okay, now she's getting in and the driver's shutting the door. It's the same limo she used this evening when I tailed her to the Village—Quality Limo Service on the door."

"It's the one she uses all the time, yeah."

Vine cut the wipers and sat with his head still and just his eyes moving as the limo started up and came on past the Camry, water fanning out from under the tyres.

"You still—"

"Yeah, Bernie, they just drove past me." Vine flicked his eyes to the central mirror. "Going south and turning west toward Park Avenue."

"Okay, pick up the tail and keep in contact with me direct—I'm in the Buick and heading for Central Park South. Don't lose the limo!"

Behrens lowered the mike and sat thinking, something worrying him suddenly, and bad.

Why had the limo driver picked up Fontaine in the street? Why hadn't he gone to Temple Mansions for her? Hadn't he wanted the doorman to see her getting into the limo?

Behrens brought the mike up fast suddenly and started talking as Woodcock swung his head to look at him.

"Operations, I want *every* car in the area to move in to Central Park South, priority, that's *priority,* we're looking for a black Lincoln Continental with 'Quality Limo Service'

in gold letters on the driver's door—you reading me, are
you reading—"

"Affirmative, sir."

"That limo is to be located and pulled over and the
woman inside is to be protected and the driver is to be held
until I get there."

From beside him Woodcock said, "Bern? What's—"

"I gotta freaky idea," Behrens said, "and I hope to Christ
it's wrong."

"Vince," Tasha said with a laugh of relief, "you don't know
how glad I am to see you!" She brushed the raindrops off
her sleeves as the limo started away from the curb.

"I'm ashamed of myself, miss, letting you down on a
night like this."

"But you didn't! I'm here and we're on our way!" He'd
been the answer to her prayer—she'd turned and started
back to Temple Mansions when she'd realized what that
nightmare had really been about: *her own future, not
Christine's past.* But maybe she could change her fate if she
really tried, go home and barricade herself in where nothing could get at her.

But now she had her bodyguard back, and somewhere
behind them there had to be the police detective Bernie had
assigned to her, or one of them.

Nothing could happen to her now. Nothing terrible
could possibly happen to her tonight.

The limo turned west toward the park, rolling smoothly
through the rain, its soft interior lights glowing on the
sumptuous black leather.

"Vince?"

"Miss?"

"You do a terrific job. A really terrific job."

He tilted his head. "I'm glad you think so, Miss Fontaine.
Not many would, after what happened tonight."

* * *

The Buick Regal moved north through the rain, swinging into the park and gunning up again. At this hour and in this weather the traffic was very light, and visibility way down.

Behrens said into the mike, "Where's Vine?"

"We're trying to raise him, sir."

"Bernie?" Woodcock said. He wanted to know about this 'freaky idea.'

"Just watch for the limo."

Another ten seconds and Behrens was asking them again. "Where's *Vine?*"

"Still trying to raise him, sir."

There was silence inside the Buick, just the sound of the motor and the steady scrape of the wiper blades.

"He's lost it," Behrens said. "He's lost the limo."

Tasha leaned back against the soft upholstery, watching the trunks of the trees swinging past in the rain. She didn't ask Vince why they were going through the park instead of north up Madison Avenue; he knew all the short cuts, was a magician in traffic, his wisdom not to be questioned, especially tonight. Tonight he could do no wrong.

He hadn't spoken for a while. He never spoke first, unless it was to ask for directions. But now she saw his head tilting upward an inch as he looked into the mirror.

"I meant to ask you, miss—I hope you received the orchids?"

Thinking she hadn't heard him right, or wanting to disbelieve his question, Tasha said, "The orchids?"

"Yes."

She remembered Bernie at the boutique, his tired, bloodshot eyes serious as he'd watched her face. *"This is very, very important. You get orchids, you call me."*

Her hand went to the telephone in the console.

"No," she said. "No."

"But I delivered them myself."

The windshield wipers swung . . . clicked, swung . . . clicked in the silence.

"When?"

"Earlier tonight." He sounded puzzled, even vexed.

"No," Tasha said. "No, I didn't get them." Everything felt like it was moving away from her, getting smaller, quieter, leaving her in the center of a vacuum as she sat with her hand on the telephone, her fingers numb, unable to lift it. "Who were they from, do you know?" Even her own voice sounded far away.

Vince was suddenly turning the wheel of the limo, sending it churning through the trees with the springs flexing over the bumpy grass. When it stopped at last, he switched off the lights, and Tasha heard his voice again.

"They were from me." He was getting out of the car and pulling her door wide open, staring in. "And I'd like to ask you something, Miss Fontaine." His voice had a monotone, as if he'd rehearsed this, had said it before, many times. "Now that we've got to know each other a little better, would you allow me to take you out one evening? Say for a modest dinner somewhere?"

Without understanding why he should have asked her such a thing, Tasha answered in the only way she could.

"No. I—I don't think so."

For a moment she was surprised by a look of heartbreak in his wide gray eyes, of utter desolation—then rage broke in the man like a sudden storm and she called his name once, twice, trying to shield herself with her hands before she knew it would be impossible and she'd have to get away somehow, pushing the door open on the other side and pitching headlong into the trees and running, running as hard as she could with the rain stinging her face and a scream coming out of her, the scream she'd heard so many times before as she ran and ran with her feet slipping on the wet grass as the man came after her, close now, very close, his breath grunting as Tasha tripped and went down and twisted 'round and saw the long blade of the knife raised above her, thin, bright, glittering against the dark of the leaves.

Behrens used a head shot.

As the headlights of his Buick swung across the grass he hit the door open and came pitching out, moving into the stance with his arms locked in a triangle and putting the first shot in, seeing the man's hands fly upward and the knife go flickering into the bushes as Behrens put another one into the head and the next into the body as it reeled like a drunk, his finger squeezing carefully and rhythmically until all six shots were in and Woodcock went loping across the grass to help the woman up.

"Well hello, Jack," Behrens said softly, the gunsmoke sweet as a nosegay on the air, "and goodbye."